T0277814

ONE HOUSE LEFT

ALSO BY VINCENT RALPH

Secrets Never Die

Lock the Doors

14 Ways to Die

ONE HOUSE LEFT

VINCENT RALPH

WEDNESDAY BOOKS
NEW YORK

This is a work of fiction. All of the characters, organizations, and events portrayed in this novel are either products of the author's imagination or are used fictitiously.

First published in the United States by Wednesday Books, an imprint of St. Martin's Publishing Group

For information, address St. Martin's Publishing Group, 120 Broadway, New York, NY 10271.

www.wednesdaybooks.com

Designed by Devan Norman

The Library of Congress Cataloging-in-Publication Data is available upon request.

ISBN 978-1-250-88218-9 (trade paperback)
ISBN 978-1-250-88216-5 (hardcover)
ISBN 978-1-250-88217-2 (ebook)

First Edition: 2024

10 9 8 7 6 5 4 3 2 1

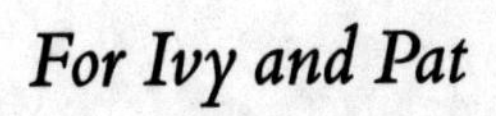
For Ivy and Pat

ONE HOUSE LEFT

The shadows worked silently, crowbars glistening in the moonlight while heavy breaths bloomed then splintered like the wood slowly cracking before their eyes.

When the board covering the door gave way, wings slapped the sky and a distant howl sliced through the muggy air, leaving a sliver of icy terror to stroke their spines.

Four of the shadows stepped back, while one crouched by the rusted lock, humming a lullaby until it finally stood, arms outstretched, then bowed.

The front door clung to its warped frame as they pushed, and then it sailed softly open, allowing them to hurry through before creaking closed.

As they lit their candles, the darkness shrank to the edges of the hallway, like the blur of old-fashioned photographs, ready to snap back the moment the flames were snuffed out.

The five friends came into focus, all with the same fragile smile. If they hadn't known one another so well, they might have seen relief or happiness or excitement. Instead, they saw only terror.

Their words were fractured, their faces like crumbling Halloween masks, their bodies leaning toward the door they had just broken through.

But they stayed, until the fear was replaced by a nervous excitement that showed itself first through tics and giggles, then through voices shattering the silence.

They shouted and they laughed and they bounded from one room to the next. Then they blew every candle out and sat in a circle, chanting words they had read online, feeling braver than they had any right to feel.

They didn't hear the whispers stirring above them. Or the scratching behind doors no one thought to lock anymore.

Their chatter drowned out the creaks that houses make when you're not alone, heavy feet resting almost silently on each step until there was no escape.

The flames came fast, pushing them into a front door that wouldn't budge.

They screamed until thick smoke forced its way deep into their throats and throttled every sound.

Then they wished, silently, desperately, hopelessly, that they had listened to the boy who warned them not to come.

Part 1

Every town has ghost stories.

Usually, they are urban legends whispered around a campfire or tales to make kids behave. But my town was different.

We only had one story, and few people laughed when they told it. It sat in the corners of conversations, a shadow we fought hard to ignore. It hung over Belleview and everyone who lived there, and when we left, we took it with us.

When letters arrive, they go to Cherry Tree Lane, but when we told the story, we called it Murder Road.

The first murder—like most murders—took everyone by surprise.

It was a calm spring night in 1963 when the little girl walked into the street and screamed.

That noise made a tear so deep that it has never been repaired, its echo lingering even now.

Porch lights flashed on, painting a warm glow over the blood. Then people came running, pulling the girl into tardy embraces, like handing shields to dying soldiers.

"What happened?" they asked.

"Are you okay?"

"Whose blood is this?"

She only answered the last question.

"It's Mommy's."

The pitch-black doorway sent shivers down everyone's spines.

And then, one by one, they walked through it, calling, praying, but knowing, deep down, that they were too late.

They found the woman in the bathtub, lying in a shallow red lake.

They found the man in the garage, swaying softly back and forth.

They never found the boy.

Until I knew the whole story, that's what haunted me the most. It wasn't what was left that terrified six-year-old me. It's what was taken.

That was *my* bogeyman story, the tale my brother gleefully sent me to bed with. My nightmares were all about a boy stolen by a monster forty-six years before I was born.

He'd sit at the end of my bed—a nine-year-old with a sadist's smile—and tell me that the boy wasn't taken. He'd say that he ran to the house at the end of the road, escaping a father who had finally snapped and a mother broken beyond repair.

Legend has it that the boy found something—in a building no one had lived in for decades—and together they cursed the whole street.

Every household that had turned a blind eye to his family's suffering down the years was unknowingly and irreversibly cursed. All the cuts and bruises ignored on the sidewalk; all the radios turned up to drown out his father's rage—they would pay for that.

At some point, "tragedy" became "pattern" and then, most horribly, "tradition."

Every few years, on the same spring night, another house on that cursed street was targeted . . . and no one came out alive.

When people started moving, and the killings continued regardless, the story morphed from one of heartless neighbors getting their comeuppance to one of innocents paying for the sins of strangers.

But a child's rage is rarely well planned. It is messy, and the

Hiding Boy's was messier than most. He saw those houses, with their windows like portals into impossible worlds, and he hated them.

My parents weren't born when the bloodstained girl and her vengeful brother changed everything. But I can tell you about every single death that followed, because when you move so close to a place they call Murder Road, you do your research.

You watch every ancient news story and read every rumor—cringing as they switch between ignorance and denial.

They should have known that a curse is a curse, no matter how you spin it. But the deaths were far enough apart, and dissimilar enough (barring the obvious), to be written off as a twisted coincidence.

I never knew our dad's parents. They were faces in boxed-up photographs, minor characters in moments rarely mentioned. His father died first and then, less than a year later, his mother followed, leaving us a house on the edge of a horror story.

It had enough bedrooms for us to have one each, plus an office for Mom and a backyard twice the size of ours. So, we moved. And we stayed there longer than we should have.

If you are selling a house, you must disclose it if someone was killed there. That doesn't put off as many people as you might think. But it's a lot harder to sell a place on a road *full* of crime scenes.

Eventually, the buildings on the road next to ours looked as old as the people inside, and when those people died, their families had an inheritance they didn't want.

Some rent them out to scare-chasers, others reluctantly moved in but always make sure they're away on the same night every year, and some block their lawyer's number.

When we first moved away, we drove past Murder Road and shivered. At the exact same moment, as we passed those houses for the very last time, Rowan, Hazel, our parents, and I all silently swallowed our fear.

No one spoke because that's the thing about real scary stories—whatever you say only makes them worse.

Sometimes it came out in the gaps between our words, in the tiny tears in our daily scripts that we rushed past before it could burst right through.

Sometimes I saw it in a flash behind the eyes; a memory wrestled back into its cage.

And sometimes I saw it in the mirror. Because Murder Road scarred everyone. Even those it didn't kill.

2

"We move too much," Rowan says, and Mom sighs and replies, "We move as often as necessary."

"What's the formula for that?" my brother asks, and Dad glares at him.

"Don't be a smart-ass. You know why we're moving."

A shudder transfers from Hazel's shoulder to mine in the cramped backseat. My sister's long blond hair hides the stare I imagine burning holes into the stained mats beneath our feet, and I lean even closer to the window.

I catch Dad's eye in the rearview, but he looks away before I can fake a smile.

"This time will be different," Mom mumbles, as though she's talking to herself.

No one replies, because no one agrees. The only way to outrun your past is to keep running, and we tire easily.

Our new home looks a lot like our last one . . . and the one before that. When we arrive, it's not quite big enough for the five of us, but we squeeze in and keep our complaints to a minimum.

The front garden is overgrown, the window frames are stained green, and the driveway is covered in clumps of moss. When he opens the door for the first time, Dad treads dirt into the hall and that's us in a nutshell. We stain things because we are stained.

"It's nice," Hazel says, her eyes refusing to focus on the grimy carpets or the peeling plaster.

"Thank you," Mom replies.

Something silent and subtle passes between them, the briefest moment when they look almost identical. Then Rowan barges past with a huge box. "You should know by now, little brother. Don't come in without your arms full."

I go back to the car, where Dad is staring up at our new home. When he sees me, he sighs and says, "It's a fixer-upper, right?"

"Something like that."

We used to live in a beautiful house. It was an expectation—for the streets surrounding Murder Road—as though perfectly tended flower beds and freshly painted fences could hide the stench of our neighbors' dirty secrets.

"Nate?"

Dad's hopeful face slowly comes back into focus before I say, "Sorry. I just want it to be different this time."

"It will be," he says. "I promise."

Parents do that a lot—make vows they can't possibly keep.

It won't be different. It will be exactly the same because, eventually, someone in the town we now call "home" will realize where we came from.

They will go looking for the place we're running from, no matter how much we tell them not to. And they will end up dead.

3

When we've finally moved every box into the right rooms, and scorched our tongues on microwave meals, Dad makes a big deal of stretching, then says, "Good night."

Mom cringes, while Rowan mumbles under his breath, and I watch our father's shoulders straighten then surrender before he leaves the room.

He uses words that don't belong together anymore. Force of habit, I guess. Even after everything we've seen.

It's been a long time since we used "good" and "night" in the same sentence.

Our mother kisses each of us on the forehead, then silently follows Dad upstairs.

If I concentrate, I can hear murmurs through their floorboards. But if I do that, I'll try to piece together conversations we are not meant to hear, their words fragmented like essays forced through a shredder.

Hazel leaves first, the few words she utters in our company saved exclusively for Mom.

Rowan opens the living room curtains and peers into the street.

"Will she be okay?"

Our brother grunts in response, his finger drawing lines in the condensation already forming on the window; then he stares at me until I look away.

"She'll be fine," he says. "Eventually."

I hate that word.

Rowan's right eye twitches and he quickly looks back through the glass. Then he mumbles, "Will *you* be okay?"

My head swells and I breathe as calmly as I can, the way Hazel taught us before we were forced to leave the last place.

"There's nothing out there," Rowan says at last. "You can go to bed."

He knows better than to say "sleep."

"I'll stay up with you," I say. "If you'd like."

He rests his chin on his thick arms and shakes his head.

I wait a few more minutes, watching him peer into the black; then I go to my room.

Four boxes are piled in the corner—my name printed neatly in Mom's handwriting on three of them, my brother's angry scribble screaming it on the fourth.

What is important becomes less so the more times you are forced to take it with you. Now my whole life fits in four small boxes that, tomorrow, I'll unpack then fold neatly and leave under my bed.

I lay a sleeping bag over my mattress, putting another layer between me and the uncoiled springs, then imagine what it feels like to close your eyes and just . . . drift . . . off.

Wind rustles through the vent above my bed, while the sounds of plugs and switches click and clack against the far wall.

Rowan must be there now and I could go to him. All three of us could spend tonight together, hoping that we've finally run far enough; praying that what always follows us will, this time, give up.

But we stay in our own rooms, in separate silences that expand as the hours tick by, until I wake with a start, half exhausted and half relieved.

We don't talk as we eat just enough breakfast to satisfy Mom and delay the inevitable.

Dad leans against the countertop, car keys clanging as he tosses them from one hand to the other.

Hazel bristles at the sound and I wish she'd snatch them from him and take us to school herself. But she waits until I'm ready, then follows me to our parents' beat-up SUV.

Rowan stands at the top of the stairs while Mom waves weakly from the front door.

It's not until he pulls onto the main road that Dad says, "I slept okay in the end."

"Good for you," I reply, focusing on all the unfamiliar sights that are about to feel like home. If we're lucky.

4

Our latest school doesn't assign tour guides or temporary "friends."

Montgomery-Oakes High leaves its new students to fend for themselves—our schedules thrust across the desk by a secretary with better things to do; a campus map too small to understand.

Hazel stuffs hers into her pocket and I mumble, "Good luck," as she slips away.

I'm on my own now. I prefer it that way.

I smile at the scowling secretary until she shakes her head and disappears into the back office. Then I watch from the doorway as kids fill the corridor, some stumbling, others soaring, but most simply taking up space.

Best to keep quiet, small, easily ignored.

Each class is a lesson in minimalism. If I don't raise my hand, lift my eyes from the desk, cough, it's almost as though I'm not here.

I eat lunch in the farthest corner of the sports field, under a tree that drops small yellow leaves at my feet. Then I watch as a group of boys look over then away, one of them nudged until he tentatively stands.

He says something and what happens next is vital—if his friends smile, laugh, show the faintest glimmer of glee, I'll refuse to be the punch line. But they don't.

One of them gives a solemn nod and his friend trots over, words forming on his lips as his shadow spills across my legs.

He has three friends but I guess there's space for one more. And maybe I would join them, if things were different.

I quickly pack my food away and stand, his eyes narrowing as he realizes what's happening. Then I turn and leave before I can hear whatever he's prepared.

When you're running from something horrible, the last thing you need is anyone holding you back. That's why I refuse to play the game. I won't make friends here. I won't let anyone in.

I'm doing this my way, because the alternative is terrifying.

5

It's harder to see what secrets a house holds once you've filled it with your life. That's why our bigger boxes remain unopened.

I'm lying on the thrift-store couch Mom bought two moves ago, familiarizing myself with the history of our new town.

Hazel sits on the huge armchair opposite—the one we all try to shotgun. It's the only comfortable thing we still own and she has it, for now, her feet tucked under her body while a low hum ripples over her lips.

She used to do this alone, but these days it's less a hobby, more a vital part of her existence.

She's been meditating a lot since we left the last place and I can't blame her. We all have our ways of getting through the day.

Mine is to learn every detail about wherever our parents make us live. After all, there is the history our teachers and books tell us, and then there's the rest.

The couch groans as Rowan sits next to me, his eyes greedily snatching at my phone.

"Found anything juicy?"

He's mocking me, but he doesn't know what I've just read.

"A guy murdered his daughter's babysitter," I say. "On this street."

"No shit?"

"Seriously. She'd known the family for years and one day he just . . ."

I snap my fingers and Rowan shivers.

"They released him from jail eighteen months ago."

Rowan's hand brushes the curtains as he says, "Don't tell me he still lives here."

"He did until he died. Natural causes. Last June."

"Monsters don't deserve to die peacefully," Hazel says, startling Rowan so much that he lets out a high-pitched giggle, then slaps my leg because he can't reach hers.

"You look so weird when you come out of your yogi state," he says. "What happens to you in there?"

Her eyes narrow but, like always, she doesn't respond.

Rowan's smirk morphs into a somber smile as he picks the dirt from his fingernails.

Hazel's shoulders sag and I wish she felt better for longer. She fiddles with her phone and I think of the boy she left behind.

If she had her way, she'd still be there—in the town where she met her "soulmate."

Her words, not mine.

I wish I believed in that stuff but it all seems so . . . unlikely.

Hazel goes to the backyard and I watch through the window as she paces back and forth, then taps her phone and holds it to her ear.

She shouldn't be calling him. But maybe his voice will ease her heartbreak.

Rowan watches me watching her; then he nudges my shoulder and says, "It won't last forever. She'll meet someone else one day."

His smile slips as he realizes what he's said. The future is a forbidden topic in our house.

"How are you sleeping?" I ask.

"Fine," he replies. "For now."

He's done being hopeful. Our brother's default setting is angry pessimist.

"Tell me if that changes," I whisper, glancing at Hazel one last time and imagining what she's saying to her first love now she's left him all alone.

Rowan's biceps twitch as he puts his hands behind his head. "You too."

He knows as well as I do that these walls are paper-thin. If my nightmares start again, he'll be the first to hear my screams.

He had the same nightmare whenever he was ill, his pillow and quilt expanding until they were as thick and heavy as elephants' legs.

It didn't sound scary when he said it aloud. He'd tried to explain it to his parents, how something sickly stirred in his stomach whenever he touched his tangled sheets; how he'd cower where his bed met the wall, his quilt kicked to the floor, while panic scurried around his brain.

That nightmare came with every fever and every sickness until it crept into his waking hours. Flashes, like déjà vu, that snapped him out of even his favorite moments.

He wondered if some dreams grew on people like mold.

When he was ten, he accepted it was part of him. Not nice, not welcome, but familiar.

He didn't think there were worse things. He assumed that was the recurring nightmare he'd been given by whoever, or whatever, decides these things.

He was wrong.

Whispers stir in the part of my head where all the dark things lurk. Distant hisses slowly morphing into high-pitched taunts.

"Ready or not. Whatever you do. The Hiding Boy is coming for you."

I fight against the sleep tugging on my eyelids, but this is my only lullaby now: an army of invisible children chanting horribly familiar words, until I lose my grip and tumble into the black.

Icy fingers stroke mine in the gloom, pulling me into a dance I don't have the strength to resist, and we twirl until nausea swells in my stomach and my legs burn.

"Ready or not."

Their voices grow louder.

"Whatever you do."

Splintering into echoes that reverberate around my skull.

"The Hiding Boy is coming for you."

The shapes surrounding me are a blur, and when the circle finally breaks, their sniggers scatter like rats into the shadows.

I know I'm dreaming, but that doesn't help. If anything, it makes things worse.

The hand holding mine lets go, hot breath singeing my ear as something whispers, "*Ready or not.*"

Stop! I want to scream. *I'm not doing this anymore!*

But the Hiding Boy doesn't listen, and neither does his twisted choir.

"He's coming for you."

The words sting like paper cuts and I picture my pillow soaked in blood.

Something coils around my wrist, its claws piercing my skin, but I stay still and silent.

It's worse if you fight back.

Eventually, the children will grow bored and the Hiding Boy will slip further into the shadows.

I clench my teeth as the claws dig deeper, waiting until the chant finally softens.

When my eyes spring open, I reach for my wrist, where five crescent-shaped dents cover my throbbing skin.

My lamp hums on the bedside table, my door not quite closed, everything exactly as I left it.

I listen for the deep murmurs of my brother or the wails of my sister, for the different ways we deal with the same nightmare, but the house is deathly silent.

I run my fingers over the marks on my skin, not noticing the exact moment when they vanish. And I stay sitting until early-morning birdsong stirs me from an ache-inducing half sleep.

I pass Dad on the landing, his humming stopping abruptly when he sees me.

"Hey," he says. "You're up early."

"So are you."

His smile crumbles and I should apologize. He's trying his best. But my body and my mind are still prickling from the nightmare, the distant murmur of that horrible song clamoring to break back through.

Instead, I go downstairs and wait for Hazel to join us, watching as she grabs the keys before Dad can, a single slice of toast snatched from the table then tossed, uneaten, onto the backseat of the car.

I lean into the headrest, watching the other kids in our neighborhood amble toward revving engines; then I let my eyes close as we make the ten-minute drive to school.

I wake with a start as Hazel nudges me, Montgomery-Oakes High stretched out in front of us.

"Thanks," I say, and she nods, her fingers dancing quickly across her phone.

The dull ache of a broken sleep smothers my brain as I walk into the main building. It's not until I notice the kid next to me, staring, that I realize I'm humming the chant from my nightmare.

"The Hiding Boy, right?" the guy says. "That's some creepy shit."

"I guess."

He grins and nods, like we're sharing a joke. But he's the only one who thinks this is funny.

"Do you believe it?"

I stare at him until doubt clouds his face. Then I feel the horrible creep of terror that hung over Murder Road like a force field and mumble, "Yes."

My new school's least subtle bully scans the corridors for teachers and victims with equal vigor, ready with a kiss-ass smile or a slap to the side of the head, depending on which he finds first.

He laughs to himself because he has no friends to share the "joke."

This boy with hair like wet worms walks through a crowd that parts not because anyone is scared, but because they refuse to share his space.

He looks for people on the periphery, people like me. We exchange a look, my fists tightening the way Rowan taught me—thumbs on the outside, muscles loose—and then he sees someone smaller and shoves them against a locker.

The boom is lost in our classmates' cackles, the kid frozen, the bully already strolling away.

Every school has these small moments of extreme violence. Before we started moving houses, I didn't notice them. But now, always the outsider, I can easily see who enjoys their education and who doesn't.

Identifying the assholes is the first trick. That way you stay out of their firing line.

"New kid," someone says behind me, and when I turn, I see a smile and nothing else.

The rest comes into focus slowly: her brown skin, her sharp eyes, a single blue streak in her straight black hair, and the two boys standing awkwardly behind her.

I step back but there's nowhere to turn. I can't escape this latest friend attempt without coming off like a dickhead. So be it.

"I'm Max," she says.

One of the boys clears his throat and she grins. "You can introduce yourselves."

Looking back at me, Max whispers, "I like your T-shirt."

Mom told me not to wear it. She said it would give the wrong impression, but that's what I wanted.

No one talks to the boy with a top that reads WHAT'S YOUR FAVORITE SCARY MOVIE? Most people don't get the reference.

But Max does. When I look closer, I see that her jacket is covered in buttons filled with quotes. DO YOU WANT TO PLAY A GAME? IN SPACE, NO ONE CAN HEAR YOU SCREAM. I FEEL THE NEED, THE NEED TO READ.

I shake my head, breaking apart the unhelpful thoughts forming as I try not to stare at her.

"We've seen you around," Max says. "You don't like other people much, do you?"

It's not that simple.

A playful grin duets with her eyes as she whispers, "We don't like other people much either."

"I'm sorry. I don't . . ."

I've said it before—told someone to their face that I don't need a friend. But this feels different.

No one's ever looked at me the way Max is.

"That's okay," she says. "No pressure. If you change your mind, we'd happily welcome you into our little clique."

One of the boys behind her scowls at me, while the other kicks the floor.

"Whatever you decide," Max says, "stay away from Jayden."

She nods at the guy who has just pushed another kid into the wall and I wonder how long she's been watching me.

"If you make friends with the bully, you're safe, right?"

She laughs, turns to her friends, then says, "You're judged by the company you keep."

My skin prickles as I realize I've let this go on too long. In school terms, she's already an acquaintance.

"I'm honored but . . . no, thank you."

Max tilts her head and sighs. "Your loss."

As I watch them leave, the corridor expands somehow, until the crowd is pushed to its outer edge and I feel almost alone.

She says something and one of the boys throws his head back and laughs; then he high-fives a man-mountain in a letter jacket and the whole school snaps back.

I need to be more careful.

And yet, something hums at the back of my brain—a warmth that fills my chest until I'm smiling.

"Shit," I say to myself, because I already want to see her again.

Thoughts are baggage, feelings are baggage, friends are baggage, and when you are running from an urban legend, it's best to travel light.

8

That evening, I listen to Hazel talking on her phone, pressing my ear against the wall when her voice softens.

She hid that she was in love for as long as she could and I don't blame her. It must have been nice, to feel light when our house felt so heavy.

I never asked how she met him. I *should* have, but it's too late to be interested now. Asking questions about the boy she calls every night would be like picking a scab that covers her heart.

Instead, I think about Max—how her face slips into the patterns behind my eyes; how, if I concentrate, I can hear snippets of her weirdly familiar voice.

The plan was to be invisible. But she saw me regardless.

There's a knock on my door and I quickly step away from the wall.

Dad's eyebrows knot as he peers at me; then he smiles and drops a pizza box on my bed.

"One more day," he mutters, turning to leave before I clear my throat and say, "Do you really think it will be different this time?"

He looks back, his mouth hanging open as his mind catches up.

"I do," he says. "Because if I don't . . ."

His lips tremble and I wonder what it would be like to hug him. Would he pull me closer or step back in surprise?

Mom told me once that she'd always want to hold my hand, even when I was "too old for that." So, sometimes, if no one else was around, I'd slide my fingers between hers and watch her secret smile.

When we were kids, she would cuddle us in bed; first Rowan, then me, then Hazel—the length of those hugs measured by our sister as she counted from one to fifty then sang, "*My turn!*"

Hazel's hugs never got a countdown, but we didn't complain.

Dad doesn't do physical contact. I think it scares him, and now that fear feels hereditary.

Instead, he does gestures, like leaving steaming take-out boxes on his children's beds because Mom isn't ready to cook a "real" dinner yet.

"I hope you're right," I say, grabbing a slice then pushing the rest toward him.

He nods and sits next to me, and we pretend not to hear Hazel's voice get louder before she ends the call.

Eventually, her sobs fade away; her voice is calm as she calls him again.

She talks to her boyfriend with such warmth, and I think of the times she spoke to us like that. Now, the few words she utters are cold, and her silences are even colder.

The front door slams, and I hear Rowan say something to Mom before he bounds upstairs, stopping when he clocks Dad.

"Mom wants to know where you are," he says, sitting on my desk chair and opening the box that's all for him.

Our father's shoulders sag as he stands, and then Rowan tilts his ear toward Hazel's voice.

He can't hear her from his room. Mine is in the middle, which means I get the emotional breakdowns on one side and Rowan's late-night workouts on the other.

"How do you cope with that?" he asks, the cracks in his bravado running deeper than he thinks.

"There are worse things," I say.

And better things, like blocking out all the hidden moments that happen in the rooms around me with thoughts about a girl I've only just met.

The next morning, I scan the crowd for her face but don't find it until third period.

Max stands by her locker, talking to the same boys she was with yesterday. She looks over and, although there's a mass of people between us, heat fills my cheeks as I turn away.

I see her again at lunch, walking quickly into a cafeteria that swallows her whole. She isn't at any of the tables, and I buy my food then head for a new spot behind the bleachers.

A boy dressed all in black sits at the opposite end, a sketch pad spread across his legs and a look of angry focus on his pale face. If this is *his* space, I'm sorry. But I'm running out of places to feel alone.

I don't see Max again until the next day, earlier this time, striding through the school gates then stopping to chat with the teacher on duty.

They look happy to see each other and I think of my old school, where the staff knew me, where I was defined by my history and my achievements, where I belonged.

Belleview Academy was my safe space, with friends who understood what it was like to live in the shadow of a horror story. I was never cool, but I was always happy, and that felt more important.

If things had been different, I'd still be there. But I've attended and left three more schools since then.

Montgomery-Oakes High is the farthest we've been from "home." With each new town, I lose myself a little more—the pieces that want to be liked or loved, that want to impress or to learn.

I thought that here I'd be nameless: that kid no one remembers on the edge of someone else's yearbook photos. But then *she* spoke to me.

Max talks just as excitedly to the librarian, dropping off two books and collecting three more. Then she stiffens as two girls meet her in the corridor—their hair as straight as the necks they arch as they pass.

Max's lips purse and I wonder what that's about. She obviously isn't nice to everyone and I feel relieved. If she's one of those uber-friendly weirdos picking up strays, I should run. But if she selects her friends as carefully as I used to . . .

"What are you doing?"

One of the boys she's nearly always with stands directly behind me and I step away, my skin growing sticky as I feel her approaching.

"Hey," Max says. "You talking to us now?"

The boy's stare narrows and she laughs.

"Ignore him. He's protective, is all. So . . . you want to be friends?"

No . . . and yes.

I could leave again. Or I could stay, for the briefest while, and see what happens.

"Okay," Max says. "This is the obligatory intro sequence. You know. The one where I point out all the social cliques while they do something cliché to match their title. Are you ready?"

When I don't reply, she snorts and says, "Second thoughts, let's scrap that. We're the only group you need to know. Me and the silent twosome."

Both boys are here now, but only one looks me in the eye.

They lift one hand each in unison and I do the same. Then Max shakes her head and says, "Do you want to hang out or are you happy going solo? We won't be offended. You just . . . seem like a good fit."

Something about the three of them feels weirdly safe . . . or safely weird.

"Sure," I say.

Max grins. "Awesome."

The boys step forward then, the white kid with thick orange hair clearing his throat for a second time before he says, "I'm Seb. It's nice to meet you."

He turns to his friend—a black boy with a baseball cap pulled toward his furrowed brow—who straightens his glasses, sniffs, then says, "Tyler."

"They warm up," Max says, but Tyler looks me up and down when he thinks I'm distracted, searching for red flags. I don't blame him. I've done the same with them.

"Where are you from?" Max asks.

"I guess, now, I'm from here." That's my standard response.

"Well, *here* is lucky to have you," Max replies. "Let's go. Next period is in five, four, three, two . . ."

She points at the ceiling just as the bell goes, then looks at my schedule and says, "English with Ms. Hewitt. Enjoy. We meet at the Hell Hole for lunch."

"Where's that?"

"You'll see. It was nice to meet you, new kid. I think you'll fit in just fine."

Max strides away, Seb and Tyler hurrying to catch up, before all of them are lost in the crowd.

Three days into my time at Montgomery-Oakes High School—despite my best intentions—I think I'm part of a quartet.

The weirdest thing—I kind of like it.

10

The lunchroom is packed when I arrive: the sound of trays hitting tables, jokers hitting punch lines, gossip hitting greedy ears.

To some people, I guess this could be a "hell hole," but I can't see Max or the boys anywhere.

For a few stupid seconds, I imagine the three of them on a table of their own, eagerly waving me over. But every single option is full to bursting.

Montgomery-Oakes doesn't seem to have an outcasts section, or one for the new kids who never lost that label.

No one pays me any attention as I get my food, then carefully tread between the outstretched legs and forgotten backpacks.

I walk from one end of the room to the other, thinking back to the moment Max was swallowed by this place. And that's when I see it.

The space in the corner narrows into an unlit hallway, the sounds behind me muffled as I step farther inside.

For a few moments, there's nothing; just a strange silence that doesn't belong here and yet, somehow, fits perfectly. Because that's what schools are, right? They are simultaneously alive and dead—full of the promise of never-ending tomorrows and forgotten yesterdays.

My heart quickens as I anticipate walking headfirst into a teacher. Whatever this place is, it's not where you're supposed to have your lunch. Then noises drift through the air, the unmistakable sound of Max's voice and the new sound of Seb and Tyler talking back.

". . . and you just draw the face and wait."

"Wait for what?"

"The monster, obviously. Or the psychopath. Or whatever it is that's out there."

The voice in my head tells me to turn around. I can eat somewhere else. I can still be the loner. But I'm not sure I want that anymore.

"Hey," I say. "The Hell Hole, I presume?"

"New kid," Max says, and I say, "It's Nate, actually."

"Okay, then, Nate Actually. Join us. Tyler was telling a story."

The boy adjusts his glasses and bristles slightly. "Are you sure about this?"

"Yes," Max replies. "It's about time we had some new blood. I'm getting bored of you two. Joke, obviously. But look at him. He's perfect for this."

"Perfect for what?" I ask. "Is this a cult thing? Am I your sacrifice?"

I'm kidding, but no one laughs.

Max points at the upturned crate next to her and says, "Sit."

"What is this place?"

"It used to be a storage space for all the janitor's equipment. But, as you've probably noticed, Montgomery-Oakes High is shiny and new these days. A lot of the old is gone but this is . . . a bit of history, I suppose. It's preferable to eating out there."

Max gestures down the corridor that seems even longer from this end.

"Why do you call it the Hell Hole?"

"Sticking with the theme. We're a club. The Hell Chasers. Have you heard of us?"

Before I can answer, Tyler chuckles and Max grins.

"Of course you haven't," she says. "But we like it that way."

"You're a secret society?"

"We have a shared passion for urban legends."

You're kidding me.

I back into the corridor as Seb mutters, "Chicken."

Max glares at him but he's right. I *am* a chicken, if that means being smart. I come from a place where the rules don't apply. The rules that say that it's not real, that spooky stories can't harm you.

On the news, when tragedy happens and the neighbors say, "You wouldn't expect that to happen here"? That's not how Murder Road works.

That place is stained by nearly a century of death; so much that the stain is all you can see. If Seb is wondering why I don't want to join a club called the Hell Chasers, he should check my old area code.

"I should probably get back," I say.

"Back to what?" Max replies.

We stare at each other until my cheeks burn. Then she says, "Is that what you want? To be on your own? Because, from where I'm sitting, it doesn't look like much fun."

It's not. But it's been a long time since fun was on my to-do list.

Being alone *was* what I wanted, or what I was *told* to want. It's easier that way. But that was before I met her.

"I'm sorry I called you a chicken," Seb says. "There's nothing sinister about what we do. We're the good guys."

"People," Max replies. "We're the good *people*. So, are you in?"

"What do you do, exactly?"

She stares at Tyler until he coughs and says, "Do you know the story of the Face in the Glass?"

The only "urban legend" I'm interested in is real. We lived it or, more specifically, we lived *next* to it.

I can't say that now, so I shake my head and Tyler grumbles. "If you want to join us, you need to know your stuff."

He has no idea, but I let him think he does. Ignorance isn't just bliss; sometimes it can save your life.

Max and Tyler share a look like the ones Mom uses when she's pissed with us in public—a silent shout—and then he sighs and says, "Okay. I'll start over for the latecomers."

A loud scrape fills the space as Tyler shuffles his crate forward, its echo settling in my ears along with the low rumble of machinery hidden even deeper in the school's belly.

"This one must be done in a secluded area, but you also need a road, so somewhere near the woods is ideal. It won't work if it's easy to save you. It also needs to be dark and cold. And there must be at least eleven minutes of complete silence before you draw the face."

Max is studying me, searching for a reaction. Do they think I'm scared? Do they think this is the worst life gets—lunch-break ghost stories and intense looks?

"Once those eleven minutes have passed, you breathe on every window, then trace the shape of a face with your finger—a circle, two eyes, one mouth. There have to be six faces in total—one on each side window, one on the back, and one on the windshield. But the circles must be incomplete. There has to be a gap. That's how it comes in."

"How what comes in?" Max asks.

I've never heard something more scripted.

"No one knows exactly what it is," Tyler replies. "It could be human. It could be a monster. I personally think it's a spirit . . . and that gap you leave allows it to break into our realm. Once all six faces are drawn, everyone in the car looks out of their window and says, 'I see the Face in the Glass.'

"That's when you'll see the shape in the darkness. It will bang on the car, begging to be let in. It will use different voices. It will try everything it can to get to you. That's why I'm saying this bit last—so you remember.

"If you *do* ever try this, make sure you lock the car."

"So," Max says to me, "are you in?"

"In what exactly? A storytelling club?"

It's not supposed to sound snarky, but that's exactly what happens, and I think I've lost them already—this strange collection of people who, for some reason, want to be my friends.

Max grins as she says, "The stories aren't the fun part. What are you doing on Friday night?"

"Why?"

"Because that's when we're drawing the Face in the Glass. We're going to see if it's real."

11

The three of them pile the crates in one corner, collect the trash from their lunch, then head back down the darkened corridor.

I close my eyes and breathe as slowly as I can, stepping back in my mind, trying to meditate the way Hazel does. That's how my sister deals with our life—by taking temporary trips away from it.

When *I* try, the tranquility teases me, sitting just out of reach, and then the screams surge through my head, ripping my eyelids open, reminding me that, for some, there's not even a brief escape.

Rowan handles it through violence. Wherever we go, the first thing he does is join the closest karate or judo or boxing club.

His teachers think he's a natural. They don't know that with every punch, every kick, every guttural yell, he's taking aim at someone . . . something.

"You coming?" Max's voice echoes in the dark, shaking me out of my daydream and forcing me into a decision.

They are standing at the mouth of the Hell Hole, our classmates illuminated by the overhead striplights, their words one long hum.

"Where are you doing it?" I ask, and Max says, "We can pick you up. We don't want you getting lost."

"No. I'm happy to meet. Give me directions."

"Stranger danger," she replies. "I respect that. We could be psychos for all you know. But then, it would probably be easier to get away with it if we didn't drive over and say hi to the family. Whatever you prefer."

"I'll walk."

When you walk, it's easier to run.

"Pass me your phone," Max says, quickly sending herself a message then handing it back. "I'll give you all the info. But remember, it must be in the middle of nowhere. That's not the kind of place people walk to."

"I'll be fine."

As the bell goes for next period, Seb stares at me, his eyes scarily serious, and says, "We choose who joins, so don't bring a friend. And don't tell anyone what we're doing."

"I don't have any friends," I reply. Except, I guess, the three people standing in front of me.

"Neither do we," Tyler replies.

They don't feel quite real. It's as if they are playing characters and they're testing me. Should I be laughing at them? Do I play along? Or should I just wait for the act to slip?

"Has anyone ever said no?" I ask.

"Just once," Max replies. "But they don't go here anymore."

12

Mom has filled the house with our stuff but it will never feel like home.

The same things come out every time. The crystal cube with Hazel, Rowan, and me inside—our 3D baby faces captured forever. Our parents' wedding photo—when Dad had hair and Mom looked like a movie star. The painting our grandma did, of the scene from her nursing-home window—the golden beach and the vast sea beyond it full of people enjoying what she no longer could.

These are the things our mom treasures most. They are, to her, what makes a home.

It takes a little longer each time—for Mom to find the strength to build one. But she's good at it, using our distant past to cover the cracks in our present.

My bedroom walls are still blank and my mind is racing with all the things I could have done. I could have said no. I could have been a prick, because no one wants one of those in their secret club. I could have hit Seb when he called me a chicken, ending our friendship before it had even begun. But Max . . .

There's a glimmer behind her words; there are unspoken certainties in the safe spaces between them. No one's ever looked at me like that. Most don't look at me at all.

I've felt scared, lost, hopeless, for so long. But with her, this girl who is not quite a stranger, those things disappear.

So, I said yes, and I don't completely regret it. Not until Rowan strolls in and says, "Rating from one to ten. Go."

"Four," I reply, because it's always four.

The houses our parents find are slightly below average. They are damaged in superficial ways. They are just in our budget. When you move as often as us, there isn't time for your home to grow in value.

I don't know how much money they've lost, in lawyers' fees and moving trucks and the rest. But I do know Dad's work hours have grown to match his worry lines, while Mom wastes less and less time before finding a job in every new town we discover.

"How was school?" Rowan asks.

"It was fine."

"You made any friends yet?"

I shake my head, because that's the answer my brother expects.

"Give it time," he says, staring at my bare walls. "You need to decorate, Nate. This place is deeply depressing."

"What's the point?"

"The point is, if you make your living space nice, you *feel* nice."

"How's that working for you?"

"I'm getting there," he mumbles.

He's nineteen. Three years older than me. And all he's done since we arrived is join a gym and arrange his vinyl.

Like always, it's not sorted by artist. It's by mood.

"I think it's a two," Rowan says.

He doesn't justify that score with an explanation. Instead, he slumps on my bed and closes his eyes.

"Was it better before?" I ask. "When you could go to school?"

When he doesn't answer, I picture my brother at Belleview Academy, then the three schools we went to after that. Every time, he'd reinvent himself—the confident kid, the quiet kid, the teachers' pet, the teachers' pest.

I'm not sure he had a favorite role. I think he loved the opportunity to be a little bit of everyone, while Hazel and I have always stuck to what we know.

On cue, our sister walks to my door then quickly away.

"What's up, sis?" Rowan says, the scaffolding of our brother's fake confidence crumbling on the last word.

She stops for a moment on the landing, then goes back to her room and slams the door.

Rowan counts down from five to one, then shakes his head as our sister's faux-cheery voice hums through the cracked plaster-board.

"She needs to stop calling him," he says. "It's not doing her any good."

"She wants to hear his voice."

"But it's not just that, is it. She wants to go back and live her happy-ever-after. She's in denial."

Max's face fills my vision as I say, "Have you ever liked some-one? Like, *really* liked them?"

Rowan's thick eyebrows scrunch as he says, "Of course not."

The thought of our brother in love forces me to stifle a laugh and I wish we could make fun of each other without the threat of something bigger.

We used to. But, these days, Rowan is better in rings or on mats, with referees and rules.

If we fight, only one of us will get hurt.

Hazel's door opens again and she hurries downstairs. She's a senior now and I make a promise to look out for her tomorrow.

Rowan has these rules, unwritten but never forgotten, and one of them is to keep away from each other at school. But he's not there anymore, so I guess, if we wanted to be the siblings who talk in the corridors, we could be.

I picture Hazel at our last school, her sentences coming out like songs, her smiles genuine, her friends hurrying around her like superfans.

I was jealous of her, and a little bit angry, but, mostly, I was proud. She had finally found a place where she could be herself and maybe be happy again.

Our brother lets out a deep breath, then stands and says, "Let's get this over with."

I follow him downstairs, where Dad is reading at the table and Mom is laying the final few plates.

"Right on time," she says. "Dig in."

Rowan leans over us, piling his dish high, while Hazel takes small amounts only from the food she can reach.

"It looks great," Dad says, kissing Mom's cheek then resting his hand on her back. And it does.

For plenty of people, this would be perfect. But, for me, every bite comes with a side of fear.

We've done this first-proper-meal-in-a-new-home thing so many times and I'm sick of pretending.

"Don't get comfortable." That's another one of Rowan's rules. "We won't be here for long."

So that's what Hazel did, until the one time she didn't. And I wonder, as I think of Max and Tyler and Seb but mostly Max, if this is the time that I don't listen to our brother either.

When we're nearly finished, Dad watches Hazel pushing the food around her plate, waiting the required amount of time, then a bit longer, before taking Mom's hand and saying, "That was delicious."

She smiles like a cashier with a broken computer and mumbles, "Thank you."

"Yes," Rowan says. "Well worth the wait."

Dad's arms tense and I can see Mom sending him a message through her fingers, tapping on his like she knows Morse code.

Hazel's fork clanks against her plate and our brother smiles at her and says, "I'll have that if you don't want it."

It's my sister's turn to tense, her glare burning a hole in the table as she takes two deep breaths in . . . then out.

She nudges the plate away and he finishes what's left in three mouthfuls.

"Right," Dad says. "We'll clean up."

Mom and Hazel stare at each other as Rowan and I help with the plates. Then I head upstairs without dessert and my sister follows.

"I'm sorry that he's a dick," I say.

A faint smile flickers across Hazel's lips as she mutters, "We all have our ways of coping."

These moments, when she chooses to talk to me, are so rare that I shouldn't risk spoiling them. But they remind me of a better time, one I desperately want to get back to. We were good—the three of us. We looked out for one another. We had fun.

Now I snatch at the tiniest thread of my sister's voice and forget what happens when it unravels.

I watch her for a few seconds, then ask, "Are *your* ways still working?"

"Some of them." Tears form in Hazel's eyes as she shakes her head.

My arm twitches as I think about comforting her, but it won't help.

I could tell her about Max, because I think she'd understand. Yet she'd also say all the things I don't want to hear; about what happens when your perfect new life, which you've built in a heartbeat, crumbles in the blink of an eye.

Hazel checks her phone, then slides it back in her pocket.

"It's okay," I tell her. "You can call him if you want."

She nods and leaves without another word. Whatever she has left, she's saving for him.

I listen for a while, then drift into a daydream that eventually morphs into sleep, images of Max blunting the claws of nightmares that, tonight at least, keep their distance.

When he was twelve, his sleep became a trap.

On the worst nights, something vast pressed against him as he whimpered in the darkness; an unbearable weight crushing his chest.

He knew, if he could call for help, that it would leave him. But all his words were broken, coming out in garbled groans that made the shape push even harder.

His limbs tensed as he fought back, every muscle in his body trying to shatter the sleep enveloping him like plastic wrap.

The groans stirred and swirled, the sound becoming a tornado that spun faster and faster until, finally, it burst out in a scream.

Sometimes, his parents were there when he awoke, stroking his wet forehead, soothing him with their whispers.

Sometimes, he was alone in the dark, relief followed by dread as he realized he wasn't awake at all.

He had to scream even harder to break out of those—so loud that he was sure his throat would bleed and his voice would be slashed into tiny pieces.

His biggest fear, even in the moments of relief when he finally fought himself awake, was that, one day, he would never escape. That he would be lost in a never-ending cycle of terror and fake solace, like a kidnap victim running, running, running, before being dragged back to hell.

13

On Friday evening, I quickly eat dinner, forcing a few mouthfuls of Mom's lasagna past the anxiety lodged in my throat. Then I say, "I'm going out. I won't be long."

Mom squints as she asks, "Where, exactly?"

"Nowhere . . . exactly. Just . . . wherever I end up. Is that okay?"

She shakes her head as Dad pats me on the shoulder and says, "You *should* explore, Nate. It will be nice to know what this place has to offer."

Most people know those things *before* they move to a new town.

Mom glances at the dimming light outside. "Don't be late. And next time, more notice would be nice."

"More notice to go for a walk?"

Her face hardens as she says, "Yes."

"Sure." I kiss her cheek to appease her, then step into the brisk evening air.

She's fine to let Rowan go to his boxing club tonight and every night, because she thinks he can take care of himself.

But I know how to look after myself too. That's why I'm not actually meeting Max, Seb, and Tyler.

I check Max's directions on my phone, then walk slowly past our neighbors' houses.

People around here don't pull their curtains when the sun goes down—not right away, at least. They're not afraid of being seen, because they don't think anyone's watching.

When we first moved in, I checked every window in our house, seeing what nighttime looks like in our latest new beginning. And this one is particularly quiet. There's no one hanging out on the corners; there are no joggers or dog walkers or late-night deliveries.

That's why it's only me walking to the end of the road and taking a left, down the hill toward the local store, then across the park where one rusty swing creaks in the wind.

I join another street, the houses set back from the road and their front gardens screaming *Look at me!*

This must be the nice part of town, and I wonder why. Is that a reaction to something, too? The same way the streets around Murder Road held a constant, unspoken beauty pageant?

The curtains of these houses *are* closed, the cars in the driveways freshly washed. But it isn't a big street. It ends as quickly as it begins, spitting me into the shadow of another building, a broken clock set in a brickwork arch and large windows made up of tiny frosted squares.

I walk over to the door and check the bulletin board, the fading announcements of years-old events held captive behind its glass.

This is a school no one goes to anymore. An elementary by the size of it—the opposite to Montgomery-Oakes High's space-station shine.

I walk for a few more minutes, until the houses disappear and fields stretch out on either side of a narrow lane. Then I keep walking until I see it—the middle of nowhere.

A dirt road snakes off to the left, hardened tire tracks crumbling underfoot. I listen for the sound of engines; then, when I'm sure no one's coming, I turn on my phone light, tread quickly through the patterns, and step away from the clearing.

As I back into the undergrowth, branches scratch my neck and dry leaves tickle my ankles.

When I'm settled, I check my cell. I'm thirteen minutes early.

Eventually, a car creeps up the road, its headlights painting a yellow fuzz over the black. Then the lights vanish and their glow slowly fades from my vision.

The passenger window opens and Seb peers out. "Nate?" he hisses. "Are you there?"

My breath sneaks out in wisps that merge with the gloom. That's the only clue that I'm here, but no one is looking that closely.

The driver's door opens and Max steps out. "Nate? We're ready if you are."

She tilts her head toward the star-speckled sky, as if she's sniffing me out. Then she shakes her head and says, "He choked."

"Maybe he's late," Tyler says, joining her in the clearing.

"I don't think so. If he was coming, he'd be here already."

She knows me. Or at least, she knows *some* of me. Maybe I *am* that easy to read, because I've never been late for anything.

I'm here for me, not for them. I was tricked into saying yes in the Hell Hole. If Tyler hadn't caught me that day, I'd still be watching Max from a distance, so I've come to see if I can trust my new "friends." And what better way to do that than to watch them in the dark?

"Okay," Seb says. "Let's get started."

Tyler and Max get back in the car and close their doors. Then nothing happens for a long time. Eleven minutes, to be exact.

That's how long they said it needed to be completely silent—before they draw the faces.

On cue, I watch breath-clouds fill the windows, then lines quickly drawn—circles not quite complete, two eyes, one mouth.

I imagine them whispering the words they said in the Hell Hole—*I see the Face in the Glass*—and then a pair of real eyes look at me through the window and it feels like Max is staring into my soul.

My back stiffens and my legs almost give way but I steady myself. It's not me she's looking for. It's whatever she thinks will come when you do this stupid ritual.

Other people might be nervous that it's true. They might be more worried about what's behind them than what they can see. But there's no monster, no man, no myth lurking in the shadows at my back. There's nothing and no one ready to tap on Max's windshield and beg to be let in.

There's just me, quickly realizing that their invitation *was* harmless. They really *do* want me to join their urban-legend-worshipping club. They just want another person's breath for their windows, another finger to draw the faces a bit quicker, another whisper for their words.

Max's face pulls back from the glass and I wonder what they are saying. Are they disappointed? Or relieved?

How many times have they done this? Trying different stories they've heard, attempting to find some truth in the biggest lies?

One of the back doors opens and Tyler steps out just as Max yells, "What are you doing?"

"It didn't work!" he shouts back. "It never works."

While his first sentence soared toward the trees, his second falls at his feet. That's where he looks as Seb tentatively steps out, eyes darting and fingers twitching.

"It could still happen," he says. "We should get back in and lock the doors . . . just in case."

"Come on then!" Tyler yells. "If you're out there, what are you waiting for?"

Goose bumps surge over my skin as I wait for him to call my name. How does he know I'm here? But it's not me he's looking for.

"We drew your face! We called your name!"

Max's door opens and she strides over to Tyler, clamping her hand over his mouth.

She whispers something and Tyler stiffens. Then the three of them edge back to the car, their doors slowly clicking shut, and I hear it.

Ready or not. Whatever you do.

I push my palms against my skull, softly pleading for the song to fade. And it does, instantly—the forest wiped clean of the words like a shaken Etch A Sketch.

Did Max hear it, too? Is that why they retreated? Or are they still more fearful of a make-believe man than a bona fide nightmare?

I'm suddenly aware of the woods encasing us, the countless spaces for bad things to hide. But the only sounds now are the thick branches creaking in the wind and the hoot of the owls whose eyes glisten in the moonlight.

The doors open again and all three of them clamber out.

"I'm sorry," Max says, and Tyler shrugs.

"No, you're not."

"I said I am, so . . ."

"You're the pessimist. I'm the optimist. Don't go changing now."

Tyler holds the back of his head in his hands and slowly paces the clearing. Then he runs between the trees, disappearing for a few seconds each time, before bounding out somewhere totally different and making his friends jump.

"Quit it," Seb says, although, in the moments when Tyler vanishes, his eyes search the shadows for every possible exit.

"The Face in the Glass is pissed now," Tyler mutters from the gloom, and I creep back, worried he's going to walk right into me.

He's masking his disappointment by playing the fool. I can see that, even from here. But I can't help smiling as Tyler grabs Seb from behind, then darts over to Max and says, "Too bad Nate couldn't come."

"I know what you're thinking," she replies.

"I told you so?"

"Why do you still have to say it?"

"Because I like being right," Tyler yells, as he jumps on a felled tree and scrambles from one end to the other. "Come on, Seb. Climb with me."

His friend reluctantly steps forward, then clambers awkwardly up and shimmies over to Tyler.

"It's better just the three of us, anyway," Tyler says.

I like the look on Max's face—the one that says he's wrong. Maybe I'll never actually be friends with these people, but it's nice knowing I could be.

That may be enough. If I let it. I could know that good, albeit slightly odd, teenagers would be happy to hang out with me.

Some people don't even get that.

I can't leave my hiding place now. The first thing they will do is shit themselves and the second thing they'll do is hate me, because how do I explain that I was watching them?

How do I say I wanted to see behind the act?

The song stirs again and I clench my fists until it fades. Then I watch Max throw her head back and laugh, so loud and so long that nothing else matters.

What are the chances that I would walk headfirst into a group obsessed with urban legends? Is this one last sick joke from the universe? And what if, despite everything, I try to let them in?

14

I could see part of Murder Road from my old bedroom window, and for a long time, that was as close as I got.

Sometimes kids on our street would stand on the crossroads and dare one another to place a foot onto Cherry Tree Lane. But mostly we watched the people going in and out of their houses, their cars edging past us as we gawked, and wondered why they didn't look permanently terrified.

"People pretend all sorts of things," Rowan told me once. "Those are pretending to be happy."

Our street was called Pennyforth Avenue. No nasty nickname. No sordid history. Just a boring road in the shadow of a cursed one. But that song. It haunted me then and it haunts me now.

Kids chanted it while they skipped on the chalk-dusted sidewalks. It replaced the counting of hide-and-seek. It slipped into the wandering minds of strangers as they hummed.

If there was ever a breeze in Belleview, the Hiding Boy's song would drift along on it. And now, somehow, it had found me in the woods as I watched Max.

"Where have you been?" Mom asks as I open the front door.

"The middle of nowhere."

She leans in until her breath burns my neck. "Don't be snarky with me."

She steps back as the top stair creaks and Dad comes down in his bathrobe.

"Hey. See anything interesting?"

"No."

He walks straight past us and I watch the fridge light wash over him in the darkened kitchen.

He takes a handful of something back to their bedroom, Mom keeping her eyes down until he's gone.

"Be careful," she whispers. "Until we get our bearings . . . you have no idea what's out there."

I nod, picturing Max laughing at Tyler's jokes, and Seb's face right before his friend jumped out at him.

At first glance, there's *nothing* out there. Nothing harmful, anyway. Just someone who I'm desperate to find out all I can about, despite everything inside me screaming no.

15

When I open my locker on Monday morning, a sheet of paper flutters out to fall at my feet.

Faceup, in red writing, it says: *You can't run forever!*

I stamp my sneaker over it, quickly checking whether anyone else has noticed. But my classmates are caught up in their own mundane moments. Even if they weren't, I'm the last person they pay attention to.

Pretending to tie my lace, I snatch it from the immaculate tiled floor. Montgomery-Oakes High doesn't do litter, so if I let it, this would stand out like a corpse in a kindergarten classroom.

I scrunch my eyes closed, then slowly prize them open, but it's still there—the four words that prove someone knows exactly what is coming for us.

Anxiety twists my stomach like fists wringing out a washcloth; then I see her, and it's almost enough to force my terror aside.

Max marches toward me from the opposite end of the corridor and I swear I can feel the ground move.

"Where were you?" she asks, her eyebrows creased and her hands fidgeting in her pockets.

"What?"

"Friday night. You stood us up."

I push the note to the back of my locker and slam the door.

The sound makes Max step back, while the kids closest to us glance over then turn away.

I look for a guilty face in the crowd, someone lurking in plain sight. If I know anything about people who want to get a scare out of you, they love to watch.

"Is everything all right?" Max asks.

Far from it.

"Sure. Did it work? The Face in the Glass?"

She chews her bottom lip, then shakes her head. "Tyler isn't happy."

"What about you?"

"For me, it's more about *dis*proving. The world is too gullible, if you ask me. Tyler's convinced that, one day, we'll open the Hellmouth or something."

"And that's a good thing?"

Max grins. "That depends how quickly we close it."

I edge away from my locker, distancing myself from the warning inside.

Without her, that's all I have here—anonymous messages, expanding fears, and tiny spaces in classrooms and crowds that I slip in and out of just to get through the day.

"Did you leave a note for me?"

"Pardon?"

"A note," I repeat. "In my locker."

I search Max's narrowing eyes for guilt, but all I see is confusion.

"I don't understand," she says. "Did you get something? Was it a love letter?"

She smirks, her lips folding together when she notices the blush creeping up my neck.

"Forget about it," I mumble. "It was nothing."

"I didn't mean to embarrass you."

"I said, it's fine."

Sympathy washes over Max's face, but I wish it wouldn't. That's worse than the other thing, because I don't want her to feel sorry for me. Girls don't feel sorry for the boys they like. And those boys don't burn from the inside out at the slightest mention of love.

"I should go," I say. "I'm sorry for standing you up."

"Why did you?"

For a split second I want to tell her I was there, but I know how that would sound.

Better to walk away with that question unanswered than to always be remembered as a weirdo.

"Good luck opening the Hellmouth . . . or *not* opening it."

Max nods, like she knows that's the best she's going to get.

When she leaves, I quickly open my locker and stuff the note in my bag. Then I go to the bathroom, lock myself in the farthest stall, and stare at the words.

You can't run forever!

A whistle echoes off the tiled walls and I hold my breath. I should be in class now, but I'm not ready for that yet. I need to study the writing a little more. I need to search my memory for any suspicious faces in a sea of strangers.

I wait for the flush of a toilet or the splash of a tap. But there's nothing except the low groan of a few stragglers followed by the distant yell of an impatient teacher.

When I am sure I'm alone, I turn the note over. There are no imprints of other things, no finger marks, nothing except a clean white sheet on one side and four neat words on the other.

"I can," I whisper, and the whistle comes again.

I snatch my words back, pressing the paper against my chest.

Who is in here with me? Someone else ditching class? Or something worse?

You don't call out. You never ask, "Who's there?" You stay silent and still . . . for as long as it takes.

Eventually, the assholes who lurk in high school restrooms to torment the kid who thinks this is a safe space get bored of playing. Eventually.

The whistle is soft now, just someone blowing out air, and then it grows louder until it fills the room—the tune that is stitched into my soul.

I stand and slowly open the door, because someone is screwing with me.

The words of the song fill my head as the whistle reverberates around the room.

Ready or not. Whatever you do.

As I step out, the sound stops.

I stare at my reflection in the wall-length mirror but there's no one else here.

One by one, I push the cubicle doors open, my heart pounding as I count them down in my head.

Five—empty. Four—the same. Three. Two.

I stare at the final door, my ears ringing in the suffocating silence. Then I reach out and softly push.

It creaks open to reveal an empty stall. Except it's not quite empty. On the closed toilet seat, there's another piece of paper, which blurs in my trembling hand.

He's coming for you!

16

That evening, I eat dinner in silence, ignoring Dad's attempts at small talk and Rowan's messed-up face.

Our brother's left eye is brown and puffy, his bottom lip swollen, a deep scratch running from his ear to somewhere beneath his T-shirt.

I'm used to him with bruises, but this looks different. For once, I don't think he won.

Dad catches my eye, then looks at Mom and says, "Tell them."

"Tell us what?" Rowan asks.

"I got a job," our mother tells the kitchen floor, before our father adds, "In record time."

"That's awesome," I say. "What is it?"

"I'm a barista now."

Rowan's eyes leave his plate just long enough for him to ask, "Do we get freebies?"

"I don't know yet. Maybe."

"But it gets you out of the house, right?" Dad says.

Mom flinches as he touches her arm; then she takes her plate to the sink even though the rest of us are still eating.

Dad has worked the same job for as long as I can remember. He designs websites and works from home, which is useful when that home keeps changing.

Mom takes whatever she can get, which means she can do practically anything now.

She's been a teaching assistant, a doctors' receptionist, a waitress, a landscape gardener. Before we left Belleview, she was an engineer.

Hazel drops her cutlery and looks at our brother. "What about you, Ro? You got a job yet?"

Our parents' backs straighten as Rowan stares at the table. Then he shrugs. "You know the answer already."

"So, what . . . you're just going to do nothing."

Rowan's eyes meet hers, his brow creased as he slowly chews his last mouthful.

Mom hurries out of the room, the downstairs bathroom door clicking shut and the lock sliding across.

"I don't do *nothing,*" Rowan says.

Hazel shakes her head. "Of course not. You fight."

"I channel my emotions. You know all about that."

Our sister stands, her chair toppling as she grips the table with both hands.

"I do," she says, and I should tell her to meditate or call her boyfriend. I should pull her into a hug that squeezes all the anger away. But I don't. I sit in silence while my siblings size each other up like predators.

"You want me to get a job?" Rowan asks. "You think that will help?"

Hazel drops her plate in the sink then disappears upstairs.

Rowan doesn't move for a long time. His fists clench and unclench, thick veins throbbing against his skin. Then he stands, gently rests his dish on the countertop, and opens the back door.

I wait for rhythmic thuds to fill the air, but what comes is far more erratic.

Dad's eyes leave his newspaper long enough to catch mine, his bottom lip twitching before he shakes his head and looks away.

Eventually, Rowan walks past us and heads straight to his room.

The silence expands as Mom slips back into her seat, her fingers massaging red circles into her cheeks.

"It will be okay," Dad mutters, like a toy with one catchphrase.

I wait a few minutes, then go to the garage, where Rowan has fitted a homemade punching bag to the ceiling.

He's taken some of the crap the previous owners left behind—PVC pipe, plywood, old carpet, duct tape—and made his own private gym.

He's smart . . . when he wants to be.

I gently tap the bag, then take one big swing that vibrates up my skinny arm until my shoulder throbs. Things like this are not meant for people like me.

I look beyond it, at the dents in the wall still crumbling under the weight of Rowan's fists.

Sometimes, punching bags aren't enough for all the anger coursing through our brother.

I could go to him, but when Rowan and Hazel light each other's fuses, it's best to stand well back.

Instead, I go to my room and take the notes from my backpack. I've tried to keep them as flat as possible, because there must be a clue somewhere.

I could scrunch them up and toss them in the trash, but that wouldn't help me. Someone at my new school knows what we're running from and I need to figure out what that means.

Each time I try to hide them somewhere—under the mattress, behind my empty bookcase, at the back of my stale-smelling closet—I pull them back out and stare at the words until my eyes water.

I keep doubting myself, wondering if the notes are a hallucination and the whistle was just a harmless sound remixed by my paranoia. But they are here, and it was real.

When my eyes droop, I push the notes into my pillowcase, lie back, and stare at the ceiling, exhausted by the worry that churns my stomach.

Then I'm suddenly back in the Hell Hole, Max sitting opposite me, grinning in between huge bites of her sandwich.

Her eyes sparkle as she tilts her head and says, "Stop making excuses not to be my friend."

I try to say, "I'm not." But the words are too distant to reach, my mouth hanging open until it feels like thorns have filled my throat.

"What's the matter?" Max asks. "Don't you like me?"

I do. More than I should.

"Good," she says, as though she can read my mind. Then she looks past me, down the hallway that leads back to the cafeteria. "Seb? Tyler?"

A tiny shape sits in the center of its shadow—a young white boy shivering in shorts and a T-shirt.

Thin plumes dance in the space between them as Max edges closer. "Are you okay? What's your name?"

It's the Hiding Boy. But she doesn't know that.

Pain surges through my body as I swallow over and over, desperately trying to find a single word.

Stop.

The boy reaches for Max's outstretched hand, and then he vanishes.

"Weird," she says with a smile, her shape slowly evaporating until I crash back to the real world with a gasp.

I down the glass of water by my bed, then check my phone. It's nearly 3:00 A.M., the house silent except for the faintest shudder whenever a vehicle drives past.

I close my eyes, trying to find the doorway into my dreams. I want to see only the best parts of that one.

But as I lie awake, dread surging through my veins, I wonder if Max knows more than she's letting on.

Because she came to *me.* She'd been watching. And, almost as soon as I let my guard down, someone, or some*thing,* began tormenting me.

17

I stare at my locker as people race past, each crash of metal or screech of excitement making me shiver. I watch Max while my hands work the lock then slowly pull it open.

She is talking excitedly with Tyler and Seb at the opposite end of the corridor, her laugh on a different frequency from the heavy hum of our classmates.

I feel it before I see it, how it brushes my arm as it twirls toward the floor. A black-and-white image that lands faceup on my left sneaker.

I keep my eyes on Max as I kneel, searching for greedy glances through the gaps between everyone else. But she doesn't look my way for a second.

Someone's leg knocks me off-balance and the paper slips from my hands. I grab it, close my locker, and hurry into the quietest corner I can find.

The photograph is of a house on Murder Road, and the headline reads:

CARNAGE AT SWEET SIXTEEN
AS CURSE CONTINUES

The date on the newspaper clipping is April 7, 1973.

Hayley Osborne—that's whose party it was. Maybe her family hadn't been paying attention, or maybe they believed it wouldn't happen to them. But that was the year the Hiding Boy came for the fifth house on the street.

That's when shit got real, because that many bodies make headlines across the entire country. Suddenly the legend of Murder Road was being whispered and altered and feared from East Coast to West and everywhere in between.

> Seventeen bodies have been found in the latest tragedy to befall the residents of one street in the otherwise quiet town of Belleview. Police were called to Cherry Tree Lane after screams were heard at the property, which was hosting a sixteenth-birthday party for the owners' eldest daughter.
>
> When emergency services arrived, they found what has been described by Sheriff Prescott as "a massacre."
>
> Police are asking anyone who was in the location on the evening of April 5 to contact them immediately.
>
> "Not for the first time, this neighborhood is suffering unimaginable pain," Sheriff Prescott said. "Our thoughts and prayers are with the victims and their families."

Thoughts and prayers, over and over. Nothing tangible, nothing helpful. Just the easiest things to offer in a moment of inconceivable pain.

I carefully fold the article and tuck it in my pocket. It's undeniable now—someone knows we used to live within touching distance of Murder Road. More importantly, they know no one ever escapes.

I hold one hand in the other as they quiver; then I close my eyes and breathe, trying to force the fear away.

"Are you okay?"

Max stands directly in front of me, her eyes a mixture of doubt and confusion.

"Why are you following me?"

A stilted laugh slips out. "I'm not. I'm seeing if you're all right. But if you'd rather I didn't . . ."

My fists tighten around my tremors, my shoulders aching, but she doesn't move.

"What's wrong?" she asks. "Seriously. You look terrified."

I touch my clammy face as if searching for proof.

"I'm fine," I reply. "I have the shakes sometimes. That's all."

"I get it," Max says, even though she doesn't. "New schools can be scary. So, the offer's still there. I know you ditched us the other night, but you've seen our secret lair, so we can still hang out in the Hell Hole. If you want."

I thought I knew what I wanted—to keep my head down, to be a loner, to get through whatever happens on my own. But Max is a blip that keeps expanding.

I like her, like I've never liked anyone. But she's also a suspect.

"I asked you before . . . if you put something in my locker."

"You did."

"And . . ."

"I didn't."

There are ways to tell when you're being lied to.

Some people itch when they bullshit you, which means increased fidgeting. Or the muscles in their vocal cords tighten, making their voice higher.

Eyes might look away at a key moment, hands may be hidden in pockets. Words like "truth" or "honestly" could be used more than usual.

But Max doesn't do any of those things.

"I don't know what's going on," she says. "But we're here, if you need us. You're not alone."

The barrier that holds my emotions in place sways then steadies, tears stopping millimeters from my eyes.

I don't want to walk away from her again. Not yet.

"I didn't come that night because I was worried," I say. "I don't know you. At all. Why would I follow you into the middle of nowhere? I've read those stories about people doing horrible shit to their friends. So, who knows what they'd do to a stranger."

A smile spills over Max's face. "You thought we wanted to kill you?"

"Probably not. But what if it was the other way around? What if *you* were the new kid and I'd come up to you? Would you have gone?"

Her grin grows even wider as she says, "I see your point. But now what? You don't think we're murderers after all?"

"It's becoming increasingly unlikely."

Max looks over her shoulder, then leans closer and says, "I think you're like us. That's all. I'm sorry if I scared you. And it was *me,* right? I can be a bit intense sometimes."

Her face shifts, the confidence replaced by something much more real. It's how my sister looks when she thinks no one's looking.

As I follow Max back into the main corridor, I check to see if Hazel is around, but I can't see her.

Tyler slouches over to us like his cat has died. "Why are you talking to him?"

"Because he's not as dumb as you," Max replies. "He didn't trust us. That's why he didn't come. But . . . if we promise not to kill him . . . maybe he's up for a do-over?"

Tyler pushes his shoulders back and stares at me as he says, "Cool."

"Where's Seb?" I ask, and he says, "It's his Miss Kittle time."

What the hell does that mean? These people talk like I've known them for years.

"She's the school counselor," Max says. "Seb is her most loyal customer."

"Is he okay?"

"Are any of us?" Max replies.

I don't know how to answer her, so I don't say anything. Instead, I wait until she fills the silence.

"Hell Hole at lunch?"

"Sure."

Max didn't sneak those things into my locker, but that doesn't mean I trust them all. I need to see their faces when I pull the note and the article out, and the best time to do that is when they feel untouchable.

18

I'm relieved that we don't have any of the same classes. I'd rather sit quietly, only speak when spoken to, disappear the way some people do.

Even the teachers avoid me: too busy to learn another name; too set in their ways to look in a new direction.

Montgomery-Oakes feels like every other high school I've been to. It may be more modern than most, but the students and staff are no different. Except for one.

The same moments are displayed in the cabinets and on the walls—different clothes, different faces, identical feelings. The same dramas rumble under the surface. And the same sense of unease follows me from one class to the next, because these people have no idea.

Their lives are so nice, so carefree, so safe.

When they've had enough tragedy, they put down their phones or switch off the TV. They turn away from it and, immediately, it's gone. Except it isn't. Bad things are still happening, everywhere, all the time.

I don't think I envy them. I can't be sure, but if I had the choice, I think I'd rather live with all the horrors in my head than be ignorant.

People swarm past me, barging, charging, never apologizing. Sometimes I stick out a leg or arch my elbow, hoping to hurt at least one of them the way they hurt me. And sometimes I don't have the energy to fight back.

No one notices my tiny victories and I get no pleasure from them. I hate always being the one in the way, the shape without a name or a place in this giant asshole factory.

There it is: the rage that rumbles under *my* surface.

I hate moving this much. I hate not having a history. At least not one to be proud of. I hate being torn between making friends and being alone.

It must be nice growing up in one safe place. It must be cool having Max's confidence. It must be one hell of a feeling being part of the school-corridor surge, filling a space rather than always being in the way.

Maybe I do envy them, after all.

I wait until Max, Seb, and Tyler are all sitting in the Hell Hole, their lunches spread across the makeshift table between us. Then I gently place the article about the sweet-sixteen massacre faceup on it and watch their reactions.

"What's that?" Max asks.

Tyler reaches for it with a greedy grin. "That's Murder Road. Our boy *does* know his urban legends after all."

I offer a shallow smile in return.

"That's the cursed street, right?" Seb says, squinting at the words in Tyler's hands then going back to his sub.

"Hell, yes," Tyler replies. "You know the song. 'Ready or not. Whatever you do.'"

"Stop," Max says.

"What? This place isn't abandoned, is it? They're just words here."

"Maybe."

"Have any of you seen that before?" I ask, nodding at the newspaper clipping.

Seb and Max shake their heads while Tyler slides the clipping back onto the crate.

"I tried it once," he whispers. "At the abandoned house on

Swanfield. Me and my sisters stood outside and recited that song. But nothing happened."

There's the truth . . . and then there's the lore.

When stories spread, they alter. Mention Murder Road to most people now and they'll tell you that if you stand outside an abandoned house and repeat the chant, one of you will be possessed by the ghost of the Hiding Boy.

He'll kill everyone, including the host.

"What if it was real?" Max asks, and Tyler chuckles.

"Luckily nothing happened. But Cherry Tree Lane? That shit is *definitely* real. You know how many homes have been targeted over the years? They kept saying it was a coincidence, all those deaths. But the Hiding Boy won't rest until he's left blood in every house on the street."

I stifle a shiver, because Tyler's not wrong.

"If you want to do that one," Max says, gesturing to the tabletop, "you're out of luck, Nate. I'm not summoning that fucking kid. They say you see him right before you die. He stands statue-still, picking which person to possess. Can you imagine that? Watching him choose which of your friends or family is going to slaughter you?"

Three stony faces stare at me in the half-light and I'm suddenly certain that none of them snuck anything into my locker.

It doesn't help. But it makes one thing clear. I'm sticking close to them for as long as necessary, because someone *is* messing with me, and I might need all the friends I can get.

19

That afternoon, I do my homework at the dining table while Hazel paces the room above me, the ceiling creaking under the weight of her frantic footsteps.

Every few minutes, Mom stares at the cracked plaster overhead, her entire body deflating before she finds the energy to go again.

I don't ask Mom if my sister will be okay, because, unlike Rowan, she won't lie. Instead, we pretend in silence. That everyone is happy. That none of us is broken.

When the front door opens, Mom's shoulders tense. And they stay tensed when Dad and Rowan walk in and dump overflowing bags of groceries on the countertops.

Our brother tosses his wallet and keys on the sideboard, then sits next to me with an exaggerated groan, the arms he holds behind his head covered in bruises.

"We got everything you requested," Dad says, wrapping his own arms around Mom's waist and only moving when she nudges him aside.

"Thank you," she mumbles, quickly emptying the bags and adding even more stuff to our already crammed cupboards.

After a couple of weeks in a new place, there are no more empty spaces.

The bruise around Rowan's eye has turned from a single shade of brown to a mess of purples and reds and black, the skin nearest his cheek engorged like a misshapen water balloon. When I look closer, I see that scabs and cuts cover his lips.

"What?" Rowan says.

"I didn't say anything."

"You didn't have to."

"It's just . . . you usually win easily."

Mom laughs and, without turning, mutters, "Do you want to tell him?"

"Stop it," Dad says. "Please."

But Rowan's button has already been pushed. Again. I have no idea what's going on but it can't be good.

Mom faces us, rage flickering in the corners of her mouth. "Your brother didn't get those injuries at a boxing club or a dojo. He doesn't do that anymore, do you, Rowan?"

When he doesn't reply, our mother snatches his wallet and empties the contents on the table.

Twenty- and fifty-dollar bills splay across the stained wood like playing cards—more money than I have ever seen in my life.

Mom's stare burns into the top of Rowan's head as she says, "You're doing it again."

"What's happening?" I ask.

Dad stands behind me, his hand heavy on my shoulder. "It's nothing."

"It's not 'nothing,'" Mom replies. "Your brother fights for money. There's no boxing anymore, Nate. No coaches, no competitions, no trophies. Just brute violence. Last person standing."

"It's still me," Rowan says, the remains of a smirk on his busted lips. "I still win."

"Look at you," Mom whispers. "If that's what it takes to win . . . you shouldn't be playing."

"Really?" My brother's voice suddenly fills the room. "If *that's* what it takes."

"Stop!" Dad shouts. "That's enough."

"Forgive me if I don't want our son getting the shit beat out of him."

Rowan stands, the veins in his arms pulsing through his skin. "I know you care. Really. I know. But I'm not going to stop."

Mom watches him leave, and then Dad removes his hand and hurries over.

"I'm fine," she says, walking out before he reaches her.

He stands awkwardly for a few seconds, then follows her upstairs.

Even if I wanted to tell my family about the notes and the newspaper clipping, I couldn't. Not with everything else that's going on.

I can't stay in this house when no one even tries to pretend. I need to get out of here; to block out the horrible thoughts that creep in when I'm alone for too long.

I've already agreed to meet Max and the others tonight. And any doubts I had have been snuffed out by a family with more fuses and flames than I can count.

20

I wait alone on Main Street, the stores all lit by separate lampposts, their window displays beckoning like a stranger's curling finger.

Compared to the last place we lived this town feels like a Hallmark movie. Everything feels neat and tidy and, most important, real.

Belleview *tried* to be perfect, but only to throw a sheet over the morbid history of Murder Road.

There's a lightness to Montgomery-Oakes that I'm growing less suspicious of every day.

When people smile at you, they mean it. When they stop to chat with their neighbors, there's no half-hidden desire to escape. And sitting here, the sunset painting pink and orange swirls across the sky, I feel strangely, wonderfully content.

I wait on a bench dedicated to Iris Lowe. The plaque says she was a grandmother, mother, sister, daughter, and friend. That's a lot of things for one person to be.

A dog sniffs my sneakers, its leash too long to comply with my rules on personal space.

The owner grins and says, "Sorry," and I hold back the urge to kick it.

It was Rowan who told me about the rage. He said you can't live that close to all those murders and not breathe some of them in.

I didn't understand immediately. But then I saw him at a tae kwon do tournament, his pupils like pinpricks and the anger coming off him in waves.

It was channeled. It was allowed. But it still scared me, because that wasn't the brother I knew.

The Rowan I'd grown up with was gentle. He probably hurt a few flies but that was as bad as it got. Until he became angry.

Now I have it too. When it comes, it's quick. As though someone has crept up behind me and taken control, like I'm the tool of a vengeful puppeteer.

My parents don't have it. At least, not that I've ever seen. But the rest of us do. Rowan the worst, Hazel now and again, and me, more often than I'd like to admit.

Is it guilt? Living so close to death? Escaping a place so many didn't? Or is our brother right, and the worst moments really do spread like mushroom clouds, scarring some, merely touching others?

I feel stupid for not knowing where Rowan goes every night, then guilty that he has no choice.

I close my eyes and try to picture an underground fight club—a ring of cheering bodies splattered by other people's blood.

I wish it was still enough for Rowan to win a trophy and yet, if I'm honest, it never was. The gold or silver glistening in his hands at the end of every competition was a bonus he had no desire to revel in.

For him, it's always been about the violence. If he can make some money out of it now that he's no longer in school, why not?

A bell rings behind me and, when I turn, I see an old man closing up. It's a candy store, and hundreds of childhood memories race back as I look through the glass.

That's all there is here. No shutters, no bars, only glass.

Every store on the street is just a brick or a kick away from losing everything. But the man isn't thinking like that. He only sees the good in people.

"Evening," he says, nodding as he walks slowly past.

"Hi."

He stops at the corner, touches the street sign, then vanishes into the black.

I could sit here every night, because this is my kind of calm. Not quite silent, the buzz of the streetlights and the whir of the distant highway nestling in my ears.

It softens everything—the rage and the fear and the uncertainty. And it makes me hope, no matter how foolishly, that we can have a home here.

"Yo! Yo!" Max yells from the other side of the square. "He actually made it."

My sense of calm vanishes in an instant. "Where are the others?"

"Seb parked around the corner. They didn't believe you'd be here so they refused to get out of the car."

I laugh but Max shrugs like she's not kidding. Then she looks past me, smiling at the storefronts. "It's beautiful, isn't it?"

"It's certainly got character."

"When I was little, this place was the center of my universe. My mom and I would spend every Saturday morning here. We hardly ever bought anything but that didn't matter. She called it 'window shopping,' which is a nice way of saying we were dirt poor."

Max walks to the candy store and rests one palm against the glass.

"This was my paradise. Mr. Taylor runs it and he'd always sneak me some candy when Mom wasn't looking."

"I think I saw him," I say. "He just closed up."

"You'll meet him properly soon," Max says, walking back across the square before I can ask what she means. "Come on. The boys will wonder where I am."

I run to catch up, crossing a pristine patch of grass with a sign that reads NO BALL GAMES.

Tyler is leaning out the passenger window, relief washing over his face when he sees us. And I realize something. What if they're scared of me? What if it's only strength in numbers, or Max's blind faith, that is stopping them from doing what I did the other night?

Max gets in the back and I do the same on the other side.

"Hey," I say, and Max hits the back of Seb's seat and says, "I told you he'd come."

Seb doesn't reply. He just puts the car in drive and slowly pulls away.

"Where are we going?" I'm trying to silence my panic, because Seb isn't driving to the same spot as last time. We're way past that, heading toward the highway and the smaller towns scattered left and right like unwatered seeds.

"The middle of nowhere," Tyler says. "I thought you knew that."

Only, this is a different nowhere, one I haven't researched. If things go south, there will be no easy escape.

Max smiles and I copy, unsure if either of us means it. Then I stare out of the window, thinking of all the times people made decisions that only proved to be bad once it was too late.

Eventually, Tyler mumbles, "Here," and Seb crawls down a narrow lane for five drawn-out minutes, then kills the engine.

Max gets out and the boys look at each other, then follow.

The breath they need for their silly legend creeps out of me, its tendrils narrowing to nothing. Then there's a tap on the window and Max grins through the glass.

"Come on!" she shouts.

I step into the darkness as the three of them disappear between the trees. Max is chattering excitedly, but that's not the noise I'm drawn to. It's the sound of something else that pulls me into the gloom then quickly out the other side.

The call of the water.

Waves lap gently below us, the lights from the shoreline of the bay sprinkled like glitter from a toddler's hand. I step closer to the cliff edge and rest my palms on the rails.

"It's beautiful, right?" Seb says.

It takes me a moment to realize why he looks different. He's smiling.

Tyler takes a stone from the ground and throws it into the darkness. There's no splash, no telling where it lands, but he looks satisfied.

"Montgomery-Oakes is surrounded by a lot of crappy places," he says. "But it's also got some hidden gems."

I've always loved water, especially the ocean—its sounds, its size, its sense of infinite calm. That's strange, I guess. That something so wild can feel so restful? But that's the beauty of it. I could listen to the waves for hours. It's the only thing that wins every time, a universal weapon against my fears—a rock, paper, and scissors all rolled into one.

I stare across the water, wondering what this place looks like to the people on the other side. Do they watch us with the same reverence? Because so many things look perfect from a distance. It's only when you get closer that you notice what's not quite hidden.

We stand there for a long time—silent and happy—and then Tyler sighs and says, "We should do this. If it doesn't work, we'll come back and enjoy the view some more."

"What if it *does* work?" Max replies, mischief in her smile.

"Then we don't leave the car until we're home."

"We could always just . . ."

"Chicken out?" Seb says.

He glances at me then away.

"I saw a couple of empty-looking places on the way over here," Tyler says with a grin. "Who's up for stopping off and summoning the Hiding Boy before we head home? Two legends for the price of one."

Max stares at me while she shakes her head. "Let's see if this one works first."

Tyler nods and follows Seb back to the car, but Max's eyes are fixed firmly on the distant lights across the water.

"I have two brothers and a sister over there," she says. "Well, half siblings. The half that doesn't give a shit."

I look where she's looking, trying to imagine the strangers she's got in her head.

"What's your family situation?" Max asks.

"One brother, one sister, two parents."

"That must be nice."

"Not always."

She turns to me, the distant reflections like jewels in her eyes.

"I read that no two kids have the same parents," she says, "even if they're siblings. The first kid has the parents who are figuring everything out for the first time. The second one has the parents who've learned from their mistakes but are also caught up in raising two kids. The third one has the parents who have two already and have all this experience and are like, sure, climb everything, you'll be fine. Which one are you?"

"I'm the baby," I say.

"So, you don't see your parents the way your brother and sister do. Three kids. Three totally different experiences. To me, my dad's an asshole, because he left when I was three. But to the people who live over there, he's a legend, because he chose to love them."

"I'm sure he . . ."

"He doesn't. And I don't need you to make me feel better. I'm just telling you a story."

"Okay."

I guess this isn't everyone's perfect view after all. But I can relate to that. If you didn't know the history of where I came from, you'd only notice its beauty. Once you've seen through a facade, you can't redraw the curtain.

Max and I walk to the car, and the boys offer her uncertain smiles that she widens with a grin of her own.

When we're all inside, the car locks slam down with a jolt that makes me jump, and Max giggles. "You okay, Nate? That isn't the scary part."

I nod, then watch as the three of them hold their fingers to their mouths.

Eleven minutes of silence. That's how this starts. So, I close my eyes and wait.

Max's breathing slows and, when I glance over, she looks so peaceful. Her lips are slightly parted, wisps of life snaking through the car.

Seb's stare fills the rearview. I try to smile but what comes out is fragile and incomplete.

I retreat into my darkness, fighting off some memories and welcoming others. I want to be back by the water, not playing silly games.

That's the kind of distraction I need—one that makes me forget, if only for an hour or two, that someone in this town knows what we're running from.

Respite normally comes in the few fragile months before we start hearing the distant thrum of its footsteps. But now, because of the notes and the newspaper clipping, I don't even have that.

Heat prickles the skin under my jeans while goose bumps cluster on my neck. Then I risk a second look at Seb, who is still staring, unblinking, before he leans toward his window and softly blows.

The others copy, so I do the same, filling the glass on my side with hot breath. I quickly glance at Max's then draw my own circle, careful to keep it unfinished. Two silent stabs for eyes. One swift slash for a mouth.

Our voices shatter the silence. Seven words—even when whispered—somehow bigger as they are spoken in unison.

"I see the Face in the Glass."

I stare past the shape I drew, into a darkness so removed from the beauty just around the corner. I can't wait to see that bay again. It may remind Max of a life she didn't get to live, of people who got the dad she'd never recognize, but, to me, it's spectacular.

It's proof that my parents may have got it right this time; that they have brought us to somewhere worth fighting for.

When tonight is over, I'll ask Tyler about the other hidden gems, the places I can go where nothing matters except the moment. But for now . . .

"What was that?" Tyler says.

Max leans forward and looks out of his window. "I don't see anything."

"I swear," he whispers, "something moved."

"Animals," Seb says under his breath. "It's always animals."

I watch them as they stare out of their windows and can't help but smile. This is how to escape my family and my fate; to bury our awkward dinner-table moments in something harmless and fun; to try to forget one urban legend by pretending I care about another.

"Are you okay?" Max asks. "What's happening to your lips?"

"He's smiling," Tyler says. "That's a first." He waits a few seconds, then adds, "So we *have* seen something unimaginable tonight, even if the Face in the Glass proves as elusive as ever."

Seb snorts as I hold one hand over my mouth.

"It's okay to enjoy yourself," Max whispers.

She touches my arm and I fight against my flinch. It feels nice, her weight on mine.

"How long until we call it?" Tyler asks.

"That depends on how brave you're feeling," Max replies.

She hasn't moved her hand and I wonder if she likes that fact as much as I do.

"We failed," Seb says, squeezing his door handle just enough for it to click.

"The abandoned house it is," Tyler sings and, all at once, the three of us say, "No!"

We wait in silence for a lot longer than they did the other night.

Eventually, Tyler glances at his watch and says, "Time of no death, ten twenty-three."

He gets out and stares at the sky until Seb joins him. Then I try not to breathe too frantically as the reality of Max and me alone in the car sinks in.

"I'm sorry again for the other day," she whispers. "When I said about the love letter. That was a joke."

"I know."

"Do you have someone?"

"I'm sorry?"

Max clears her throat then says, "A significant other."

When I laugh, she nudges my shoulder with hers.

We left Belleview when I was twelve, with plenty of friends, one or two crushes, but nothing even close to serious.

Until now, I haven't looked at any of our temporary towns and seen the prospect of anything more.

As Tyler gestures for us to join them, I open my door and say, "No."

We watch Tyler dance between the trees until Seb is the one to disappear.

"Hey," Tyler says. "Where *are* you?"

Uncertainty spreads across his face as he searches the shadows. Then his friend bursts out and Tyler yells, "Shit! What are you doing?!"

"Returning the favor," Seb says.

Max giggles as they compete for the biggest jump scare, Tyler winning when he literally leaps out of a tree. Then they walk back to me and sit amid the dry leaves.

"One day an urban legend *will* come true," Tyler sighs. "But, until then, this isn't a bad way to spend the evening."

"Have you thought any more about your future?" Max asks, and Tyler tosses a small stone that lands harmlessly at her feet. "Sorry. I couldn't resist."

"This would be a good future," he says. "Feeling this free."

"You want to be a wood wanderer?" Max asks with a snort.

"I don't want so much pressure on me that it feels like I'm going to explode."

"*Im*plode," Seb mumbles.

Of the three of them, he seems to be having the least fun.

Max turns to me and says, "Tyler gets pulled in lots of directions. His coach thinks he's guaranteed a soccer scholarship. Mr. Conrad says he's, quote, 'the most promising physicist Montgomery-Oakes High has produced in . . .' How long?"

Tyler cringes as he says, "Twenty years."

"*Twenty* years!" Max's voice echoes as wings slice through the trees. "But Tyler is a family man. And what a family it is. Picture. Fucking. Perfect. So, he has some big decisions to make. Sports star, scientist, or hometown hero."

Gray clouds cover Max's eyes as she stares into the distance.

I'm used to silences like this. Our house is full of them. But the leaves crackle as Tyler slides over to her, his hand resting perfectly in hers, while something unfamiliar stirs in my stomach.

"What was that?" Seb whispers, his eyes darting toward the woods.

As he stands, there's a groan from the shadows and he freezes.

Max stands beside Tyler and I wait for the punch line: There was another kid all along—a fourth friend I somehow didn't see. This is some twisted trick they like to play on new arrivals. But all three of them look terrified.

Max's fingers fidget as her foot kicks a widening hole in the dirt. Seb's shoulders tremble while his eyes dart from one patch of black to another. Tyler steps forward, then back, his bravery blunted by three false starts before he finally heads for the woods.

"It's probably nothing," he says, just as something heavy rustles through the undergrowth and he turns and bolts for the car.

We all follow, the doors slamming shut and sticky breath filling the space.

"What the hell was that?" Max asks.

Something crashes against the car's trunk and all our heads snap to the rear window.

"That's not an animal." Tyler's voice cracks on the final word, but no one disagrees with him.

Max rests both hands on the seat between us then peers through the glass.

Her breath comes out in sharp bursts and I realize that, for every inch she moves closer to the window, I'm edging further the other way, until I'm pressed hard against the back of the driver's seat.

I steady myself, waiting for another bang. I can still hear echoes of the last one, the sound of something hard against metal so loud that there must be a dent. But what comes next is worse.

I'm not sure what it is right away. It's too small and too distant. Then it comes closer—the sound of scratching against the side of the car, the high-pitched scream of something digging its claws deep into the paintwork.

The noise rips through my ears until I push my palms hard against my skull. Max and Seb copy but Tyler is following the sound, his head pressed against the door before he moves into the back, clambering over Max as she slides awkwardly into the middle seat.

"It's real," Tyler whispers, right before the door handle is pulled so hard that I picture the end of him.

"I locked it," Seb says. "We're safe."

Whatever is outside tries the handle again, gentler this time. Then there is movement before it yanks hard on the opposite door.

"Fuck," Max spits. "We need to get out of here."

Tyler shakes his head. "We've prepared for this. The doors are locked so we're . . ."

"*Let me in,*" something hisses. "*Let me in. Let me in.*"

One of Max's hands finds mine in the darkness and I focus on that, desperately trying to ignore the whispers outside. But they keep coming.

"I'm not here to hurt you."

Seb's knuckles are pressed hard against his mouth as he sits on the center console, doing all he can to distance himself from the doors. Tyler continues to follow the sound around the car until Max whimpers, "Go."

"Let me in."

The words crawl over my skin like spiders, burrowing greedily into my ears. Then another sound replaces it—faint and rhythmic, like raindrops tapping slowly on the glass. Except, it's not raining. The more I focus, the more I imagine fingers rapping on the window.

Tap, tap, tap. Tap, tap, tap. Over and over, the same sound, biding its time.

The car rocks, then settles, briefly shunted by a raging wind. And yet, there is something within that roar—words that almost find their way to resistant ears but shatter and fall before they can be deciphered.

Seb scrambles back into the driver's seat and pulls away, his tires spinning in the dirt before propelling us forward.

I stare back, braver now that we're moving, but all I can see is black.

"Did you hear that?" Max asks. "Tell me you heard that."

I think she's going to hyperventilate, but then a laugh slips out between the panting.

The first one is nervous and out of place. Then, after a minute or so, that's all she's doing. Laughing and swearing and staring at me like I'm the missing piece of a puzzle she's been stuck on for months.

"Holy shit," she says, not taking her eyes off me. "The Face in the Glass is real."

"It can't be," Tyler mutters as he wipes the steam from his glasses.

"It *can* be," Max replies. "I heard it. We all heard it."

She hasn't looked away from me since we started driving.

"Who's going to fix my car?" Seb says from the front.

"Who cares about your car?" Tyler replies. "We nearly died."

I search each word and every movement for the hint of a lie. But all I can see are three terrified teenagers. Four if I look in the rearview mirror.

"Just tell me," I mumble, "please. Are you messing with me?"

"No!" Max shoots back. "Whatever that was, we had nothing to do with it."

Except that's not totally true, because if the Face in the Glass is real, they had *everything* to do with it. We drew the faces. We said the words. Whatever is lurking in the woods is only out there because we opened the door.

21

"Can we go back?" I ask, suddenly realizing something. "To the overlook, I mean. Can we still go there, or is that . . . thing waiting for us?"

"Do you *want* to go back?" Max replies.

I do. I want to watch the waves crashing against the shore while she tells me everything about her life. But, like so much, that's ruined now.

"We shouldn't," Tyler says from the front seat. "If we really did summon something . . ."

He turns back and stares through the windshield, our combined silence expanding in the gloom.

I should have known this was too good to be true. As we sat in the woods, Max beaming at her friends like a proud mother, I felt truly, unbreakably, happy.

And that's when life goes to shit.

All the horrible things I've been holding back suddenly crush me like a landslide—Murder Road and everything we're running from, the person stuffing warnings into my locker, the family whose cracks are turning into craters, and now this, a ghost in the woods to go with all the ones in my nightmares.

"Where do you live?" Max asks. "We'll drop you home."

"No need," I mutter. "I'll walk."

It's the last thing I want to do, but what choice do I have? I'm not bringing them straight to my front door.

"Don't be stupid," she says. "It's no trouble."

"I'd rather do that. I need to clear my head after . . . you know."

"You'd rather walk? In the dark?"

I'd prefer to be alone in my bedroom but that's not possible right now. I shouldn't have come in the first place. I knew that. We keep to ourselves and then we run. But now there are other things chasing me—whispers in the woods and girls who want my address.

"Just tell us where you live!" Seb shouts.

When I don't answer, he swerves onto Main Street and says, "Fine. Here you go."

"Stop being a dick," Max says.

"*I'm* not," Seb replies. "I want to go home and process what the hell just happened. So, if Nate wants to walk, let him walk."

When Tyler opens his door, Seb laughs and says, "You, too?"

"No, I'm . . . checking the damage."

I stand next to Tyler and follow the jagged scratches that run the length of Seb's car.

"They look like claw marks," he says, pressing his fingers into the grooves.

Seb hurries over, then starts pacing with his head in his hands. "What am I going to tell my parents?"

Max puts her arm on his shoulder as she says, "The truth?"

He laughs, but a tear still creeps down his check before he pushes it away.

"I don't understand," he says. "What is this? The *sixth* time we've tried it?"

"Seventh," Tyler mumbles.

"Whatever. Nothing *ever* happens."

Seb glares at me until I look away.

I wish it were that simple. But he's got the wrong idea if he thinks I'm involved.

I'm as scared as they are, more so, pinning my eyes closed as panic and uncertainty fill my brain.

What would they say if I told them I once lived on the street next to Murder Road? What would they say if I explained that, no matter how far you run, some legends always catch up?

Has it come early this time? Is it playing with us in new and twisted ways? Or is the Face in the Glass a different kind of monster from a vengeful boy?

Rowan's right. We stay on the periphery. We keep to ourselves.

Max was . . . Max *is* . . . something better. She's a very welcome distraction from an extremely shitty life. But I've been kidding myself. And something out there is punishing me for it.

"I'll be fine," I say. "I can look after myself."

"Whatever," Seb mutters, glancing one last time at his wrecked paintwork before getting back in the car and revving the engine until the others follow.

"Message me when you get home," Max says.

I nod, watching as they drive quickly away.

The beckoning storefronts are like time machines pulling me back to the quiet moments before Max and the others turned up.

I don't head home immediately. I sit on the bench and wait, daring myself to stare into the darkest corners of this town.

I think of the scratches, the tapping, the whispers, and I fight against the fear stroking my ankles.

After spending so much of my life close to Murder Road, I shouldn't be surprised if other urban legends are true.

Panic and confusion swirl through my head until it feels like I'm underwater.

I'm the good one, the son who does what he's told, the brother who never makes a fuss when his siblings take all the attention.

I don't rock the boat, even when it's sinking.

But where has that got me? Alone, in the dark, and haunted from every direction.

I try to focus on something else, picturing this town when it wakes up. I imagine the candy-store owner, the florist, the barber, everyone taking their place in a scene rehearsed to perfection.

I think this is another gem, less hidden but equally precious. Even before tonight, I knew that liking where you live is dangerous when there's no guarantee you can stay. But it's worse now.

This place isn't perfect. Nowhere is.

I block those thoughts out as I walk home, my shoulders tensing at the thought of someone behind me. I wait until my neck stings, then spin my head around and see nothing, over and over until I'm home.

Then I stare up at the windows, Mom and Dad's curtains drawn, Rowan's pulled wide.

Don't hide any more than you have to. That's what he says.

So, he wakes with the sunrise and, if you're passing late at night and he's still awake, you can see him shadowbox or karate kick or, like now, stare back at you, with fresh cuts held together by Steri-Strips.

I hold my hand up and he does the same. Then I think of what Max said about families.

It must be nice. That's what she said about mine. But we run so often that when we stop, it takes time for our pieces to settle. It can take an age for the "nice" to find its way back.

I creep upstairs and walk past Rowan's open door. Then I stare at the old ceiling of a child who liked stars, their thick yellow bodies glowing in the dark and impossible to budge.

Did they try? Did someone stand on a ladder and slide their fingernails under the sharp plastic edges that move just enough to draw blood?

Or did they forget the stars were even there—a moment left in childhood like the Spider-Man stickers battling along the baseboards?

I close my eyes and think about how Max looked at me once we were safe.

I should have told her not to rely on me. I should explain that, one day, I'll vanish with no explanation. But I *liked* that look. I liked being part of something; being a part of her.

I should message her like she asked. But if she's better off without me, we'll start now. That's why I stare at her number until it blurs, then delete it with one quivering finger.

If I really am the reason another urban legend just came to life, Murder Road stained me even more than I first thought.

22

Not all darkness feels the same. Every town, every house, every room is slightly different.

The darkness in my new bedroom is speckled with shards of light peeking through claw-ravaged curtains.

Sometimes I imagine kittens hanging from the cloth; those same cats lounging on the sun-trap windowsill when climbing lost its fun.

In the day, this room is hot. At night, that heat lingers like a stalker.

The dull glow from the plastic stars on my ceiling rests behind my eyelids, imprinted from hours of staring. When I open them again, I peer into the darkest corner until all remnants of light are snuffed out.

And that's where I keep looking—this place that is murkier than my mind—until my eyes grow heavy and sleep stubbornly arrives.

The darkness in my dreams is a blanket twisted around my limbs. The more I struggle, the tighter it becomes, so I submit.

I imagine a game of hide-and-seek, my sister rushing to me in seconds, my brother leaving me to wonder if I will ever be found. But it's been a long time since we played like children.

My breath is hot and jagged, my sweat merging with the gloom until I am part of it. When I move, the darkness comes with me. When I finally fight free there's no respite.

I stand alone in the clearing, Seb's car next to me but no one inside. "Hello?"

The trees creak as one, their heavy heads dragged back and forth by a growling wind. Then something crackles in the darkness and everything stops.

The bushes in front of me shake, their leaves cast off like droplets from a soaking dog. Then claws creep out of the gloom—yellowing and razor-like.

I turn to run, then freeze as circles slowly form on the car windows, the screech of invisible fingers dragging long smiles across the glass.

"Are you messing with me?" I say, then louder, yelling into a wood that snatches my words and holds tight to their echoes. "Who's doing this?!"

Bodies appear behind the glass—Max, Tyler, and Seb—their eyes as black as oil.

Max presses her palm against the window, smudging the face she's drawn, and I try to move closer.

My feet are stuck to the spot as her face slowly drips down the glass, leaving nothing behind. Then the world flips, sending me crashing into the dead leaves, as a starless sky fills my vision.

Footsteps crack against the rotting mulch, and then I stare into the empty eyes of the Hiding Boy.

Something hard presses against my chest, forcing the air from my lungs.

I push back, tensing every muscle in my body, picturing Rowan punching holes in our garage wall until I know I've found the strength to break free.

Then I scream as loud as I can, bursting out of my nightmare as all the perfect pieces of Max's face scatter like confetti, while the Hiding Boy stands at the end of my bed, slowly counting my days away on his tiny, translucent fingers.

23

"Fuck!"

I blink and the ghost is gone. But I don't feel any better.

My ribs ache as I pant in the early-morning haze, my forehead sticky, my eyes scrambling for clues that he's still here, lurking under my bed or behind the gaps in my closet doors where the wood doesn't quite reach the frame.

Slowly, methodically, I put my peace back together, until I can look at the foot of my bed without trembling. Then I stand in the space where he was—the ghost that broke free from my nightmare—and freezing fear surges up my spine.

Is it a warning? A reminder from Murder Road that, whatever we summoned last night, it is nothing compared to the grieving boy who despises an entire street?

I should never have befriended Max.

My phone lights up with a message I assume is from her—*Emergency meeting. Get to school early*—and thank God she doesn't know where I live. If she did, she'd probably be throwing stones at my window, desperate to talk about last night.

Mom is alone in the kitchen and I wait a few moments, listening as she sings softly along with the radio. Her voice is wasted on us, on the lullabies that still stir when I lie awake in the dark.

Before us, she sang in bars and small clubs and had dreams and then, with each new child, those dreams had less and less room in her heart.

When the music stops, Mom keeps going, adding melodies to

the song in her head, humming and riffing until Dad walks into me and says, "Sorry, bud. I didn't see you there."

Mom looks up, wraps her arms tight around her waist, and says, "What do you want for breakfast?"

"I'm not sure," I say, opening the cupboards before she can, getting my bowl and my spoon and the milk one millisecond before our mother swoops in.

I know why she does it. If there are enough small things in your day, enough moments when you can forget why you have moved for the fourth time in three years, your life almost feels normal.

But if Mom takes all those moments, there are none for the rest of us.

"Did you have fun last night?" Dad asks.

I look away from Mom's intense stare as I say, "Yes, thanks."

If they know that I'm lying, they don't correct me. But it isn't all a lie. Some of last night *was* enjoyable and, on another day, in another life, I'd tell our parents about the illuminated storefronts and the view across the bay.

If they know about the magical pieces of this town, perhaps they'll explore for themselves, lifting some of the extra weight off this already-crumbling house. But I don't want to share them, not when they are the only things preventing the horror of last night from overwhelming me.

"I don't like it," Mom says. "This habit you've got into . . . of wandering the streets alone."

Images of Max and the boys flash into my mind before I push them aside. "It's calming. And I haven't come across a single axe murderer yet."

Dad's grin dissolves as Mom glares at him. Then she shakes her head and says, "Have you made any friends?"

There it is again. Just like Rowan, she wants to know if I've done what you're supposed to do when you move somewhere different.

"No."

Mom shakes her head as Dad mumbles something I can't make out.

Hazel slips into the kitchen, gray stains of sleep smudging her eyes, and kisses our parents—Mom on the cheek; Dad on the top of his shaved head.

"You ready?" she asks, and I nod.

"What's the rush?" Dad asks, but my sister doesn't answer.

For him, there's no rush at all. But we can't wait to get out of the house. With Mom working now, it's only him and Rowan at home. That's why he clings to us like a child. Minutes aren't enough but they are all we're willing to give.

I kiss Mom as I pass and it feels like she tries to pull me back, the arm of my sweater stretched then released. But I ignore it, like I ignore so many things.

In the car, Hazel turns her music up but doesn't sing along. Whatever she inherited from our mother, a good voice isn't on the list.

I watch her, eyes front, hands firmly on the wheel, and wonder what she would do if I opened up.

The anonymous notes and the newspaper clipping are still tucked in my pillowcase. Showing her those would only do damage. But I could tell her I'm being taunted, or that last night we fled something we've never encountered before.

I could. But I don't.

"How are you feeling today?"

"Better," Hazel says. "Thanks for asking."

Her phone sits in the storage space between us, not lighting up or vibrating for the whole journey.

Does Mom ask my sister if she's made new friends here? I doubt it. She saves that question for me, and the real answer turns my stomach.

"What do you think of the school?"

Hazel's eyes don't leave the road as she mutters, "You don't need to do that."

"What if I want to?"

"Then you should be prepared for a disappointing answer."

She increases the volume on the radio, then glances at me before reaching back and turning it off.

"Sorry," she says. "I think our new school is very much like every school we've ever been to. Except for one obvious thing. And that . . ." She wipes her eyes and breathes slowly in and out. "And that makes me feel incredibly shitty."

"I know you miss him."

"Don't," she replies. "Don't ever try to understand. Just be you, Nate. And let us be us. I don't want to start hating our rides to school as much as I hate everything else."

"Okay."

I turn the music back on, my fingers tapping along, while Hazel's dig holes in the steering wheel.

That is the most she's spoken to me since we moved.

When we arrive, I leave her alone in the parking lot. Whatever she needs to get through the rest of her day, I'm not part of it.

Max is leaning on one of the columns by the main entrance, its bricks built into a tornado swirl.

Whoever designed Montgomery-Oakes High did it with big ideas and deep pockets. Everything catches your attention—the stained glass windows above us, the immaculate tiles below, the giant murals that fill the hallways, the names of former valedictorians calligraphed into the library's walls.

I try to merge with the crowd but she is already hurrying over.

"Still alive, I see."

"You, too," I reply.

"I'm not going to lie. I was shitting myself when I got home. I must have checked my closet at least twenty times for monsters."

"Did you find any?"

Max laughs as she pulls me aside. "Look . . . I know this is a lot. But nothing like that has ever happened before."

I think of last night, when she spoke about her broken family as if she'd known me for years.

There's so much I don't understand about people; there are so many questions that would probably be answered if I had time to properly get to know someone.

Is that how other people feel about me? All the ones I talked to in the towns we've left behind? Do they ever wonder what happened to that Nate kid? Do they ever think I could have been something to them, if only we'd stayed?

"I still can't believe it," Max says. "It actually happened."

"I wanted to talk to you about that."

She frowns as she says, "Okay."

"I want to keep my head down, just settle into this place in my own way, and last night . . . That wasn't what I had in mind."

"It wasn't what *any* of us had in mind, Nate. But it happened. We came face-to-face with a real urban legend and we were so terrified that we didn't even film it. We'd be rich if someone had whipped out their phone. I'm kicking myself."

She licks her lips and something greedy settles behind her eyes.

"Seriously," I say. "I like hanging out with you all but . . . I don't think I can anymore."

As I look over her shoulder, the Hiding Boy stands in the parking lot, vanishing as a group of freshmen run past.

Max's hand brushes my shoulder as she says, "It's okay. That's understandable. But we're in this together."

No. We're not.

Seb drives in and Max grabs my hand and drags me over. My cold skin sits uncomfortably in her warmth but I can't pull away. Snatching myself back would make this something it probably isn't. Instead, I try not to sweat and hope she doesn't comment.

That's the worst, when someone tells you how cold you are—as if you didn't know.

Tyler gets out of the passenger side and looks at the ruined paintwork, his bottom lip pinched between his teeth.

Sunlight catches the ragged scratches as Max crouches next to them, one finger running along the metal until she pulls it back with an "Ouch."

She watches the blood spread, then licks it off, her thumb pressed against her finger until she rummages through her bag and pulls out a pack of Band-Aids.

"Always come prepared," she says.

I wonder what else is in there, because she'll need a lot more than Band-Aids if that thing comes back.

The sound of scraping metal rips through my head and I shake it hard, the way I do whenever something horrible breaks through. Sometimes I twitch so much that I'm sure others have noticed, but whenever my eyes refocus, no one is looking at me, nobody cares.

Seb slams the driver's door and marches over.

"Did anyone actually sleep last night?" Max asks, her eyes darting between the three of us.

Tyler shakes his head while Seb stares into the distance.

"Nate is having doubts," Max says. "He wants to break up with us and go solo."

"Fine by me," Seb mutters.

"Ignore him," Tyler says. "He's grumpy because his car got mangled."

"Tell Nate that we need him," Max says. "He's the magic member."

"I'm not," I say quickly. "I appreciate you taking me in, but . . ."

"If you can't finish that sentence, there's no justification in going."

Max looks proud of that one. The only problem is, I *can* finish the sentence. I just don't want to.

"I still can't believe you walked home," Tyler says, holding his hand up for a high-five that I reluctantly accept with a feeble slap. "You're braver than I am."

"Or dumber," Seb says.

Max nudges him. "Seriously! Nate has done nothing to you, so stop pretending to be an asshole."

Seb's cheeks go crimson as he glares at the people pointing at his car.

"What happened?" someone asks, and he shouts, "None of your fucking business!"

"Sebastian!" Tyler says. "Find better words."

Slivers of happiness spread across Seb's face before all three of them start laughing.

"What did I miss?"

"You'll see," Max replies.

I close my eyes and pull on the strands of last night's memories.

Let me in.

"There is another explanation," I say. "*You* did it."

Tyler's shoulders tense as he eyeballs me. "I'm sorry?"

"Maybe you're playing a joke on the new kid. It wouldn't be the first time."

I think of Anthony Morgan, so small and lost when we met, so different when he tossed me in the trash. What were the odds that two new kids found each other on their very first day? That a pair of thirteen-year-old loners with their heads down crashed into each other when there were so many obstacles in our way?

He was a good friend, with a wicked sense of humor and great taste in comics. I didn't keep my favorite things a secret from him, because he was one of them. But I guess I wasn't one of his.

He soon got new friends, with "secret" handshakes performed while they looked me straight in the eye. His jokes changed to fit his audience, the punch lines leaving bruises.

Anthony stopped being the new kid quickly but, thanks to him, I never did.

"We're not screwing with you," Tyler says. "This *means* something to us. Why would we ruin it just to get a scare out of you?"

Because that's how some people think.

"I thought you *liked* urban legends. You're the one with

fifty-year-old articles about Murder Road. Where the hell did you get that, anyway?"

"Where did *I* get it?"

"You brought it to us, remember?"

Tyler pulls a face, and then Max's expression softens as she says, "Was that . . . ? Did someone leave that in your locker?"

"No. We're not talking about that anyway. We're talking about *you* . . . and last night. It's a coincidence, right, that you took me to the middle of nowhere and then . . . *that* happened."

Tyler opens his mouth but Max holds up a finger.

"You're right," she says. "It's strange. But I promise you, Nate. We're not fucking with you. Whatever happened out there, happened."

Nasty people have cracks in their faces where the glee falls out. The three people in front of me look genuinely scared.

"Okay," I say, because I'm desperate to believe her.

"We could go back and record it," Max says, but for once, she sounds doubtful.

"We're not doing it again," Seb mumbles. "We tried. It worked. We're done."

"We're *not* done," she says. "We're moving on. There are plenty of other urban legends."

Max carefully touches the paintwork one last time; then she points at the sky as the bell sounds.

"How do you always know?" I ask.

"Intuition. Please think about it some more before abandoning us. I know we've only just met but you can trust us. I swear it. And whatever happens next . . . safety in numbers, right?"

I glance at the parking lot, where my sister is talking animatedly on her phone. Eventually she stops, stares into the sky, then ambles over.

"I should go," I say. "But I'll definitely think about it."

"You can't ghost us, Nathaniel," Max calls after me. "This is a small town. I can easily find out where you live."

I stop dead, turn, then say, "Okay. We're still friends."

"That simple?"

"Yes."

I leave before she can say anything else, then watch from behind a pillar as Hazel drifts past like she's another stranger in a sea of them.

I wait for her to meet someone; to be a part of something. But she slips into the building alone.

Then I watch Max, Tyler, and Seb join the masses heading to first period.

When they're gone, I wait a few seconds, seeing if the ghost who haunts my dreams is still lurking. But there is only a teacher I haven't seen before, his thick tie flapping against a coffee-stained shirt as he hurries us to class.

Someone trips on the top step and curses under their breath. He glares at them before bellowing, "Find better words!" and I smile.

I had every intention of leaving Max alone. But I don't think I can do that anymore.

Did she mean it when she said she'd find my address? Was she telling the truth when she claimed they had nothing to do with last night? And what happens if I keep dreaming about her, only for the Hiding Boy to take a hammer to my happiness?

24

As I stare through my teacher, blocking out the voices of classmates whose names I'll never learn, distant wails slowly peel the skin from my ears.

The noises crammed into my head are soundtracks to horror movies I haven't seen; unfamiliar ghouls taking refuge in my brain.

Behind those sounds, footsteps play on a loop—from soft to heavy; from distant to close.

I sit at the back of every class, the wall as near to my back as possible. That way, when the hot breath spreads over my neck, when my limbs tense as a shadow uncoils in the last layer of space between me and nothing, I know it's not real.

What we're running from will find us eventually. A part of it is buried inside us all—a beacon powered by our terror—and I hate myself for thinking that this time might be different.

I accidentally make eye contact with the teacher, his grimace morphing into a smile as he focuses on the boy directly in front of me. Then I spend the rest of the class filling my book with random sketches, both sad and relieved that I can.

When we go, the teacher hands me an envelope with a room number and a time inside.

"What's this?" I ask, but he's already talking to someone else.

Would he answer me if I talked a little louder, if I stood here until everyone else had gone, if I screamed?

I don't know and I don't care. Instead, I go to the room on

the note and stare at the plaque. The name sounds familiar. But I know so many names, from so many stories that I wish I'd never heard.

The door opens and Seb's laugh dissolves when he sees me.

Behind him, a small white woman with cropped black hair looks from me to him and back again, then says, "Can I help you?"

"I got this."

She takes the note from me and nods. "Nathaniel?"

"Nate."

"Hello, Nate. I'm Miss Kittle. I'm the counselor here and, alongside other things, I help new students settle in."

Seb stares at the ground, his neck glowing red.

"I'm okay, actually," I say.

"Others have found it quite useful."

"No, thank you."

"It might help, if you have any questions about the school . . . or your future."

I do have *one* question. Why won't you take no for an answer?

Seb kicks the ground while Miss Kittle grins at me.

Tyler said Seb is this woman's most loyal customer—whatever that means. Did he accept her invitation and never leave? Does she begin by answering your questions and then tunnel away with her own?

"Is it compulsory?"

"No."

"Then I'll think about it."

Miss Kittle nods, calm settling over features that were beginning to rupture. Then she turns to Seb and says, "Same time next time."

Her laugh stops short when she sees his face. Then her eyes narrow as she studies me.

"Do you know each other?"

"Kind of," I say, stepping into the crowd before she can ask anything else.

I thought I could avoid the adults here by being me. In my experience, they don't have the time or the desire to bond with the quiet kid. But Miss Kittle is different.

Maybe Seb and I are more similar than I first thought.

I walk quickly to my locker then stop dead.

Nothing is out of the ordinary and yet I know, somehow, that there is another warning inside. The hair on my arms bristles and sweat seeps from my pores as I work out my next move.

What happens if I never use my locker again? Will it eventually burst open under the weight of a stranger's torment?

A tiny part of me wants to know if we're still in the middle of a horrible game, so I step forward, my legs like concrete blocks, and carefully open the door.

When nothing falls to the floor, I gently breathe out. Then panic surges up my spine as I see it lying in the darkness.

They haven't forgotten me. Not yet.

The clipping feels brittle, like a layer of sliced-off skin.

I check to be sure no one is watching, then lean in to read the headline.

MOTHER'S HEARTBREAK AFTER NANNY SMOTHERS TWINS

The paper is dated 1985, but I already knew that. Out of all the Murder Road stories, this is the one that lingered longest when I read about it more than thirty years later.

> The mother of murdered twins Eloise and Tammy Witchell has spoken of her anguish after their trusted nanny of five years smothered them while they slept.
>
> The killings—the latest in an increasingly long line of tragedies to befall the residents of Cherry Tree Lane—rocked the entire country earlier this month.
>
> Martha Harkness had worked for the Witchell family since

their children were born. With a career spanning forty years, and numerous glowing references, she was the last person most would suspect of murder.

Speaking after the coroner ruled two cases of asphyxiation, Mrs. Witchell said, "Our lives ended the moment our beautiful angels were taken from us. The person we trusted the most with our children stole them. The only minuscule blessing we can take from this is that Tammy and Eloise remain together."

Who the hell is doing this to me? At every other school I've been to since leaving Belleview, I have been ignored.

I press the article between my thumb and finger, gently rubbing until the ancient paper begins to crumble. Then I slide it carefully into my math textbook.

This is an ancient artifact, a collectors' item. These things aren't left lying around the house or conveniently found at yard sales. They are kept. On purpose.

My hands start to tremble and I slip as far into the corner as I can, a few kids casting puzzled looks as they pass, but most ignoring me altogether.

I need to think, so I hurry through the shrinking crowd to the only place that feels safe right now.

No way am I going back to those stalls. Instead, I look through the closed lunchroom doors, then creep inside, the sound of chattering cooks sneaking through the metal shutters.

I march toward the Hell Hole without looking back. If Max is right, and everyone else ignores it, this is the only place in school where I can get my shit together.

I slump against the bare-brick wall, slowing my breathing as everything I know about the Witchell twins rustles through my head like pages caught in the wind.

Theirs was the eleventh house on Murder Road—targeted more than two decades after the Hiding Boy's curse.

Two five-year-old girls were smothered in their sleep, someone forcing their favorite teddies over their faces until four thin arms went limp.

During the autopsy, they found traces of artificial fur lodged in the victims' throats. The same type they pulled from the fingernails of the woman entrusted to look after them.

At first, the police assumed the nanny took her own life, but, like Tyler said, the Hiding Boy kills everyone, including the host.

If you believe the legend, he possessed the nanny, killed the kids, then finished the job. Another house ticked off the list.

I freeze as footsteps echo in the corridor linking the cafeteria to the Hell Hole.

No one comes down here, I tell myself. *Nobody except us.*

The sound grows louder, then stops.

I wait for a teacher to clear their throat, or pull me out of the shadows with a gotcha grin, but there is only an expanding silence that squeezes the air from my lungs.

It's your imagination. You're safe here.

Even when the whistling starts, vibrating off the high ceilings and swarming through my ears, I don't believe it.

I've had them before—waking dreams, lucid lies. I'm alone and I am safe. That's all that matters.

The footsteps start again, stopping after a few seconds before a metallic *bang!* rings out.

My head jolts back in shock, crashing against the cold wall.

As pain fills my skull, someone steps slightly closer, then *bang!*

I picture the busted lockers lining the unlit corridor like scolded children.

Another door smashes against rusted metal, squeaking on its hinges before it finally comes to a halt.

I slink further into the gloom, edging along the wall until my fingers find something wet. I flinch, holding my hand to my nose but smelling nothing.

When I listen closer, I hear water dripping from one of the pipes zigzagging across the ceiling.

Another locker door crashes against its frame. Then another.

Nowhere is safe in a new school, in an unfamiliar town. Everything is a potential trap and I should know better.

"Who's there?" I stutter, but no one answers.

They edge closer to me, the whistle ringing in my ears.

"I said, 'Who's there?'"

I pull my knees into my chest, waiting for the inevitable. At least I'll know soon—who it is. And why.

Bang!

My body reverberates from the force, my heart beating so fast that I imagine it bursting from my chest. Then I dash into the only space I can see, a janitor's closet filling my vision moments before I squeeze inside, gently closing the door as the cold metal scrapes my lips.

The feet move again, two steps—*click . . . clack*—calm and patient.

My fingers search for a weapon in the darkness, wrapping around a thick wooden stick attached to something that softly clanks against the mess all around me.

I'm not particularly strong. Not compared to Rowan, anyway. But sometimes you only need to be strong enough.

I wait. For the door to spring open. For whoever is tormenting me to show themselves. But no one comes.

Instead, as someone whistles the last line of the Hiding Boy's song, footsteps head back down the corridor until all I can hear is my frantic panting.

I charge into the Hell Hole, tools crashing to the hard ground behind me, and then I burst through the black and stare into the empty cafeteria.

The door opens with a hiss, before I'm staring into the classrooms on either side of the main corridor.

Am I in one of those rooms? Sleeping through another pointless lesson? Is any of this real?

I try to pinch myself, then slam my palm against the side of my head.

"Am I dreaming?!" I yell.

The kids in the nearest class stare at me as their teacher steps out.

"Where should you be now?"

"I don't know."

His eyes grow warmer as he says, "Are you okay, son?"

I nod. "English. With Ms. Hewitt. That's where I should be."

"Best be off then."

The teacher watches me pass, killing his students' giggles with a single word. "Enough."

I'm scared. Like always. Yet, this time, it's so much worse.

25

That evening, I put the article about the murdered twins with the other clipping and the notes.

He's coming for you!

I know that. It's inevitable. But those warnings usually lurk in my nightmares, not in my locker or empty bathroom stalls.

Rowan strides in without knocking and I quickly smooth my pillow while trying to look as calm as possible.

The brother he used to be would have listened. He would take those four sheets of paper seriously. But now it's not only his battered face I struggle to recognize, it's also his heart, grown cold and indifferent.

He lies on his back, tossing balled-up socks into the air, until I ask, "When did you start fighting for money?"

He sits up, broken veins painting his right eye a watery pink. "Last year."

"And when did Mom find out?"

Rowan chuckles. "Almost immediately."

We're good at keeping each other's secrets, and I wonder if our mother knows more of mine than she's letting on. Does she know about Max and the Hell Chasers? Has she found what I've hidden in the bedding she usually leaves us to strip?

"Is it worth it?" I ask. "You look awful."

My brother fixes me with an unblinking stare. "There are different types of pain, Nate. I prefer this one."

"Does it get easier?"

He pauses for a moment, then sighs. "No."

I don't follow him downstairs. Instead, I think of Max, wondering if she's my way of coping, just like Rowan and Hazel have theirs.

I used to think *my* way was keeping quiet, remaining small. But Max is the only thing that makes sense to me right now. Even after that night in the woods, when something dragged its claws along Seb's car, my strongest memory is her hand in mine.

"Dinner!" Mom yells.

I silently take my place at the table, all the ways I could say what I'm feeling jumbled into a thick ball of twine with no obvious ends.

"I hate this," I mumble, and Mom's fork pauses halfway to her mouth.

"What did you say?"

"I said, 'I hate this.'"

Only Rowan is still eating now, his cutlery scraping loudly against his plate. Between mouthfuls, he smirks, because, for once, he's not the cause of an explosion.

"You hate *what,* exactly?" Mom asks.

"*This,*" I say. "Sitting *here.* Pretending everything is okay. Ignoring all the horrible moments that, let's face it, are basically all the fucking time."

"Nathaniel!" Mom yells.

Dad's hands rise then fall, his eyes fixed firmly on his newspaper.

"What's this about?" Mom asks. "Is it Rowan's bruises? Or have you seen something out there . . . on one of your walks?"

She makes it sound like when the old folks at Grandma's nursing home took an afternoon stroll.

"It's *this* place. It's suffocating. And school . . ."

It feels like I'm back cowering in the Hell Hole while something nasty crawled toward me.

"Do you ever think what would have happened if we'd stayed in Belleview?"

"No more!" Dad shouts, every plate on the table clinking with the force of his fist.

When I glance up, tears creep down Hazel's cheeks, while Rowan's broken face is blank.

"I'm glad you've all got your ways of coping," I say as I leave. "It's time that I focused on mine."

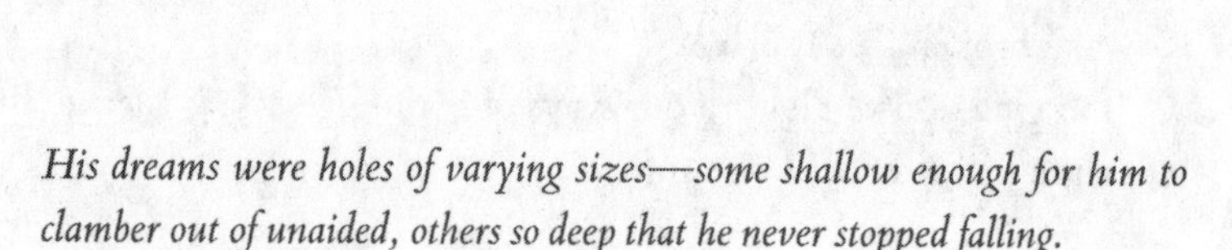

His dreams were holes of varying sizes—some shallow enough for him to clamber out of unaided, others so deep that he never stopped falling.

Sometimes his fingers found respite in the darkness, his nails peeling from his skin as he clung to a crumbling ledge.

Blood trickled down his quivering arms, tickling, teasing, until he fell once more—a never-ending cycle of tumbling terror and brittle hope.

He hated those dreams. He despised that sensation, the moment before he was finally dragged back to the waking world, when he was falling so quickly that his soul came away from his body.

In those moments, right before he landed, he saw the bloodstained girl, her arm outstretched.

Her mother was murdered. Her father was gone. Her brother had vanished. So, he went to help her, because that was what he had been taught to do.

As his fingers touched hers, he felt the sticky warmth of someone else's blood. Then she gripped his wrist and dragged him toward the house that started it all.

His heels left tracks in the dirt as she pulled, the dust he kicked up landing sharply in his eyes.

"I'm here to help you," he said, and she stopped dragging.

Red splatters fell at her feet as she shook her head and whispered, "It's too late for that."

When he awoke, he looked for her—in all the usual places and all the less obvious ones. He searched until his parents stumbled in, wiping sleepy confusion from their eyes.

They stared at the ruins of his bedroom—the upturned furniture and strewn clothes, the computer table pushed clean over.

Then they stroked his hair until his eyes cleared and he asked, "What happened?"

"You had a bad dream," his mother said. "You're safe now."

He nodded, staring at the ghost hiding under his bed, then whispered, "I hope so."

26

The following Tuesday, Max lies on one of the benches dotted around the school's huge courtyard, her hands behind her head as she sighs at the sky.

"After you've come face-to-face with an actual urban legend," she says, "the next few days are a bit anticlimactic."

For her, maybe. But I'm still studying every classmate who passes by and eavesdropping on every whispered conversation. Someone here is reminding me of Murder Road's horrors, and I'm scared of what comes next.

I haven't found anything in my locker for a few days. And I've managed to avoid the main bathrooms, sneaking into the forgotten stalls behind the science block whenever necessary.

For a few nasty nights, the Face in the Glass made cameos in my dreams. But whatever was out there, it hasn't come for us . . . yet.

"What is it?"

Max waves a hand in front of my face until I realize I'm staring at her.

"Sorry. I zoned out."

What I want to say . . . what I'll never say . . . is that being with her is the only thing that stops me being afraid.

That has its own problems, but for now I ignore them and hope for the best.

Max has barely mentioned the Hell Chasers since it happened and she suddenly jumps up and starts pacing.

"You want to do another one, don't you?" I ask, and she laughs.

"You think I don't have a life? You think I literally spend every minute waiting for it to get dark?"

"It seems like that."

Max leans toward me, tilts her head, and whispers, "Appearances can be deceiving."

"So, what else do you do?"

I want more of the Max that she was that night—before we drew the faces; before whatever that thing was begged us to be let in. *That* Max is the closest I've had to a genuine friend.

Am I being foolish? Have I mistaken one moment of honesty for something else? Maybe she would have told anyone about her father that night. Or perhaps she really does see something special in me.

"You want to know what I do?"

I wait, think, then nod.

"What are you doing on Saturday?"

"Haven't we been down this road?" I ask.

Max smiles and says, "Not this one. This is a daytime activity. Are you free?"

"I *can* be."

"Okay. I'll show you what else I do then."

Her grin stirs something in my stomach—not butterflies, because they can't survive inside me, but excitement.

Two girls walk past, their fake laughs shrill enough to break a dog's eardrums as they stare at Max then scuttle away. In response, she lets out a low growl.

"What was that?" I ask.

"That's what bad blood sounds like."

"Friends of yours?"

"Never in a million years."

Max watches them for a few more seconds, all the while picking tiny patches of black nail varnish from her thumb. Then she nods and says, "Do you have enemies?"

That's hard to define.

"I have people I hate."

"Close enough. That's Demon in Chief Helen Keane and her minion Stephanie."

"Okay."

"They made my life a living hell in middle school."

"What did they do?"

"What all mean girls do: enough to make you feel *this* small but not enough to get caught. She leaves me alone now. Tyler thinks she's scared of me. I think she's scared of Tyler."

"School can be shit," I say.

Max laughs into the sky. "It really can."

"If you ever want to talk again, about your family, I'd like to listen."

Max nods, stares at me until I look away, then says, "I will."

I wish I could tell her something in return. Instead, we sit in silence. In my head an entire conversation plays out. I tell her where I lived before, why we left, who didn't get that chance. I tell her all the things that cling to my insides like leeches.

27

The woman's weak breaths fill the stale air, rattling, crackling, nothing like normal breathing at all.

"How old is she?" I whisper, and Max says, "Eighty-two."

Max's neighbor is in bed, her eyes frantic, like she's woken up in the wrong place. But it's not the room she's uncertain about, it's me.

"It's all right," Max says. "This is the friend I was telling you about. Nate, come say hi."

My legs stiffen, then submit, as I slowly step toward the woman and mutter, "Hello."

It sounds like a question, and Max smiles, touches my arm, and says, "It's okay."

I love how calm I now feel in her company; how calm *everyone* feels.

The woman's bed sits in the center of a large living room—her fingers gripping one of the metallic rails and her tiny body lost beneath the sheets.

I look at the television, the photo frames, the cabinet full of well-read books, and the half-finished sudoku puzzle on the arm of a chair. In the corner, I notice another seat. One that almost belongs in a waiting room but not quite.

Below the thin black legs and the removable plastic cushion is something I quickly look away from.

An image of my grandma shoots through my mind—when she was losing so many things, her strength and her shine and her memories.

When I was ten, I pointed at Grandma's new commode and asked, "What goes there?" And she replied, "My dignity," for the briefest moment as sharp as a tack.

"How are you, Bella?"

Max's voice brings me back as the woman, lifting her words like dumbbells, says, "I'm fine."

"Glad to hear it."

Through the large bay window, I see a man stepping carefully through the garden, his back slightly bent and thin purple flowers in one hand.

He sees us and waves, no uncertainty on his face, no concern that a stranger is standing over his wife. It seems Max's word is enough for this family. If she vouches for you, they will shake your hand and offer to make tea. Because that's exactly what the man does next.

"Henry," Max says. "Let me."

"Guests don't make drinks," the man calls from the kitchen, his words a lot lighter than his wife's. "Guests sit."

Max grins. "Some do."

She holds up one finger to me, then leaves the room.

I think about sitting, but that feels wrong here. This seems like the kind of room you can only relax in when others are already relaxed. So, I stand. And I wait.

When I catch the woman's gaze, her eyes look pleadingly at me. At least, I think that's what they're doing. I don't spend long trying to interpret the look. My heart is pounding and I feel sweaty under my clothes, so I step back and study the photographs.

Bella, that's what Max called her. And that's who she looks like in the images that line the windowsill. She looks like a person with a great life, a stunning smile, and a husband to match.

Now, the elderly lady who lives three doors down from Max is lost behind her wrinkles and confusion.

Grandma used to say age is a gift but it's also a thief, stealing the parts of you displayed in frames, hiding your favorite moments, making you a victim over and over until, eventually, you submit entirely.

When you are running from something that lives to kill, that's what scares you the most. And yet strangely, foolishly, I'm afraid of getting old too.

I don't want to forget things the way my grandmother did. I don't want to know the fear that swelled in her big wet eyes.

Max and Henry's laughter leads them into the room, and I breathe out, relieved to have someone else to look at.

The man puts a small vase filled with the purple flowers next to his wife, while Max sits beside me, smiles, and says, "Are you making friends?"

No.

"I guess."

"I told you that you'd meet Henry for real," Max says, looking from me to the man and back again.

"Pardon?"

"The candy store. You saw him leave the other night, didn't you?"

I look closer at the man opposite; at the lines etched on his warm face, the tanned hands softly lifting a glass to his wife's cracked lips, the white wisps on his head, dancing in the faintest breeze from an open window.

It was so calm sitting in the square, as a stranger locked up and wished me well. But this is anything but calm. I feel out of place, and the worst part is that Max can't see it.

"You'll have to come by when we're open," Mr. Taylor says. "Do you have a sweet tooth?"

"Who doesn't?" Max says, before I can reply.

"You've got a great friend here. Max has been looking after us since she was tiny."

Mr. Taylor's smile softens as he turns to his wife, and I try to imagine Max as a little kid, puttering around this house.

"That's not quite right," she says. "I'm just repaying a favor."

I don't reply but they seem happy to sit in the silence. Neither of them explains, because they don't have to. They know their story by heart and I don't have the courage to ask for more.

Instead, I listen to them talk, always including Bella in the conversations, even when she doesn't speak back.

They laugh for her, remember for her, while faint tremors ripple across her face.

When she falls asleep, Max whispers, "How is it coming?" and Mr. Taylor grins and says, "See for yourself."

"Come on," Max says. "You'll love this."

I follow them down the cobbled garden path and into a large shed, where paintings rest against every surface and an easel stands covered in the far corner.

When Mr. Taylor removes the cloth, dust motes dance in the sunlight. Then his wife's face comes into focus—the one from the photographs, with the huge smile and electric eyes.

Henry twirls a paintbrush between his fingers as Max steps closer.

"It's amazing," she says. "Bella will love it."

I think of the woman wheezing in the living room and hope, with all my heart, that she does love it.

Sometimes we did things for Grandma that we were sure would help—treating magical memories like time machines, then crying when she didn't leave the room.

Both Max and her neighbor have the hopeful look that Mom used to have when she believed something would help. I'd hate for that hope to shatter.

"Henry has a plan," Max says. "He's painting this for Bella's birthday. I picked the frame. We're almost ready to go. He has three weeks for the finishing touches. Not that he needs it."

Mr. Taylor leans in to the painting, wiping away something invisible.

"It's amazing," I say. "Really amazing."

Max looks like she wants more but that's all I have. Her pride in these people radiates off her, and I wonder what they did to deserve it.

"We'll leave you to it," she says. "But don't tinker too much. It's already perfect."

For the first time today, a shadow falls over Mr. Taylor's face. Then he follows us back into the house and busies himself with his wife.

"I know you can't see it," Max whispers, "but she used to be so alive."

Back on the street, she turns to me and says, "Thank you. Those people are my family. They saw a single mom and a little kid move in and immediately made us feel welcome. They made a shitty time a lot easier. So, I'm trying to do the same for them."

28

"That's my house," Max says, pointing to a single-story building on our right.

I tense at the thought of going inside. It's one thing meeting her neighbors, but I haven't prepared myself for her mom.

If she's anything like *my* mother, she will ask too many questions and try so very hard, and that combination always brings out the worst in me.

"When are you going to tell me where you live?" Max asks.

"You think I don't trust you?"

She laughs. "I *know* you don't."

"It's not that. We move a lot. I've never had a friend to bring home, so . . ."

"It's not in your nature to share?"

"Something like that."

Max walks past her house and stops at the end of the street.

"I've got one last thing to show you," she says. "If you don't have anywhere better to be."

By this point, that's rhetorical, so I silently follow her down a narrow lane that leads into a small parking lot.

To the right, a church spire pokes the sky and a large metal latch holds a wooden gate in place.

Max lifts it and gestures for me to go through. Then she closes it and points to the thick stone steps leading into a graveyard.

"What is this?" I ask.

"Let's call it research."

She walks ahead and I follow, careful not to step on the small squares set flush with the ground. As we go farther, they are replaced by much larger headstones, some weather-beaten and barely legible, others shimmering in the sun.

We pass a woman replacing old flowers with new, and then I step aside as a dog bounds past, its owner smiling apologetically before they both disappear through a gap in the fence.

I think of the last time we visited a cemetery—Rowan laughing, Hazel silent, and me in between, my giggles quickly swallowed by uncertainty.

There were one headstone, two names, and three mysteries.

I hadn't wanted to go but Rowan can be persuasive.

Maybe Hazel could have stopped him, but she came too. Out of boredom, perhaps, or curiosity, or simply to tell her friends that she'd been.

The first victims of Murder Road were names carved into stone—Harriet and Eli Souter, beloved mother and cherished son. But her son wasn't with her, just his name.

That was the first mystery: Where was the boy whose body they couldn't find, the brother of the girl drenched in blood?

The second mystery, to me at least, was the father, who had swung back and forth from the garage rafters until the police cut him down. Where was his body? Where was his name?

And then there was the biggest mystery of all. What had really happened to them?

Stories swirled around Belleview, and my parents shielded me from them as best they could. But they couldn't protect me from playground gossip, or the morbid fascination of our brother, who by the age of nine believed he was an authority on all things horrifying.

That night, after he dragged six-year-old me to the graveyard, Rowan told me the truth about Murder Road. He said I was old enough to hear the story of the Hiding Boy, who made a pact with a devil.

"Are you okay?"

I snap back to the present, to Max's eyes filling my vision. "Sure."

She crouches next to a smaller grave, the stone pot full of plastic yellow flowers, and I read the words as she traces them with her finger.

Diego Soto—Born June 30th 1989;
fell asleep July 1st 1989.

I don't notice my tears until Max stands and wipes them away.

"Who were they?" I ask.

"I don't know."

We wait in silence for a while, and I wonder if this is the biggest tragedy in a sea of them. How many people in this graveyard lived a suitably long life?

I hear Dad's voice when I think that, remembering when he tried to ease the pain of Grandma's passing by focusing on her existence rather than its end. But you can't do that when a life is measured in hours.

Max walks away, then points at a grave tilted to one side, as if the ground has been disturbed from below. Grass creeps over the lower edge of the granite, and small green stones fill the overgrown bed.

There's no name on this one; not anymore.

"This is the next one," Max says.

"The next what?"

"The next urban legend. We're leveling up."

"I thought we were here to . . ."

I can't say the rest, because I don't know what I expected. But it wasn't this.

"We *can* do both," Max says. "We can think about the lost, and we can keep living."

She doesn't need to tell me that.

"Seb is terrified of this one," Max says. "Tyler says he's not, but we'll see."

She crouches next to the grave, where the stone comes away from the ground, and rests her hand on the moss. Then she pulls it away to reveal a hole.

"You want to reach inside?"

She grins, although nothing about this is a joke.

"Are you serious?" I ask.

"Why not? It's just a hole."

"Into a grave."

"Exactly. That's the legend. You come here on a full moon, reach inside, and . . ."

"And what?"

Max replaces the moss, stands, then says, "It's called the Corpse's Grip. There are different stories. Some say it holds your wrist until your whole body goes cold, then it lets go. Others say it tries to pull you in. One kid had to go to the hospital with a dislocated shoulder. Another lost two fingers."

"And who told you this, exactly?"

She huffs out a laugh. "A friend of a friend? The town gossip? Who knows how these things get out? We've done it before, but . . ."

"You think I'm some kind of urban-legend summoner?"

"There's only one way to find out."

"No."

I hold my features steady as she looks at me, uncertainty turning to playfulness as she says, "You're getting confident, new kid."

"I don't want to do another one. Messing with this stuff is dangerous."

"Do you speak from experience?"

Max's grin wavers as I figure out my reply.

"We *all* do. Don't forget how scared you felt when we were in the car. Just because life is 'back to normal' that doesn't mean you should keep playing."

Max looks at the tilted grave and sighs. "If you feel that strongly about it, you can sit this one out."

"Why can't we just hang?"

She twirls the blue streak in her hair between her fingers as she watches me. "That's what we're doing now."

"But there's an ulterior motive. You're scoping out the next Hell Chasers project. I thought that was over."

Her brow creases as she asks, "What made you think that?"

"Because of Seb's car. Because sometimes I still hear those whispers as if they burrowed into my brain. That wasn't fun."

Max shrugs. "It's what we do."

"And the others are okay with it?"

"They don't know yet. But they will be."

Max walks back to the baby's grave, touches it, then heads for the church.

Why can't this be enough for her? If it's just the two of us, filling our days with beautiful normality, I can almost forget the notes and the articles, the Face in the Glass, my fractured family, and the unending horrors of Murder Road.

I need Max. Now more than ever. But if I stay, I won't let her railroad everyone.

Safety in numbers—that's what she said. And sometimes it's about protecting people from themselves.

The church doors are open and I step inside. It feels small and big at the same time—the pews close together and the ceiling stretching upward.

Max stands to the side, her head bowed, so I walk over to the flat white candles flickering in the breeze and light a new one.

One isn't enough, not for all the victims of Cherry Tree Lane that I want to mourn. But there isn't a candle for every person taken by the Hiding Boy, so I group them all together in my mind and hope that's not an insult.

Max's sleeve brushes mine as she lights one of her own and I wonder who she is grieving. I hope it's a grandparent, because, while all loss is heartbreaking, the cracks heal quicker when the rules aren't broken too.

The rules that say that old people die first; that children outlive their parents; that Time kills more than Tragedy.

"Amen," Max whispers, before we step back in unison, then leave.

As we approach her house, my nerves stir, but Max stops a few doors away and says, "I'll see you at school."

Disappointment fizzles in my stomach as I say, "Sure."

I watch her walk up the front path and disappear behind a bright red door. Then I go back to the church, where an old woman sits with her head down.

I've never prayed. Not once. The closest I've come is talking to myself and wondering if someone is listening.

Mom said that *is* praying, but I don't think it's that simple. Because praying is *believing* someone is there or, at the very least, *hoping*. It's not enough to wonder. There's a certainty to prayer that I've never had because I'm not that confident about anything.

I sit a few rows behind the woman and wait for her to finish. As she leaves, she stares at me unblinking, unsmiling, and I think of my grandma's face before she forgot us—always young, always happy.

I could try talking to her now. The connection to wherever comes next is probably strongest in places like this. But I have no words; only regret.

Instead, I walk back to the candles and light them one after another until the varnished box is empty. Then I watch their flames sway and steady, like all our lives do, balancing on the line between here and gone.

29

When I was eight, I sat in a corner of the school field while my classmates played, listening to Annabel Jenkins and Harpreet Suman chat about last night's TV. Then Annabel's eyes narrowed as she said, "Did you hear about Mr. Goodhand's dog?"

I had. Many times. I'd both heard *about* it and heard *it* because the damn thing never stopped barking. But then, one day, it did.

Silence suddenly filled the evening air and we all assumed the dog had, as Dad put it, "woofed its last woof."

But Annabel Jenkins had a different take.

"The boy killed it," she said, glee plastered across her face. "The boy that got banned from the pet store."

It was bullshit. I knew that. And yet, Annabel wasn't a bullshitter. One time she told Freddie Avery that he was talking "the biggest lies I've ever heard" just for saying he was moving states, so, whoever told her the dog story, she believed them.

"Want to hear something horrible?" she asked, and while Harpreet shook her head and I stared at the grass, she told us anyway.

The boy lived on Cherry Tree Lane before any of us were born. He was twelve when people's pets started going missing, and thirteen when they found the first one in his treehouse.

Before that, when he was seven, he'd been banned from the pet store. The reason was a warning no one heeded: a sign pointing directly to the dead animals they would find six years later.

"Everyone starts somewhere," Annabel said, her braces catching the sunlight as she grinned. "That's what my brother told me."

Like so many of the Murder Road stories, it was spread by a sibling. Just as Rowan told me and Hazel about the very first victims, Annabel's brother filled her head with horror. And now she was passing it to us.

"This is nasty," Harpreet said as she left.

I could have followed. She had opened a door that I only had to walk through. But I stayed.

I didn't ask exactly why he had been banned from the pet store. Neither did I ask what happened to the animals he took from their owners. I knew, even then, that some people were twisted.

But I know that, when he was found, his parents didn't hand him over to the police. They sent him to live with an aunt who had a good heart, a spare room, and no pets.

That should have been the end of the story. But, decades later, the boy came back.

The house wasn't his anymore. It belonged to the Oswald family by then—bought at auction after the previous owners had died, their memories stripped away and painted over.

If you believe Annabel, the boy who was banned from the pet store stared past his aging reflection, into a home he no longer recognized, and he yelled so loud that every dog in the neighborhood roared back.

I don't believe that part. I think, as with most Murder Road tales, some things were added later. All I know is that he waited until midnight, when the owners woke with a start to find the Hiding Boy at the foot of their bed, and then the man smashed his way into the house and killed everyone and everything inside.

When it was done, the man dragged his victims to the treehouse, their bodies painting thick red trails down the stairs while skull fragments thudded against the carpet.

Then he sat with their remains on either side of him, stroking something that used to be alive, until the police found him; a single stab wound from a knife still held in the cold hand of Mrs. Oswald enough to take him too.

They said he acted alone, and why wouldn't they? Back then, only a few people from Belleview believed the legend of a cursed street. Maybe he did, and those murders would have happened regardless. But I've done enough research to know that the ghost was a warning they had no time to heed. If you've seen him, it's already too late.

Those words have lost their sharp edges now but, when Annabel told me, they left cuts in my mind, causing fear to trickle into my days when I least expected it.

Images of Max flash through my brain: the excitement on her face before we heard the whispers in the middle of nowhere; the playfulness when she pointed at the hole in the grave and dared me to reach in.

Her worst-case scenarios were harmless games, but things have changed. I have no intention of seeing if the Face in the Glass was a one-off or if this town really is some kind of Hellmouth.

If she pushes, I'll push back, ensuring they know that leveling up isn't always a good thing.

As I walk home, a dog yowls in the distance and another barks a response. I think about my old teacher's pet—the one Annabel claimed was taken by a monster.

The sounds sit softly in my ears, far enough away to be calming.

When I reach home, I sit on the sofa opposite Dad and run through all the things I want to tell him. But he speaks first.

"Where have you been?"

I've been to an old lady's house and a graveyard and a church. I've walked past Max's house twice, both scared and excited at the prospect of being invited in. And I've been to the past—mine and other people's—when a school friend tried her best to scare me and when a horror story was born.

What would our father say if I told him all that? He looks at me expectantly but I know he doesn't have room in his head or his heart for my problems. He acts like he does. I genuinely believe he would listen. But something inside him would break, and we're old enough to save him from that now.

Instead, I go upstairs and try to put my feelings in some kind of order. First, I reach my hand under the mattress, careful not to catch my skin on the broken springs. Then I pull out the notebook I took from Grandma's room, on the day Mom asked if there was anything I wanted.

Its cover is full of rich blues and greens, two kingfishers with orange tummies peering at each other from opposing corners.

Grandma told me it was where we would chronicle our adventures, when she finally got out of the nursing home. At first, I believed her. Later, I didn't have the heart to put her right.

I leaf through the pages until I find a blank one, and then I write some of the questions swirling around my head.

Why did Max bring me to the Taylors'?
What will happen if I go back to the cemetery?
Can I really stop her from doing another urban legend?
Am I doing the right thing?

The spaces for the answers remain empty for now. But I feel calmer for trying.

When I'm done, I slot those questions between other, heavier things, so they can't break out.

Then I stare around my room, at all the cracks and dents and stains that should be more familiar by now. They usually are. But then, I usually spend a lot more time in our new houses.

This time, Max is my distraction, her story something she seems intent on pulling me into.

But can that happen without her being dragged into mine?

The man sat in the corner of his dream, stroking something small and still, the fur on its back matted with crimson clumps that he carefully picked through, rubbing them between his fingers until they crumbled.

In another corner, an old woman stood with her back to him, her veiny arms working quickly until she turned—needle and thread in one hand and the sawn-off head of a teddy in the other.

The blood spooling from its neck lapped at the woman's bloated ankles until she stepped forward, a low hum coming from somewhere deep inside.

As she held it closer, he could see the uneven stitches she had forced into its face.

"Push it," the woman said, the bear's body suddenly in her other hand and the needle gleaming between her teeth.

He rested his thumb against the button on the bear's paw, then did as he was told.

"Say it," someone mumbled, and a child's voice rang out: "I love you, Mommy."

The sound made him shudder, but he couldn't stop himself.

"I love you, Mommy."

"I love you, Mommy."

"I love . . ."

"I . . ."

When he pushed it again, a bloodcurdling wail shattered the darkness.

In its place, he saw flames as tall as skyscrapers, and blistered skin reaching out to him.

He cowered until the hands pulled back and the fire shrank, its roar replaced by unnerving silence.

The Hiding Boy slammed his fists against the bedroom window, but he clamped his hands over his ears and sang to himself—all the songs his mom made up just for him.

He sang until he was shouting, every inch of his nightmare taken up by someone or something that had either died or killed in that infernal street.

He looked from one to the next, ticking off the horror stories he'd been forced to learn by heart. Then he saw someone new, his hand reaching for the flames that suddenly surged again, meeting the blackened fingers of the only body still fighting.

For a few seconds, they held each other—two hands trapped on different sides of the same tragedy—and then there was nothing but ash, carried away on a rising river of blood.

30

"I've told you before . . . I'm not doing that!" Seb's face contorts like a stubborn toddler's as he catches my eye then stares at the ground.

Max grins. "It will be fine."

"Remember the boy who had his arm ripped off?"

"No," she replies. "Do you?"

I think back to the graveyard, when she told me about the kid with the dislocated shoulder and the one who lost two fingers. She picks and chooses what to do with the rumors that swirl around this town; when to use them as ammunition and when to throw them away.

"There's only one night of the year when I'm going in that graveyard," Seb says. "You know that?"

"Fine," Max says. "We'll do it without you too."

There's a lot to take from Seb's stare, even in the few seconds before I'm forced to look away. He's jealous of me; he thinks he's being replaced; he's daring Max to do it because he knows (or hopes) that she's bluffing.

Of course she is. But there's still a moment when Max's nerve swells and Seb's falters and I think she's going to kick him out of this ridiculous club.

"How about if you stay in the car?"

"How about we do something different?"

Max shakes her head. "I want to do *this* one."

"Well, Seb doesn't," I mumble. "And I don't either."

Seb's anger dissolves as I watch him recalibrate his opinion of me.

"This is interesting," Tyler says.

Max's lips are pressed together and her arms are wrapped around her waist as she sways on the spot.

Tyler risks a glance at her, but I'm too scared to see what it means to not only stand up to this girl but embarrass her as well.

That's not what I wanted. But no way am I letting anyone reach into that grave, not after the noises that came from the woods the last time that we did something stupid.

"I went there," I say. "In the daytime."

"Yes," Seb replies. "That is a sensible time to go to a place full of dead people."

Tyler's smirk is shot down by a single glance from Max, but when she turns, he smiles at me.

"I'm doing it," Max says. "With or without you."

She walks away as the bell goes, but the others stay put. When I don't move, the dimple in Seb's cheek twitches before he glares at Tyler and says, "Thanks for the support."

"I want to do it," Tyler replies. "And you did, too, so what's changed?"

"You know what's changed."

The rest of their conversation happens through looks, until Seb turns to me and says, "Aren't you going to class?"

"Aren't you?"

Tyler laughs, then puts his hands behind his head and stares at the school. "Seb thinks it's going to happen again. He thinks we summoned the Face in the Glass and, if we go to the graveyard, he'll be pulled into oblivion."

Seb lets out a hiss before Tyler touches his shoulder and says, "We've always been okay, right? It's harmless fun."

There it is again—that change in tune from believing to dismissing. Did Tyler get it from Max or vice versa?

"I'm not putting my arm in," Seb says.

"Fine," his friend replies. "I'll do it."

The heavy dent between Seb's eyes softens, but he doesn't reply. I don't think that's the answer he wanted, yet it's not one he can reject either.

"We should go," Tyler says, and as we enter the main building, Seb mumbles, "Thanks for not backing Max."

"No worries," I reply.

"For the record, I'm not scared, I'm just . . ."

"Careful?"

Seb stops and nods. Then he and Tyler disappear into the science wing while I head for the music department.

I think that's what some people would call bonding, but, as with so much since we moved to Montgomery-Oakes, I can't be sure.

31

I can't shake the fog in my head. In class, I close my eyes when it's safe to do so and feel the comfort of sleep lowering itself over my brain like a blanket.

It would take me now . . . if I let it. It would pull me into the deepest slumber until my teacher's yell or a slammed fist on a desk yanked me back.

I've done that before, at other schools, after other sleepless nights. But I've yet to embarrass myself here and I'm desperate for that to remain the case.

Through the window I see a phys ed class running with varying degrees of enthusiasm around the track. At the front, bursting clear and staying there, is Hazel.

Two boys attempt to catch up, their faces contorted and then crushed as they realize, like everyone does, that you can't beat my sister in a race.

She glides past and I see the focus in her eyes—the way they look when she's deep in meditation. That's how she runs so effortlessly. Because, in her mind, she's not running at all.

I've often wondered what she pictures when she runs. Is it something she wants to reach, or something she's eager to escape? I can vividly imagine both.

The weight behind my eyes lifts slightly as I watch my sister. Then it grows heavier as her teacher brings them in and she sits away from everyone else, while her classmates smile and chat between snatched breaths.

She's alone now. Just as she was alone on the track. When you're running, that distance is a good thing; it's a measure of your talent. But when you're motionless and no one gets near you, that's something else entirely.

Ms. Hewitt doesn't notice where I'm looking. Nor does she try to involve me in the discussion that drones in the distance. I may as well not be here, and I wonder what would happen if I ditched her next class.

Could I fall asleep somewhere safe—the Hell Hole, maybe? Could I use my latest high school as a space to catch up on all the rest I'm robbed of at home?

It's a nice thought but I know the truth. If I found a quiet place, with no one around to judge me, I'd remain as awake as I am now. Sleep only offers itself when I can't take it—in humming classrooms or packed buses or the minutes before our parents wave us goodbye.

In bed, in a silent house with every door closed and a clock ticking past midnight, sleep runs away faster than my sister.

Besides, how can I sleep in this building when someone in it is taunting me?

Are they in this room—one of the nobodies I'm forced to spend my days with? Are they hatching their next plan on the desk next to mine?

I stare at the boy to my right, so engrossed in his note-taking that he doesn't stop for breath. Then the girl on my other side, whose smile turns to a grimace as I glare at her.

I'll find them because, eventually, everyone shows their true colors.

I sense the bell a split second before it sounds and smile at the thought of Max doing the same in another part of the school.

She is rubbing off on me and, despite everything, I'm pleased we found each other. If I tell Hazel, she'll understand, because *she* found someone somewhere once. But then she'll warn me off. She'll tell me this feeling isn't worth the sadness that inevitably comes next.

That's what it says in *her* journal—on the page where nothing else remained. On a sheet of scribbled-out words like redacted evidence, a single sentence survived.

The joy of now isn't worth the despair of after.

When we move, sometimes it takes me a while to find where she's put it. But there are only so many hiding places in normal houses.

I wait until the rest of the class has gone then head for the door, slowing in front of Ms. Hewitt, waiting for her to say something, anything, to the kid who never talks. But she keeps her head down, moving sheets of paper from one side of her desk to the other.

I can feel the corridor before I step into it—the way its roar causes shudders—but I brace myself and head for the cafeteria.

Someone touches my arm and my fists tighten as I turn.

"Are you okay?" Seb asks. "You look tense."

I breathe out, the electricity leaving my fingers as they spread. "I'm good. I don't do well in crowds."

"Me neither."

As we walk side by side to the Hell Hole, I quickly crush the memories of cowering alone in its shadows. If this is the only place Max and the others are truly themselves, I won't have some asshole ruining it.

Right before we enter, Seb mumbles, "Have you been to see Miss Kittle?"

His eyes escape mine as I say, "No. It's not really my thing."

I know better than to ask what *his* thing is. If he wants to tell me, he will.

"She *is* helpful," he says. "And she listens . . . which not many people do."

His eyes find mine, the strain of his stillness making his facial muscles vibrate.

"I get that. But those kinds of conversations feel like traps. Does that make sense?"

Seb nods, then lifts two crates off the pile and hands one to me.

"Sometimes they are," he replies, a red glow spreading across his cheeks. "But not always."

"I guess you three are my Miss Kittle," I say. "If I had any questions about this place, I'd come to you."

A smile pulls on one corner of Seb's mouth; then it vanishes as he says, "I'm not scared of the graveyard. I go there every year for something else. But I'm not reaching into that hole. It's disrespectful."

"Fair enough," I say, taking out my lunch so I have something to do.

"Do you know anyone who's died?"

There's another one—a simple question with an impossible answer.

I think of all the people who died on Murder Road—the ones before we arrived (just stories to us) and the ones as we grew up a single street away (memories wrapped in police tape; news spread first by distant sirens then by the fearful chatter of our neighbors).

"My grandma," I say. "She died when I was twelve. Our dad's parents passed away, too, but I didn't know them."

"How would you feel if someone reached into their grave?"

I don't correct him. I don't explain that, wherever that hole leads, I doubt it's within stretching distance of a skeleton. Instead, I say, "I wouldn't like it."

"Exactly. I don't like it either. And Max knows that."

His voice cracks as someone emerges from the shadows and says, "I *do* know that."

"Sorry, I . . ."

"It's fine," Max replies. "It's good to see you two getting along. We're not doing the Corpse's Grip. Tyler spoke to me, and . . . I don't want to fall out over this. Are we cool?"

Seb's grin says yes, they *are* cool, just as Tyler strides into the space and drags a crate over.

"Have you two made up?"

"We have," Max says, "and, as a peace offering, Seb can choose the next legend."

"The Caretaker," he says, without a moment's thought. "Can we?"

"Again?"

"It's my favorite."

I stare around the Hell Hole and think back to what Max said, how this was where the janitor used to keep all his stuff, before they built a building he now sits in between jobs, slurping coffee and listening to old music.

Max catches my eye and says, "How do you feel about breaking and entering?"

There was a time I would laugh and wait for the punch line. But now I know better.

"Seriously? Have you all forgotten what happened in the woods?"

Tyler pushes out his chest as he says, "Of course not."

"So why are you doing another legend?"

"This one's different," Seb says.

"Different how?"

"We've done it tons of times," Max says, "and we're still here."

"Didn't you say that about the Face in the Glass, too?"

"Well, it hasn't come for us, has it? And no one else has been gobbled up while hiking. So, it's safe to assume whatever we heard that night slunk away again."

It's not "safe" to assume anything.

"I'll sit it out," I say. "You should too."

Tyler chuckles. "Been here ten minutes and thinks he knows this town better than us."

But that's not it. I have no idea what lurks in the corners of Montgomery-Oakes. *That's* what scares me.

"We're getting mixed messages from you, Nate," Max says. "You eat with us every day, you sit here, in *our* domain, then you say you want out."

Of some of it. Not all.

If I'm back out there, alone, will the articles and warnings multiply? Will whoever softly whistled *that* tune while I hid up the ante? And how will I block out the restless murmurs of my past and the increasing pressure from my family?

"I don't want out," I reply. "But it *did* happen, you know? Even if there were no repercussions, even if whatever did that to Seb's car never leaves those woods. Don't let the fact that most days are safe prevent you from seeing the danger."

"We know," Max replies, resting her hand on mine. "We're not dumb."

"If something bad happens . . ."

"If something bad happens," she repeats, "I will personally hit pause on the Hell Chasers."

"Okay. I'll come."

Better to be close, just in case, than wake up the next morning and hear that everything's gone to shit.

32

Main Street is too busy to be enjoyable, crammed with vaguely familiar faces grabbing their post-school caffeine fix and elementary kids pawing at the candy-store window. But I need to clear my head before going home, so instead of getting a ride with Hazel, I walk in the opposite direction.

Someone is sitting on my bench, so I stroll around the green until they move, then quickly snag it. But that doesn't feel right either. The magic sprinkled over this place at dusk is washed away in the light.

I watch Mr. Taylor fill tiny paper bags with metallic scoops, then walk to the coffeehouse, where Mom is fixing someone's order like she's been doing this for years.

I've watched her do other jobs, in different towns, and that look of absolute focus never falters.

She wants this to be the best coffee that girl has ever tasted. Unlike so much in our life, it's something she can control.

She glances up before I can step away, uncertainty filling her eyes as the right side of her mouth rises, and she ushers me inside.

I nudge past the queue and sit alone at the farthest table, listening to all the pointless chatter from people ordering drinks with increasingly ridiculous names.

Eventually, a shadow looms over me and Mom places a hot chocolate between my fists.

"Thanks," I mumble.

"What are you doing here?"

"Can't a son visit his mother at work?"

"I guess."

We've barely spoken since I lost it that night at dinner. But, even after the worst arguments, our family finds its way back together.

Deep laughter pervades the air, dread filling me to the brim as Tyler strolls in with three other boys, all wearing mud-smeared soccer jerseys.

As he catches my eye, his huge grin slips; then he recovers, one hand quickly slapping his closest buddy on the back.

I think I know what that means. It means here, now, he's with his team, not his clique. It means there is no chance of him rushing over to me. And that's fine, because there's zero chance of me going to him either.

"Do you know those boys?" Mom asks.

"No."

Her head tilts ever so slightly as she holds my stare. Then she tugs on her apron and heads back to the counter.

I shouldn't have come. But there are so few things to distract me now—from Murder Road, from the unyielding knots that tie us to it, from the Hell Chasers, who despite my best efforts might risk their lives all over again.

Mom takes Tyler's order and he glances from her to me and back again.

The man-mountain next to him says something and their laughs come out like a thunderclap that forces Mom to step back.

"Sorry," Tyler says. "They're not housebroken."

The others laugh even louder, but he doesn't. He waits for his drink then leaves with one final, apologetic glance my way.

Mom watches me, searching for the slightest clue that I've made friends here; then she turns to the next customer, the biggest, fakest smile appearing from nowhere, and I slip out, leaving my own drink untouched.

I peer into each immaculate window display, pausing slightly longer outside the candy store.

Mr. Taylor stares at me, realization slowly dawning as he gestures for me to come in.

"On your own today?" he asks, quickly filling a paper bag and pushing it across the counter.

"I'm okay," I reply.

"Nonsense. You don't get much for free in this life. Enjoy it when you can."

"Thank you."

As the last customer leaves, he slumps on his chair and sighs. "The legs aren't what they used to be."

I pull the same faces I did when I was cornered in Grandma's nursing home—not by her, but by fellow residents desperate to be heard. Then I make my excuses and leave.

As I reach the last store on the strip, I hear heavy breathing behind me before someone grabs my shoulder.

"I think you dropped this," they say, stuffing something into my hand before running back the way they came.

They are gone before I can process what happened, a hood pulled low over their face.

As I uncrumple the paper, I see the photograph first—of the house with boarded-up windows and police tape stretched across the front door—and then the headline above:

RESIDENTS FEAR HIDING BOY'S RETURN AFTER GORY DISCOVERY

By 2021, reporters weren't ignoring the urban legend. They were plastering it across their front pages.

The remains of a man have been found in an abandoned house on Cherry Tree Lane.

Derek Thornby, 32, was reported missing from his home in

Hayschurch on August 25 when he failed to return from work. Twelve days later, police discovered his body more than 100 miles away, in what has been described as "a ritualistic setting."

The street more commonly known as Murder Road has suffered numerous tragedies since an alleged curse was placed on it back in 1963. Whether you believe that or not, there is no ignoring the horrendous acts that have taken place in the following half century.

Speaking to reporters outside number 19, Sheriff Prescott said, "Like my father before me, I have seen more horror on this street than I could ever have imagined. Please rest assured that, while there will always be speculation after incidents like this, we have working theories of our own.

"I would like to assure Mr. Thornby's wife and three children, along with the general public, that I will not rest until this crime has been solved."

I turn and run in the direction of whoever pressed this into my hands. But they are long gone.

They said I dropped it, but I've never held this article before. I've only ever seen it online.

The print smudges my fingers as I ball it up and force it into my pocket.

What the hell is going on?

I've grown up with that tale, that chant, that promise.

Ready or not. Whatever you do. The Hiding Boy is coming for you.

But I didn't used to think he had helpers.

The tremors in my hands come so hard and fast that my arms shake all the way up to my shoulders. I pull my elbows into my body, my hands pressed against my forehead, and I try to ride it out.

I see feet pass by but no one stops or asks what's wrong. They leave me to have a panic attack in the middle of the street until I fumble my way to the nearest wall and slide to the sidewalk.

Slowly, in fractions, I ease my fear, staring out at a town that carries on without me.

Where is the only person who makes me forget how messed up my life has become? Where is Max?

It's never been this bad before. Not for me. But, as I stare at Montgomery-Oakes's prized street, I start to see the stains and the scars, the bruises and the lies, and I wonder how long I've got left.

33

That evening, I drag a blackened metal trash can from our garage into the backyard, fill it with old magazines and lighter fluid, then toss the notes and the articles into the flames.

My parents watch from the patio windows as the fire crackles in the darkness, smoke merging with the fog that hangs low over the town tonight.

Eventually, Hazel joins me, throwing something of her own into the orange glow.

We stand in silence, watching our separate sacrifices turn to ash; then my sister reaches out and softly squeezes my fingers.

I love her. I love all of them. But I wish things were like they used to be.

"I'm sorry," I whisper.

Hazel sniffs three times, then releases my hand and stares at the full moon glistening through the mist.

If Rowan were here, what would he add to the fire?

I shudder at the thought, then leave our sister alone as I creep back into the house.

"I'm going out," I say. "Again."

Dad offers a faint nod, while Mom keeps watch over her daughter.

"Be careful," Dad says.

I feel freer after destroying the warnings, wrestling back an element of control.

They will come again. I'm sure of it. But what's the point in fearing the inevitable?

Instead, I meet my friends, because tonight that's what they are and it's all I need.

The abandoned school looms over us, reminding me of the night I followed Max, Seb, and Tyler into the middle of nowhere.

I respect Seb for saying no to the graveyard, and I like that Max only fought for so long. She could have kept going. She could have won. But I don't think that was ever her intention.

She's headstrong, not heartless.

The clock in the brickwork arch is still broken, the huge frosted windows daring me to look closer. But we'll see what's inside soon enough.

"My parents went here," Tyler says.

Max stares at the forgotten bulletin board, her fingers adding another smear to the glass; then she sniffs and says, "Come on then."

She walks to the side gate, the thin metal railings tipped with arrowheads that I hope are as blunt as they look. Then she kneels, locks her fingers together, and holds her hands palm-side up.

In silence, Tyler steps forward and Max propels him up. His right foot finds a gap between the spikes, and he swoops over, then grins from the other side.

Seb glances at me then trundles forward. He puts his foot awkwardly in Max's hands and half jumps as she lifts. He falls into the gate, barely making it halfway, and mumbles, "You go first."

"How are you getting over?" I ask Max, and she shakes her head but doesn't answer. For a moment, she looks disappointed in me; then she smiles and says, "Show him how it's done."

I try. But there's nothing graceful about my effort. I manage to reach the top and, for a few horrible seconds, Max pushes as I try to use whatever muscles hide deep below my skin.

As I suspected, they aren't much use. But eventually I scramble over and keep my footing.

"Hey," Tyler says. I wait for something else—a joke, a smirk—but he turns back to Seb and whispers, "You can do it."

Seb nods, steps once more into Max's palms, and does a pretty good Tyler impression, without the graceful landing or the composed expression.

"Nice job," Tyler says, as the pair silently high-five, their palms touching then floating back like barely moving bumper cars.

"What about . . . ?"

Max pulls herself over the fence and lands effortlessly between us, then puffs out her cheeks and says, "What about what?"

"Nothing."

The three of them share a smile that flashes to me like a spotlight until heat creeps up my neck.

My blushes swell under scrutiny. They turn from hot to almost unbearable and I wait for someone to comment, but Max only touches my arm and says, "That's the hard part."

They are gone before I can move and I race to catch up, slipping into a darkness that expands when I see the vast playing field beyond.

There are no lights here. Nothing to protect this building from what we are about to do.

Tyler crouches next to a boarded-up door, pulls a crowbar from his backpack, and slides it behind the graffiti-stained plywood. With a pop, the wood comes away, leaving a hole that he scrambles through without a word.

How many other people have broken into this building? And is that even the right phrase, when you can enter with so little effort?

I pause for a moment, staring at the hole that Max has just followed the others into. Who am I now?

I'm not the kid hiding in the shadows of another temporary home. I'm not timid or compliant. I'm not defined by something I've always been told is inevitable. For as long as we're here, I'll enjoy it.

I will burn every anonymous note, and next time someone whistles that damn song, I'll kick their stall in.

And I'll spend every available minute with Max because . . . who wouldn't?

"Nate!" she hisses. "Come on."

I haven't seen a single police officer since we moved here. Some people would view that as a good thing—a sign of a safe neighborhood. But what happens when things go wrong?

I make a mental note to check how far away the nearest sheriff's station is, for peace of mind, then I place my hands on the cold asphalt and slowly crawl into the school.

A flashlight gleams from the opposite end of the corridor, three shadows forming as my eyes get used to the dark.

"This way," Tyler whispers, and I follow as they stride confidently into a room on the far left.

Seb rests his flashlight on a low table and all three of them sit cross-legged on a carpet that, when I look closer, I see is shaped like a dinosaur, its long neck snaking across the floor and disappearing behind shelves full of books.

As I take in the entire room, I realize how neat everything is, and my thoughts shuffle, then rest in a new order.

"A history lesson," Tyler whispers, "for the newbies among us."

He offers me a warm grin, then continues.

"Twelve years ago, Forge Lane Elementary School closed its doors for the last time. A combination of failing architecture and dwindling student numbers meant it was simply not viable for the school to continue, despite staunch support from locals."

It sounds like he's reading from Wikipedia, but when I glance up I see that he has his eyes closed and is clearly relaying this from memory.

"Plans to knock the building down and replace it with more housing have, so far, failed. And we all know why."

Max sniggers, while Seb bites his bottom lip. Considering it was his idea to come here, he doesn't seem to be enjoying it.

Tyler's voice shifts as he turns to me and says, "Do you believe in ghosts?"

Yes.

Before I can answer, he says, "Rumor has it, that was one of the interview questions for the teachers wanting to work here. Because so many people ran away from this place screaming."

Tyler's words make me shiver, because I've seen the kind of buildings that make people scream and they aren't so easy to escape.

"Teachers didn't stay late when they worked here. They all left together, while the sun was still up. But that didn't stop things from happening. Once the kids had left for the day, if you were alone in a classroom, you'd smell cigarettes even though no one was smoking. It would start faint, as if it was creeping through the AC, and then there were voices, crackling like radio static through the vents now heavy with invisible smoke."

I glance at the wall and imagine tendrils creeping through the air and clawing their way up my nostrils.

"That's why it's so easy to break into this place," Max says. "Everyone wants to see the Caretaker."

Tyler's brow creases but he lets her interruption pass. "He never haunted the children. Not once. He would always wait until the school was full of adults."

"Who's 'he'?" I ask.

"Like Max said. The Caretaker."

When Tyler says it, you can hear the capital *C*.

"He worked here decades ago. They say he died in the boiler room."

A laugh sneaks out as I say, "Like Freddy Krueger?"

The least they could do is be original. But Tyler's eyes narrow as he says, "Freddy isn't real."

His glare stops me from pushing back. Instead, to change the subject, I ask, "How many times have you been here?"

"Five," Max says.

"And have you ever seen him? Have you ever smelled the smoke or . . . run out screaming?"

She pulls a face that she thinks is shutting me down, but the simple fact is that we only avoid the questions we don't want to answer.

"What have you noticed about this place?"

Seb's voice sounds strange in the gloom and I realize it's the first time he's spoken tonight.

I stare at all the dusty books and fully stocked pencil pots, the immaculate walls and scribble-free whiteboard.

"You have very respectful vandals around here?"

"We're not vandals," Tyler mumbles. "But yes, no one takes anything. We leave it as we found it."

"Why?"

"See what happens if you do."

I swallow the nausea suddenly bobbing high in my throat, reach out for a book on the closest shelf, then pull away at the last moment.

"I don't want to."

"Smart move," Tyler says, as he stands and leads the others out of the library.

While we walk back down the corridor, I pay closer attention to the displays showing off handwriting and art and design. How old are the people who did this work now? If this place closed twelve years ago, they must all be older than I am. Yet their childhoods are frozen in time rather than torn off walls and replaced like the rest of us.

How many of them know they are part of a ghost story? How many have crawled through that hole in the door and traveled back in time? And how many believe it?

Tyler stops at the broken door then steps quickly to the right. Whatever this is, it's not quite over, and I wonder if we would have been better off at the graveyard.

Here is a different kind of horror—one that makes me think

of the schools I went to before we started running. Then all the others that came and went as we arrived and left on repeat.

Do they remember how it felt as we huddled together in Seb's car while claws tore chunks out of the metal? Of course they don't. If they did, they wouldn't be creeping through these corridors.

But nothing followed them out of the woods that night. Eventually, after enough good sleeps, they rewrote their terror. They feel brave. They feel ready. But that's when things usually go wrong.

Seb stops in front of me while Max and Tyler disappear through large double doors.

"Are you . . ."

"Go," he says. "I'll be there in a minute."

I follow his gaze to another display board, this one full of photographs and essays about summer vacations.

The one he's peering at is titled *Vale Adventures* and the photo shows a boy on a wooded path with a thin grin and skinny legs poking out of his shorts.

"Is that you?" I ask, even though it can't be, not if this place closed over a decade ago.

"It's my brother," Seb mumbles. "He went here. Before I was born."

I look closer at the boy in the photo. He's the spitting image of Seb—the same red hair, the same long limbs, the same uncertain smile.

"How old is he now?" I ask.

Seb pauses before saying, "He would have been twenty-eight."

"Do the others know?"

"Why do you think they're leaving me alone?"

I turn to leave as Seb clears his throat and says, "Not all ghost stories are scary. They come here hoping to smell smoke or hear voices. I want to spend time with my brother."

"What happened to him?"

For a moment, I don't think he's going to answer. Then he

turns away from the wall and says, "A car accident. I got out. He didn't."

"Shit. I'm so sorry."

"No need to apologize. You weren't driving, were you?"

He manages a smile and I look behind me, suddenly keen to be back with the others. I don't want to intrude any more than I already have.

"I was seven. He was nineteen. It's safe to say our parents didn't plan it that way. But we had a lot of fun."

Seb wipes his eyes, and I watch him turn back to the photograph, then leave him to it.

Max and Tyler are waiting in a large room that seems to have once doubled as a gym and a performance space. A mural of a huge tree glows in the beams of their flashlights, its leaves filled with words like "compassion" and "respect" and "equality."

"Did he tell you?" Tyler asks.

"Yes."

"That means he likes you," Max whispers, although no one smiles.

I hate that Seb is grieving. I hate that breaking into a derelict school is the only way he can feel close to his brother. And I hate that I intruded on his moment.

Max sits cross-legged on the floor and Tyler takes the space across from her, gesturing until I sit between them. Then we wait in silence until Seb completes the circle.

He and Tyler nod at each other, and then both shut their eyes. When I look at Max, she's done the same, so I copy them.

I don't know what's happening, but I've already spoiled one aspect of tonight and I won't ruin another.

As one, the hushed voices of my three new friends say, "*Our eyes stay closed. Our minds stay open.*"

The silence that follows prompts other things to creep from my corners and twist around my brain. I could open my eyes and escape into the brisk night air, but Max and Tyler reach for my hands, anchoring me.

Their skin against mine awakens different feelings—ones that are easier to shake than the horrid grip of dread.

So, I sit until my stomach cramps, and pins and needles stir in my thighs. I sit until the smell of cigarette smoke drifts into the room and the hands holding mine tighten. I sit until Max whispers, "He's here," and every fiber of my body screams *Run!*

The smell gets stronger as it shifts from the ashen taste of a distant bonfire to the molten stench of tar. I try to lift my hand but Max holds tight.

When does this end? What are the rules? Last time, they told me everything before we arrived. This time, I had to wait until we were shrouded by darkness.

The air shifts behind me, my skin prickling and my ears doing all the work. Then something crackles from another room, a hacking sound like an old man clearing his throat.

Max's nails dig into my skin but Tyler's grip softens slightly, and I think I won't be the first to run.

"Wait," Seb whispers. When I risk the quickest look, his eyes are clamped shut, but he says it again, "Wait," as if he knows his friend's courage is faltering.

In response, Tyler's grip tightens, just as the noise comes again, nearer this time. My body hums and my temples throb and this feels so different from the car. At least in there we were shielded. Here, we are sitting ducks.

The hacking comes again, closer still, each silence a space for something horrible to step into, and the smell is so acrid I want to clamp my nostrils shut.

Is everyone else's heart beating a hole through their chest? Is everyone else's head on fire?

Icy air swipes the back of my neck, and then the gap between the sounds grows wider until it begins to feel almost safe.

But it's not until the odor fades to nothing, creeping out of the hall, leaving only the soft scent of varnished wood and rubber gym mats, that Max releases my hand.

"Fuck."

She breathes out the word, then lies back on the cold wood.

Tyler's eyes burn into me, so I stand, staring at the door that I'm desperate to leave through.

"I told you," Max says as she gets up. "I fucking *told* you. Nate is . . . he's special."

No, I'm not! I'm a lot of things but "special" isn't one of them. I'm confused. I'm terrified. I'm a mess.

My eyes scan every corner of the room, waiting for twisted shapes to crawl from the shadows. Then I settle on the only thing I know for certain: Someone in this town wants to hurt me.

"Why are you doing this?" I ask. "Get them out here. Whoever's messing with me—the fourth friend that you've somehow managed to keep secret—and don't bullshit me anymore. I know this is you."

As Tyler stands, he reaches out a hand that I slap away.

"Hey," he says. "You think you're the only one scared here?"

I look at them—at Max jigging on the spot, at Seb, who has one hand in his pants pocket and the other clasped tightly over it, and at Tyler, whose faint smile flits between cocky and fearful.

My heartbeat thuds through my skull and I don't even try to hide the tremors hijacking my hands. I'm not ashamed of my fear. It's a sign that I know what I'm dealing with.

I focus on Max and say, "You don't look that scared."

"You ever play Top Trumps?"

"What?"

"Have you played or not?"

"Sure."

Max steps closer, taking my clammy hands in hers. "Well, currently, my fear rating is maybe eighty. But my excitement is ninety-nine and rising.

"Like it or not, Nate, you've changed things for us. We've never seen *anything*. And now . . ."

"I'm not doing anything else. Not a chance! This is it. My official retirement from the Hell Chasers."

Max shrugs. "Yet you keep coming back."

"Because I *like* you. And, if you want to know the truth, I've never liked anybody."

She steps away as Tyler mumbles, "Awkward."

Seb chuckles, but I want to run from these people and never look back.

"You like *us*," Max says, "or you like *me*?"

"Does it matter?"

Her beautiful, terrifying eyes widen as she watches me in the glow of Seb's flashlight. "Quite a lot, actually."

This wasn't supposed to happen. How could I have been so reckless, especially after what my sister went through? And yet, everything about Max feels inevitable.

"I thought I could do this," I mutter, "but I can't."

Max's mouth hangs open while her eyes scramble from Tyler to Seb and back again.

"I don't want to be the reason your urban legends are coming to life. This is no way to live."

"It's fun," Tyler says.

I shout, "No! It isn't. Your selective memory is fucking alarming, truth be told. Because, if you're not involved in this, how can you hear those noises, and smell those smells, and then call it 'fun'? How many days will it be before you're back doing another one? You should take this stuff more seriously."

I quickly wipe my tears away and bury my head in my hands.

I don't know what's worse—believing coming here would distract me from my messed-up life or admitting to Max that I like her.

"Well, we're not dead, are we?" Seb says. "Whatever haunts this place never killed anybody."

Yet.

"He's right," Max says. "I think we're safe here."

I breathe as slowly as I can manage, trying to calm my heart while panic and shame swirl behind my eyes.

Seb steps onto the stage and looks down on us. How many times was his brother up there, performing while his parents beamed from the plastic chairs now piled in the corners?

We all have our ways to remember the lost. If I wanted to be close to Grandma after she died, I went to the hill where her care home sat and stared into the crystal-blue water. Now, I look at the paintings she did of that scene and imagine her fidgeting fingers stilled by the brush between them.

This is Seb's way to be with his brother, even if he was a different person back then. The boy he was before another boy came along.

"Maybe we should stop," Tyler says. "Is it really wise to piss off a whole town full of ghosts?"

"We're not pissing them off," Max replies. "We're just . . . saying hi."

"Well, I'm saying bye," I say, seizing the moment to run.

I march out of the door, then freeze, as a shadow hovers at the opposite end of the corridor. Everything catches in my throat—my breath, my pleas, my warnings. I should tell them we're not as safe as they thought. But all I can do is watch in terror, as the figure sways from side to side, then slowly steps into the half-light.

I close my eyes, scrambling for solace in my own darkness, until the Hiding Boy stares back.

Let me in, he whispers, his high-pitched giggle echoing somewhere deep inside me. When my eyes snap open, the shadow has gone, the low hum of Tyler's voice slowly filling my ears.

"Are you okay?" he asks.

"Did you see that?"

He follows my gaze before shaking his head. "See what?"

"Nothing. I . . ."

I'm scared. More scared than I've ever been.

Max stops next to me, the confidence she is usually decked head-to-toe in replaced by something more fragile. "Are we cool?"

It takes all the effort I can muster to give her one unbroken word. "Yes."

"We can talk about the other stuff when you're ready," she says. "If you want to."

When I don't reply, Max adds, "And don't worry about tonight. The Caretaker has been haunting people for decades. Finally, we got our chance to see what all the fuss is about. If you follow his only rule, he's basically Casper."

"Are you sure about that?"

"If someone really wants to hurt you, they do. They don't play games. They get on with it."

As Max's eyes drop, I flash back to that night overlooking the bay, when she told me about her father's new family.

Then I follow her into the corridor, pausing for a moment while she hurries after her friends.

Four staples clamping tiny pieces of ripped paper are all that remains of the essay Seb has taken, and I wonder if this is the last time he'll come here, and if he's forgotten that one simple rule about leaving the school's contents untouched . . . or else.

34

Mom sits alone at the kitchen table, one finger stroking the rim of her mug.

The faint smell of smoke fills my nostrils as I work out what to tell her . . . and what not to.

I shouldn't have told Max those things. What does that mean anyway? To *like* someone?

And that's not the worst part. I keep picturing the shape at the end of the corridor—the horrible thing they have tempted out of the shadows with their careless games.

There's no going back now.

"I'm scared," I whisper.

Warmth fills her eyes as she stands and pulls me into a hug. "Me too."

"I wish I had longer. I like it here. I made friends."

Mom steps back, one hand stroking my hair like she used to after all my bad dreams, then says, "Tell me about them."

It's hard to break that habit. But there's no point lying anymore.

Mom reaches for another mug, then gently reheats the cocoa on the stove. It's easier to talk when she's focused on something else—for both of us.

"They're nice."

"What are their names?"

Did she do this with Hazel when she got too comfortable in the last place? And how did my sister respond?

"You know there's a bay not far from here. You and Dad would love it."

"Okay."

Guilt and anxiety stir in my belly as I say, "Max. One of them is called Max. She's . . . interesting."

Mom looks up from the pan, her eyes wide in the half-light, and says, "Interesting is good. Your dad was interesting."

"Was?"

Her laugh catches us both by surprise, before she steadies herself and says, "Is. I mean *is* interesting."

I wish I could laugh back, but our parents aren't the people they used to be.

Dad's way of dealing with conflict was to be ridiculous. If Rowan got angry or Hazel acted out, he would put on a silly voice or re-create a scene from one of our favorite movies and suddenly, just like that, there would be no more drama.

With me, he would make funny faces or act like a dinosaur or change the words to nursery rhymes, until my tantrums turned to giggles and my frustration turned to joy.

I didn't understand what he was doing until he stopped doing it. I didn't know how good my parents were at being parents until we were forced to grow up too soon.

"I'm sorry for the other day," I say. "It's hard, being the last one. Rowan and Hazel take up a lot of space, you know?"

Mom nods then goes back to the table. The drink warming my hands is steaming while hers sits cold and ignored.

I think of that day at the Taylors' house, when Max chatted, and drank her tea, and made every second better for all of us.

If she was here now, she would sit with our mother and talk. She wouldn't let the darkness win. But she's *not* here. She's at home, thinking about my stupid confession, while reframing a scary story as a "success."

If I told her what I saw at the end of the corridor, would she listen? Should I have been honest from the outset? Explaining that, while most people love urban legends, things are different if you've lived next to one?

I've always been able to separate my genuine fears from my paranoia, my dreams from my reality, but, recently, those lines have blurred.

When I go to my room, I read a new message from Max.

Please don't feel embarrassed x

How can that be the emotion she pins on me after everything we've seen?

I imagine Seb lying on his bed with his brother's essay, staring at a boy he only knew as a man. Why did he take it now, on his sixth visit? Is it worth the risk, to own that tiny piece of his brother? Or do you care so much less about yourself when your family is already shattered?

When I close my eyes, a stranger's breath tickles my face, the chill of their skin almost, not quite, touching mine.

My eyes snap open but there's no one here. There never is. Everything bad is hidden—in the stories I was forced to learn, in the memories I fight to ignore, in the fabric of this and every town.

I think of all the people still living in their renovated houses on Murder Road. Did they erase every blemish, or were some scars from those terrifying nights overlooked? Scratches in the floorboards from frantic fingernails? Bloodstains hiding in the varnished sheen of staircases? Screams still echoing deep within the walls?

Those people believe the curse will be over once the Hiding Boy reaches the end of the street. They believe the homes targeted half a century ago are safe now. As for the rest, they lie empty, except for the bodies the police sometimes find inside—like Derek Thornby, the man from the article someone stuffed in my hand on Main Street.

He didn't live on Cherry Tree Lane. He didn't even live in Belleview.

Missing people from out of town are the Hiding Boy's favorite toys now. These days, no one else will set foot in his playground.

Our front door clicks shut, careful footsteps on the stairs, a creak on the floorboards directly outside Rowan's room.

"Hey," I whisper, watching as my brother jolts in the darkness.

He stares at me, no fresh wounds on his face, and asks, "Are you okay?"

"Not really."

As I go to Hazel's door, I listen to the words spilling out of her, the anger and heartbreak that builds throughout the day unleashed on a boyfriend who always listens without interruption.

Then I join Rowan in his room, the silence expanding between us, until he is finally the one to break.

His dreams weren't always bad. Sometimes he sat in a sun-kissed field while his mother and sister lounged on a picnic blanket and his father tossed a football to his brother.

He could feel the size of his smile; how it pushed against his teeth, anchored deep within his dimples.

His dreams were silent movies, unspoken words warming his soul like a bonfire, until those flames turned to talons, slicing the air just enough for evil to sneak through.

His family sat with frozen faces as those shapes morphed into the earliest victims of Murder Road—the mother drowned in her own blood, the family mauled by the boy who was banned from the pet store, the couple shot on their wedding night, their rings glistening on the front porch next to a note that read There is no such thing as a happy ending.

One by one, the ghosts stood before him, until a hand touched his waist.

He turned in slow motion until he was staring into the face of the boy every victim saw before they died.

He looked kind, safe, too young and innocent to be the catalyst for so much horror. But that was the point, wasn't it? He knew that, even when he was trapped in a nightmare with broken locks and dozens of dead ends.

When something so pure sees only horror, when, day after day, a child who should be playing in the sun is forced to hide in the shadows while his sister tends to their mother's cuts and echoes of his father's rage fill every room, that's how monsters are born.

35

At school, I avoid all the places Max may be.

How do you greet a person when the last thing you said was that you liked them? I don't understand the rules of situations like this, so, like always, I hide.

The tree I sat under before I had friends is taken—the group of boys I walked away from on my first day has more than doubled in size. Would I have been better off with them? Or with the goth kid under the bleachers who is still sketching, while three more toss candy into one another's mouths and nod as I quickly walk past?

Even Jayden, the asshole whose shoves have left dents in half the lockers here, isn't alone anymore. His eyes narrow as he sees a lone freshman, his right shoulder tensing, until the girl by his side says something and he smiles, the kid gently brushing his arm as he slips past.

Am I the only person still alone at Montgomery-Oakes High? And is there any other way?

"Hey." Tyler slaps me on the back, his grin slipping as I flinch. "Sorry, I . . . force of habit."

I think of him in Mom's coffeehouse, every gesture so much bigger when he's with his soccer team.

"No worries."

"How are you?" he asks, and a million different answers would tumble out if I let them.

"I'm fine."

"That was some weird shit, right? At the school?"

"I guess."

Tyler's eyes sparkle as he says, "And the other stuff. When you confessed your undying love for Max."

My skin prickles as I mutter, "That's not what happened."

"I know. I'm just messing with you. Seriously, though . . . way to go. It takes a lot of courage to tell someone you like them."

I stare at him—sports star, A+ student, with enough confidence and status to be friends with us and them at the same time—and wonder if he's ever found it difficult getting a date. "Okay."

"If there's a guy I like, and I have to talk to him about something totally unrelated, I literally turn to goo. I'm good at a lot of things but romance isn't one of them."

"My grandma used to say that you get better at love when you've got some miles on the meter."

Tyler raises his eyebrows, then nods. "I can see that."

I check over my shoulder then peer past him, because the three of them have a habit of finding one another in a crowd.

"She's not here yet," he says. "And when she is, you shouldn't hide from her. Maybe she likes you too."

"Maybe."

But what happens then?

Tyler looks behind him, his face suddenly serious. "I was meaning to say sorry, for the other day. I saw you when we were getting coffee but . . . the team and the Hell Chasers . . . I tend to keep them separate."

I imagine the situation if he *had* come over and Mom had introduced herself.

"That's okay."

Tyler frowns. "It's not really. I should be able to flit better, you know. Move between groups without being . . ."

"Embarrassed?"

"I don't mind if some people think I'm a walking cliché. I know what goes on in here."

He taps his head and I get that.

"Seriously," I say. "Don't worry about it."

"I know it can come across as prickish; especially because you're new in the group. I'm not ignoring you because I think my Hell Hole friends are lame. If anything, it's the other way around.

"Soccer is a door my family wants me to keep open. Same with the physics. And with the volunteering I do on the weekends. Although that's probably my favorite."

"What do you do?"

"Two things, actually. The best is the soccer coaching. I get to work with these incredible kids and they never stop laughing. It's like, they listen, they work hard, but they haven't forgotten how to have fun. Maybe that's why I'm obsessed with urban legends. It's the only bit of being a kid that I haven't let go of yet."

"I get that."

"Then there's the hospice," Tyler says. "Some people think it's morbid, but you see more life there than most other places. You should come by sometime . . . if you want."

I think of Grandma—who she was and what she became. As she got older, parts of this person who had brought me nothing but joy began to scare me: how she would ask the same question over and over; the doubt in her eyes each time I arrived; her panic as memories she had once held so tight fell between her fingers like sand.

"You and Max both do a lot for people."

"For different reasons," he replies. "But yeah, I guess."

"If I do come, at lunch, promise not to make fun of me."

Tyler holds up both pinkies and says, "I promise."

So that's why I meet them after all, because I want to, and because there is nowhere left to be alone.

"Roll call," Max says, "just to check none of us are dead."

I grip my hands tight, trapping the tremors.

Max's feet bounce on the Hell Hole's floor, the sound echoing in the gloom, and I imagine someone in the cafeteria following that noise back to us. But no one in that huge white hall can hear her because there is no space; not even for the ripples our bodies make in completely different rooms.

Max lays a sheet of paper on the crate in front of us and dramatically ticks another one off.

Below it, I take note of the other legends—the Laughing Water, the I Scream Man, the Boy in the Spider-Man Pajamas. At the bottom, crossed out with a thick black line, it says ~~*the Hiding Boy*~~.

In Max's messy handwriting, the other legends look almost harmless.

The memory of acrid smoke filling my nostrils makes me twitch so hard that Tyler notices.

"Are you okay?" he whispers.

"I'm fine."

"Has anything happened to anyone?" Max asks. "Anything suspicious? Anything to suggest that the Caretaker followed us out?"

The boys shake their heads.

"Good. And I assume we stuck to the rules. Leave it as we found it."

The only sound is Seb's nail cracking between his teeth, and I picture the space where his brother's essay was snatched from the wall.

"What happens if you take something?" I ask.

"You make him angry," Max replies. "That's when bad things happen."

"*Real* bad things . . . as in, you know people who have been hurt? Or just stories?"

"Why?" Tyler asks. "Did you take something?"

Seb's stare is firmly on the ground as I say, "No. Nothing at all."

"Good," Max says. "So, what are we doing next?"

"We're taking a break," Seb mumbles. "It's getting exhausting."

Max laughs. "Seriously? Exhausting?"

"Yes."

Seb catches my eye and I see his sorrow stains.

"You know how I feel," I say, my stomach twisting as I catch Max's eye then look away.

"We do," Max replies. "And we respect that decision. So, if you want out of the club . . . but are happy to hang out here . . . I'm sure everyone will be okay with that."

Seb and Tyler nod, but that's not enough.

They all need to be out. All three of them. They can't keep chasing things into the shadows and expect to remain unhurt.

"Maybe we should *all* take a break," I say. "Just for a few weeks. I know nothing happened before but, now it is, it's kind of weird being terrified one minute then actively chasing the next scare."

"That's the point," Max replies. "It's what we do."

Seb's words are small and flat as he mutters, "We can't just forget what happened the other night. Some people need closure."

"You're not using that word right," she replies, but she's wrong. He's using it perfectly, because I can imagine an eleven-year-old's handwriting tucked deep in his pocket, their photo unfolded one hundred times a day.

Seb is never going back there. He doesn't care if he broke the rules and potentially angered a ghost, because some things are bigger than that. All he cares about is the brother he lost.

I think of the words before I utter them, then change them over and over until, eventually, I clear my throat and say, "Seb's right. If you still think I'm the reason things are finally working, then you need me. And I say we regroup. Let's do something else for a while. Let's leave the dead alone."

Max's mouth hangs open, all the potential responses crumbling before they reach her lips.

"Nate wins by knockout," Tyler says, chuckling as he packs up his lunch.

The bell goes without Max's countdown; then she sighs and says, "Okay."

She leaves first, vanishing long before we step into the harsh light of the lunchroom.

"See," Tyler says. "That wasn't awkward at all." His laugh echoes as my lips rise slightly. "She didn't even mention that you like her."

Seb chuckles, then turns to me and says, "Do you want to come over after school? Just hang out?"

"Sure."

My answer comes instantly, and I wait for the regret and the worry to follow. But I want to know him better.

I watch Tyler and Seb merge with the crowd, and then, five minutes later, I get a message.

Front gate after school. Don't tell Max.

36

Seb's legs swing back and forth as he sits alone on the wall that runs around Montgomery-Oakes High.

I stay in the crowd for as long as I can, wondering what would happen if I let them push me along until I'm far from here. But I want to meet Seb's family, see his home, understand more about this quiet kid with the dead brother.

The swarm moves on without me, until Seb glances to his left, puffs out his cheeks, then lands on the path far more elegantly than he managed when we scaled the elementary school gate.

"Where's Tyler?" I ask.

"Soccer practice. You still cool to come?"

"Sure."

I follow Seb to his car, the paintwork glistening in the afternoon sun, no sign at all that something sharp was dragged from one end to the other.

When he sees me staring, he sighs and says, "My parents finally got it fixed."

"Were they angry?"

"They don't really do anger. You'll see."

Empty water bottles fill the footwell, and Seb leans over and tosses some into the back.

"Got to stay hydrated."

He sounds like my brother—except it's not water that Rowan fills his body with; it's energy drinks and Coke.

My Chemical Romance plays softly through the speakers, and Seb's fingers drum against the steering wheel.

A few minutes later, he pulls into a driveway and nods at the building in front of us. "Home sweet home."

Potted trees sit to either side of the door and flower baskets sway next to the wide front window. When I step out, I see that stone ornaments rest along the lawn's edge, while tiny bursts of color shine amid the weeds.

In one of our first new houses, Mom thought gardening would make everything better. She filled the front yard with peonies and dahlias and roses, then searched the lawn for weeds as thoroughly as she'd once searched our hair for lice.

As she stood in the kitchen, scrubbing every speck of dirt from her fingernails, her tears were carried away with the muddy water.

"That's all Dad," Seb says. "He loves his garden."

He opens the front door and I follow him inside, where framed photographs cover the walls and a strong smell of mint fills my nose.

"Mom!" Seb yells. "I'm home."

A gray-haired lady appears in the hallway, beaming as she walks quickly over to Seb and kisses his cheek. "And who's this?"

"This is Nate. A friend from school."

"Hello, Nate. Let me get you something to eat."

She disappears before I can respond and Seb leads me into the living room, where a man with the same bright orange hair as his son sits at the dining table, Lego blocks spread in front of him.

"Hey," the man says.

When he looks up, he adds an "Oh," and a smile that ignites his eyes. "You must be Nate."

"I told Dad you might come over."

When? I wonder. Did he plan on asking me before I stood up to Max? Or did he message ahead?

There are more photos in this room—one grinning boy, two grinning boys, then one boy again, the smile wiped clean from his face.

Seb's brother is everywhere, and I half expect to see the picture he took from the school in a frame of its own. But that's more likely to be hidden—an unshared memory in a house where the past is all they have.

"It looks good," Seb says, standing for a few moments behind his father before leading me upstairs.

Shelves line his bedroom walls, Lego sets and modular builds filling every surface.

"How much did all this cost?" I ask.

"A lot," Seb replies. "But Dad loves it and . . . I do too."

He won't look at me for a while, and when he finally does, his eyes are wet.

I walk to his desk, where a see-through ball hangs from a hook. Inside there are four minifigures, three with red hair and one with blond, all wearing Christmas sweaters and surrounded by plastic snow.

Seb catches me looking but he doesn't say anything. We both know who these people are.

"Thanks again," he says, "for sticking up for me against Max. She can be a bit intense sometimes."

"I've noticed."

Seb smirks and sits on his battered gaming chair. "I didn't like you when we first met."

His bluntness knocks me backward, literally. But I steady myself as he chuckles and adds, "I've changed my mind now."

There's a gentle rap on the door, glasses and plates tinkling as Seb's mom creeps in.

He jumps up and carefully takes the tray from her, resting it on his desk before kissing her cheek.

"I didn't know what you liked so I've brought a bit of everything."

Happiness and expectation bloom behind her eyes as she waits for my response.

"Thank you."

She looks a lot older than my parents, and yet parts of her seem younger. I search for the scars that grief leaves behind, but Seb's mother hides them well. Either that or she's turned them into something else in the years since her other son—her first son—died.

She stands awkwardly for a few seconds, unafraid to show her joy that Seb has brought a friend home. I know that look, because it's the one *our* mom would have, too, if things were different.

Then she clicks her tongue and says, "If you need anything, you know where we are."

When she's gone, Seb pushes the door until it's almost closed, then pulls it back so a strip of hallway is visible from where I sit on his bed.

"You don't have to eat anything . . . if you're not hungry."

I'm already picking icing from one of the cakes that I recognize from the bakery window, and Seb laughs and adds, "Knock yourself out."

As we eat, I study the intricate displays that line his walls and imagine Seb and his father building them long into the night.

Dad and I don't have anything like that. We don't bond over anything good.

"They were Joshua's," Seb says.

"Your brother?"

He nods. "He and Dad were obsessed with Lego. It was their thing. Not mine. Mostly I pulled the heads off the figures or tried to eat the pieces."

I smile at the thought of a baby-sized Seb waddling around this house, his tiny fists gripping multicolored choking hazards.

"Even when I was older, it didn't interest me. I liked being outside—running, climbing, trying to reach the horizon or touch the sky, you know?"

"Sure."

"When he died, all the sunsets and stars dimmed, so there was no point running or climbing anymore."

"I'm sorry."

"You shouldn't keep saying that," Seb replies. "Don't apologize for something that isn't your fault. Be angry. Be helpful. But don't be sorry."

"Okay. How can I help?"

The smallest smile slips across his face. "You didn't tell Max about the essay. So, you already have."

He lifts some books from his desk and shows me the photograph he took from the school.

"Aren't you scared? Max said if you steal anything from there . . ."

"What? The Caretaker will blow smoke in my face? Besides, it's not stealing. It belongs with Joshua's other stuff. No, I'm not scared. I've seen a real horror movie, when some drunk asshole crushed my brother and I had to listen to him die.

"He was talking to me in the car, telling me everything would be okay, making sure I didn't close my eyes. But I didn't say it back. Not until it was too late."

"I'm . . ."

I stop myself just in time and Seb nods.

"I liked being a little brother. You get away with a lot. And you get a lot of love. But that's not me anymore. I'm not the youngest. I don't have someone to piss off or watch out for me. I'm all there is."

"Do you think you'll go back to the school?"

"No. I'm done now. Miss Kittle says the more we travel back in time, the less we look to our future."

"Does she know you broke in?"

"Of course not. I hide my truth in harmless words."

Me too.

"Why are you telling me this?" I ask.

He shrugs. "I save my best shit for strangers."

I go to his window, where the glass in one of the panels is fractured, the cracks sending shafts of jagged sunlight across his walls.

"What happened?"

"A bird, I think," Seb says. "Flew right into it."

I look at the flat extension roof below, a pile of cigarette butts sitting neatly in the center.

"Do you smoke?"

"No."

"When did your window break?"

"A few days ago. Dad has ordered a new one."

I let the silence stretch as I stare at my distorted reflection; then I turn to Seb and say, "Was that after we broke into the school . . . or before?"

"After."

The shadow that I saw creeping at the far end of the corridor that night fills my mind, forcing my head to jolt.

"Are you okay?" Seb asks.

The words tumble out before I can stop them. "What if you *did* piss him off?"

"Who?"

"The Caretaker. He smoked, right? That's why those smells creep through the vents if you're there after dark. What if he's angry that you took something from his school and . . ."

"What? He smashed one tiny window and left some cigarettes behind."

"As a warning."

"You're paranoid," Seb says, but his hands are shaking as he clasps them together.

If I ever found the courage to tell any of them about my time living next to Murder Road, it would be Seb. He's felt the weight of loss and suffered the scars of tragedy. He has the storage space for those kinds of stories.

I glance again at the used butts, then at a friend who takes one last look at his brother's photograph before sliding it into his jeans pocket.

He doesn't stick to the same hiding place and I respect him for that.

"Be careful," I say. "Messing with that stuff can be dangerous."

"It's too late for that," he replies. "If there really is a ghost smoking outside my window."

"Do you think we can convince Max to give up entirely? Or to change things. We could only do jump scares, maybe a bonfire or two, without all the rituals."

Seb grins. "That would have been a lot easier before *you* turned up."

That night I watched them from my hiding place in the woods—if I'd told them then to stop reading twisted histories and learning ancient mantras, maybe they would have.

Seb turns on his Xbox and says, "It's not Max you need to worry about. It's Tyler. He's the one obsessed with urban legends.

"We used to hang out in the woods, build dens, climb trees, play Murder in the Dark. But there were no legends.

"Then one day, Tyler showed us this article he'd found, about the Laughing Water. He said if you recited some creepy phrase, while you all had your hands in the bay, you'd hear cackles across the water. They'd skip along the surface, growing louder as they approached. If you were all brave enough to keep your hands submerged, and the laughter traveled from one side of the bay to the other, a scream would burst from the deep."

"Did you try it?"

Seb nods. "It didn't work. But it became a thing—a fun way to start our nights out. We'd try an urban legend, play a few tricks on each other, then get back to doing what we've always done."

"But now things are actually coming true."

"Exactly," Seb says.

"Are you scared?"

He presses both hands against his mouth and stares at the ceiling. When I glance up, I see that he has the same plastic stars as me.

"I'm not sure 'scared' is the right word," he says at last. "As I watched Joshua die, I was petrified. Once he'd gone, the thought of an entire life without him filled me with dread. But noises in the woods, torn metal, unexplained smoke—that doesn't feel important enough to be afraid of."

"Can I ask you something? About your brother?"

"Sure."

"How can you drive . . . after what happened? I don't think I'd be able to."

Seb sighs and says, "Joshua used to get in his car and go. No plan, no map, just for the fun of finding somewhere new. After the accident, I hated getting into other people's cars but, by the time I was old enough to drive, it felt nice being in control.

"We used to have this neighbor who was always working on an old Chevy. He'd rev it until Mom was this close to cursing. But it never left the driveway.

"My brother told me there's nothing sadder than an unused car. He was wrong, obviously, but I've never forgotten that."

Seb's door creaks open, his mom's strained smile shining through. "Can I get you boys anything else?"

I stare at the plate of snacks, still half full, and say, "No, thank you."

When I turn back to Seb, he hands me a controller, and I remember the days when Rowan and I used to play for hours. He'd beat me at absolutely everything, although that never stopped me trying.

After an hour, I check my phone and tell Seb I should go.

"We'll do this again, right?" he asks.

"I hope so."

His father is still at the dining table when we come back down, his latest build expanding across the thick wood, his fingers dashing from one instruction to the next.

"Maybe you should do one with him," I whisper.

Seb shakes his head. "I've tried."

Before I leave, he clears his throat then says, "Whatever you think might have happened here, with my window and those smokes, it didn't."

I wish I believed him.

37

"How was your playdate?"

For a moment, I'm convinced that Max is behind me, bristling with betrayal, but when I turn, Tyler is standing alone.

"It was good," I reply, because that word feels safe. It's a nothing word, a filler, one that keeps the truth from conversations that don't need it.

"What was his dad building?"

"I don't know."

On the way in, I didn't care. On the way out, I couldn't look.

"I thought you'd be there," I say.

"Sorry. That was *your* awkward to deal with. We've all been through it."

"Did you know his brother?"

Tyler shakes his head. "Before my time. But I know *about* him. Seb lets you in in stages. You'll see."

"What about you?"

"I have two older sisters and two younger brothers. The sisters are at college, the brothers are probably napping about now. They're two."

"Seriously?"

"Seriously. My dad used to say I was his last chance for a son. It's what some fathers want, right? A boy to keep the legacy going or whatever. Then fourteen years later the twins turn up and Dad wants a refund on his wish."

Tyler stares into the distance for a moment; then he says, "I'm a shitty reminder to Seb and Max that life deals different hands. He wants his brother back, she wants a dad who didn't leave, and my family keeps getting bigger. Like Max said: Picture. Fucking. Perfect."

All three of them define themselves by their families—grieving, broken, or whole—and I wonder if that's what they expect from me too.

I told Max about Rowan and Hazel—their places in my life, if nothing else. But that slipped out in an unexpected moment and I won't do the same with Tyler or Seb.

"Some people are lucky," I say.

"Tell my parents that," Tyler replies. "They are exhausted."

I like this version of my new friends better. This is what it's like to have a normal life, with people who are happy to see you, on days that aren't filled with despair.

"How was practice?"

"It was tough. Do you play?"

"A bit . . . just for fun. My brother . . ." Shit. I've done it again. "He prefers contact sports."

"Like football."

"Kind of."

"If you ever want to kick a ball around, let me know. You might be good enough to try out for the team."

I doubt it. I'm not good enough for anything, but I let Tyler think I might be.

"Seb said he didn't like me when I first arrived."

"Me neither," Tyler replies. "It's nothing personal. I wouldn't have liked whoever was standing in front of me. We were a trio with no plans to become a quartet. But you changed that."

"Thanks for giving me a chance."

"You've got Max to thank for that."

"I know."

Something stirs at the back of my mind and I resist. Then, as Seb walks toward us with his head bowed, I say, "Why aren't you scared? If these legends are suddenly coming to life. Why are you so relaxed about that?"

"Who says I'm relaxed?"

"You look it."

Tyler chuckles and says, "If I stop, I get scared. So, I don't stop. Between school and soccer and volunteering and my little brothers, there's enough to keep me distracted. And I have a new job now."

"Where?"

"The coffeehouse. You should come by sometime. I'll sneak you a freebie. And I promise I'll talk to you this time."

I picture Mom's green apron hanging by the front door and shudder.

"Sure. I'll do that."

It's hard to hide in small towns, where the strands of strangers soon become webs.

A whisper sneaks past my defenses and I grip it until it goes limp then disintegrates on the breeze.

I'm so busy watching Seb that I don't notice Max join us from behind. She looks broken, and I know immediately that she's angry with me.

Is that how this group works—that we are one thing together and other things apart? When I agreed to go to Seb's I felt guilty, if only for the briefest moment, because I wondered if I was betraying Max somehow.

I don't understand friendships. I don't know when it's fine to say yes and better to say no.

I know Max wasn't happy when I backed Seb about the graveyard. But have I made it worse by putting a temporary stop on the Hell Chasers and then going to his house?

"What's wrong?" Seb asks.

He's staring at Max and, when I do the same, I watch a tear creeping down her cheek like the insects I used to watch in the garden.

It paints a thin track across her skin, then falls in the space between us.

"Bella's dead," she says.

"Shit," Tyler replies. "I'm so sorry."

Seb looks at me then pulls Max into a hug. Whatever he says is whispered into her shoulder and they stay like that for a long time.

I want to ask who Bella is when it hits me—Mrs. Taylor, Max's neighbor.

At least she followed the rules. At least she died old and safe in a nice warm house.

You can think that, but you can't say it. Out loud you never put luck and death in the same sentence.

Seb steps back, creating the space I know it's my turn to fill. But it's Max who comes to me, taking my hands and saying, "She'll never see that painting."

Another tear sneaks out and I think about wiping it away. Is that what good friends do?

"How's Mr. Taylor?" I ask.

"He's broken. We knew it was coming, but . . . I thought she'd hold on for a few more months."

That's what Grandma did. But how do you know what's worth holding on for, and what is delaying the inevitable?

"How can we help?" Tyler asks.

Max sad-smiles and says, "Just be here."

"We are."

I look at each of them in turn and feel something different. When we first met, I feared so many things. And I've been so terribly scared ever since. But now, in this exact moment, I think I'm proud. Because friends come together at horrible times and, as I know too well, horrible times are inevitable.

38

"I need to go to a funeral."

My parents stare at me, and I could leave it at that. But I've already told Mom about Max, so what's the point in hiding anything now?

"My friend . . . her neighbor . . . she died."

Dad rubs the confusion from his eyes while Mom busies herself with dinner.

"You can wear Rowan's suit," she says with her back turned, and I picture the five of us standing over Grandma's grave—everything I was desperate to say tethered deep within me.

"What did she die of?" Dad asks.

"Old," Rowan says from the living room. "She died of old."

Relief washes over our father's face because, in this family, we think the worst and are usually right.

"Of course you can go," he says. "Do you want us to come with you?"

No way in hell!

"It's fine. My other friends are going too."

"Do you hear that?" Rowan says. "Nate has 'other' friends. My man got popular."

I stare at Rowan until doubt fills his eyes and he looks away. "Yes. I have friends. Three of them. Which is three more than you."

"Shit, little brother. Are you biting back now?"

"Don't curse," Mom mutters.

"What if I am?"

Rowan stands, his muscles flexing out of habit.

"Enough!" Mom's hand slams against the countertop. "I am sick of this sniping. I'm sick of you three not connecting. And I'm sick of pretending that you're not smashing the living daylights out of the garage wall when that damn punching bag goes untouched. If you don't want it, pull it down."

Rowan sags, as though our mother's anger has deflated both his body and his ego.

"I'm sorry about the walls."

"I don't care about the walls. This whole place is falling apart anyway. But stop being so passive-aggressive with your brother and sister. If you're struggling that much with your anger, go back to what you used to do, because these 'secret' fight clubs clearly aren't working. Join a *proper* club . . . or two . . . or whatever it takes to stop *this*. Enter a competition every weekend if you must."

We used to watch him fight, back when we thought it was a healthy habit. Mom and Dad would stare at the glistening trophies that he brought home like they were somebody else's newborns. It's been a long time since he came back with anything except busted knuckles.

"Okay," I say, holding our mother's stare until she looks away. "I'm just emotional, I guess."

Dad nods, then rests his hand against Mom's back.

They are thinking things—maybe about Grandma, maybe not. Either way, I leave them to it.

Rowan smirks as I walk past; then he lowers his voice and says, "See. That wasn't too bad." He can't feel the fear swelling in my stomach. "Plus, you get to wear *my* suit."

The briefest laugh spills out before Rowan's lips snap shut.

I look at him, at the results of countless hours spent working out, and curse the curse of hand-me-downs.

There was a time when our bodies almost matched—ten-year-old me fitting perfectly into the faded and holey clothes that ten-year-old him enjoyed new.

But even before Rowan learned how to fight, before his limbs thickened and his shoulders spread, his body grew in ways mine won't.

I'm the "skinny" one. The one told to "eat more" even when my plate is piled high. The one an ancient teacher once looked at and said, "I've seen more meat on a chicken's kneecap."

I smiled, like I always do, while thinking *No one asked your fucking opinion!*

"How's your friend?" Rowan asks. "The one whose neighbor died?"

"She's okay."

"Grief doesn't have rules," my brother mumbles. "Let her do it however she wants. Just be there when she needs you."

I nod, watching Rowan's thoughts settle, and wish he was this version of himself more often. Beneath the snark, the anger, the bravado, he cares—even about people he's never met.

39

Seb and Tyler stand in the parking lot, smiling awkwardly when I join them.

To our left, a cloud of silent strangers hangs outside the church, and I search for Max. But all I see are unfamiliar faces painted gray by grief.

"There," Tyler says.

I turn and think it before I can stop myself.

Max looks beautiful.

The words are so big that I want to pass them on, to untangle the meaning from the letters, to get them out of my head. But there's no space for them here. There are already so many feelings bristling in the air.

I watch the woman holding Max's hand and tug on Rowan's jacket sleeves to free my own.

Tyler steps forward and Max hugs each of us in turn; quick, emotionless gestures that leave nothing behind.

"I'm Jasmine," the woman says, looking directly at me. "Thank you for coming."

I don't know how to reply, so I nod.

She touches Seb's and Tyler's shoulders as she steps past, hugging a few people closer to the church before disappearing inside.

"How are you?" Seb asks.

"Not too bad," Max replies, but there is no sparkle in her eyes today. "You didn't have to come."

Tyler smiles. "Yes, we did."

She takes his hand and I watch the slightest squeeze echo in the tips of their fingers. Then the four of us turn as the murmuring stops, and a hearse creeps slowly around the corner.

The coffin is lifted gently onto the shoulders of four men and two women—some blank-faced and professional, others leaving streams beneath their feet.

I feel jealous and proud of these people. And certain that I will never be one of them.

I'll be lurking in the shadows, like we are now. I will be watching the strength to do what's right, not channeling it.

Seb and Tyler sit on either side of me in the narrow pews. Max is four rows ahead, on the opposite side of the church, and I wait the entire service for her to turn. But the only time she moves is when she walks to the altar and reads a poem full of cracks.

Her eyes burn into the sheet of paper that quivers through each silence, and I want to be up there with her—something solid to hold as she crumbles.

I picture Mrs. Taylor, barely lifting words the rest of us tossed to one another like Hacky Sacks. Max's words aren't heavy; they are fragile.

Seb wipes his eyes and I wonder how they said goodbye to his brother. He is here, putting someone else's grief above his own. He's a good person, and I wish he didn't have to suffer.

Max stares at the floor as she retakes her seat, her mother pulling her into a hug and whispering something against her hair.

Max gives one emphatic nod, then stares straight ahead until we follow the Taylors' family and friends to the hole in the ground.

In movies, it always rains at funerals. In real life, as we watch the coffin lowered into the earth, the sun stings my neck.

Mr. Taylor stands between two women who look about Mom's age. His face is dry and blank, while tears paint mascara tracks down their cheeks.

Next to them, spread out on either end, are younger people,

some around my age, their hands holding the arms of tugging toddlers.

If they want to run, let them run. But there are rules on days like this. Some may call funerals a celebration of life, but that celebration must be muted, acceptable, with caveats the dead have no say in.

One of the women next to Mr. Taylor reads a poem; then he steps forward and drops dirt on the coffin. One by one, the rest of his family does the same, and I must tell my parents that under no circumstances do I want to be buried.

Then we walk slowly back to the car, Max carried along ahead of us—on a tide of more important people.

"Are you okay?" Tyler asks, and before I can answer, Seb mumbles, "I'm fine."

As Jasmine drives away, and Max sits in the passenger seat staring through us, I wonder why we came.

"Are you going to the wake?" Tyler asks.

"I can't."

They don't ask why. They only nod and head for Seb's car, while I wait until the parking lot is almost empty. Then I go back into the church, where someone has restocked the candles, and I light every single one.

40

The following day, our classmates hurry past like nothing is wrong. They don't care about Bella or Max or anyone but themselves. They aren't grieving for the candy-store owner's wife, because she's as relevant to them as they are to me.

These strangers, these apathetic nobodies—all they do is take up space and spoil silences.

As I open my locker, a sheet of paper slips out, two words scribbled on one side.

It's coming.

I let it fall to the floor, the warning twisting and turning until it lands facedown at my feet.

I thought it was over. There had been nothing since I tossed the other notes and clippings into the flames and I assumed, naively, that whoever was doing this had grown bored.

Whatever they think they know—it's only part of the picture. But sickness still stirs in my stomach as my hands shake and a collage of horrible images forms in my mind.

I look down and the paper is gone.

I search for it in the slipstream of the crowd, then check the bulletin boards and the rolling news display for hidden messages. But everything is the same as always.

I stumble to class and make myself even smaller than usual. Then I fill my notebook with those words.

It's coming. It's coming. It's coming.

And suddenly Max's hand is pressed into mine and we're running. As I look at her, I stumble, but she yanks me up and we keep going until my thighs burn and my lungs scream for me to stop.

"Come on!" Max says.

But I can't. I have nothing left.

"Nate!" Max yells, my head jolting up as laughter spills over me, washing my dream away.

"Late night?" Ms. Hewitt asks, her kindly smile out of place among my classmates' cackles.

"Sorry," I mumble, turning the page of my book before she can see the warnings screaming from every page.

She taps the side of her head as she strides back to her desk, and I do my best to concentrate on a lesson that isn't important, for a test that means nothing, in a school that has no idea what's coming.

41

Each day, the warnings multiply—the notes that fall from my locker stamped on and kicked aside, flyers fluttering under windshield wipers as I hurry through the parking lot, unfamiliar words creeping out from below bulletin board announcements like claws emerging from caves.

I avoid enclosed spaces now, leaving campus if I need the bathroom, my ears on high alert for the stirrings of that terrible tune.

No one whistles. No one shows themselves. But I know they are here, hiding in plain sight.

I watch Tyler and Seb from the shadows, doing their best to be happy in Max's absence, then sneak away before they can find me.

In class, my eyes grow too heavy to lift, and most teachers let me sleep. Only Ms. Hewitt thinks I'm important enough to include in conversations—even when she gets nothing back.

"Is everything okay?" she asks. "Is something keeping you awake at night that you want to talk about?"

I imagine being farmed back to Miss Kittle—so greedy for the secrets of high school kids that she made a career out of it.

"It's nothing," I say. "Honestly."

"I can't stand by and watch you sleep through my lessons, Nate. If it *does* continue, maybe we should call your parents in."

"I'll try harder," I reply, and she nods—an emphatic gesture from a face full of doubt.

As I leave, I imagine Mom and Dad sitting in this classroom—hands clenched, smiles fixed, their responses rehearsed and rewritten.

Fragments of words stir in the recesses of my brain, crawling toward each other and crunching into place.

Ready or not. Whatever you do. The Hiding Boy is coming for you.

I don't need anyone else to taunt me now. I know enough to punish myself.

"*There* you are!" Tyler says. "Are you avoiding us?"

Yes.

"Of course not."

"That's all right then. Have you seen?"

"Seen what?" I ask.

"The countdown."

Tyler points to the end of the hallway, where a huge sheet hangs overhead, the paint from the words written on it leaving thick crimson trails on the otherwise crisp white.

4 DAYS TO GO

"You can see that?"

Tyler's brow creases as he says, "Yes. Are you okay, Nate?"

Not at all.

"What does it mean?"

A broad smile plays across his face. "You'll see."

"Stop fucking with me."

"What?"

"I've been getting these notes in my locker, and seeing warnings on the bulletin boards, and now . . ." I point at the banner. "There's that. If you know what it means, please tell me."

Tyler's features soften as he touches my arm and says, "It's a game, Nate. We've *all* been getting those notes."

"Seriously?"

I close my eyes for a few seconds and, when I open them again, I focus on the people around me. I listen to their laughter as sheets of paper fall from their own lockers. I read the flyers that are no longer hiding under other announcements on the boards that line the corridor. They have broken free now, two words stuck and stapled to every available surface.

It's coming!

"Hey," Seb says. "It's good to see you, man."

When I don't answer, Tyler leans toward him and whispers, "Nate's having a moment. He's taking in . . . this."

The corridors are suddenly buzzing, everyone I usually ignore grinning or screeching or slapping someone on the back.

School spirit makes me nauseous but this feels different.

"It's back, baby!" someone yells, high-fiving Tyler as they race past.

I press my back against the lockers and picture my "happy place," Max, anything at all that could slow my heart rate even slightly. But I don't know what's real and what isn't.

These notes might be for everyone, but how does that fit with the Murder Road articles, and the warnings I was getting before?

"It's okay," Seb says. "This is probably a bit unexpected. But you know when I said there's only one night of the year that I'd go in the cemetery? *This* is that night. Well, if Max lets us."

"Why wouldn't she?" Tyler asks, his eyes widening as Seb nods and mumbles, "Fair point."

"Is this . . . a Hell Chasers thing?"

They laugh in unison, then shake their heads.

"This is a Montgomery-Oakes thing. A school tradition . . . with a twist."

"So, no urban legends?"

Tyler draws a circle in the air with his finger. "Zero. But, like we said, Max has the deciding vote on this one."

"What are we voting on?"

Everyone sneaks up on you in this place, especially today.

There's another streak in Max's hair—red this time, on the opposite side from the blue—and she has a flyer in her hand.

Tyler's lips twitch as he says, "After the funeral, we thought you might not want to, you know . . ."

"We haven't missed one yet," she replies. "Besides, Bella loved it when I told her about them."

"Seriously?"

"Yes. Henry and I joked that we'd sneak her in one day."

The cracks from Max's poem rush through her mouth and she shakes her head hard.

This is my chance, to be the something strong, but she steadies herself, the smile she offers us broken in places but enough to do its job.

"I want to go," she says.

Tyler grins. "Then we should probably tell Nate what's happening."

"He doesn't know?"

"He's been hard to track down while you were off school."

An awkward silence hangs over us until Tyler adds, "But he's here now."

Max watches me with an uncertain smile. "Are you okay? You seem nervy."

"He thought this was all in his head," Tyler replies. "I get that. For some totally unknown reason, the principal lets the social committee cover these pristine walls for one wonderful week. It's called Bloodbath. The game we play. And it's happening this weekend."

Max points at the people celebrating in the corridors. "Everyone's invited."

I know what happens when teenagers get foolish ideas. So many have camped out on Murder Road down the years, thinking there was nothing to worry about. They were excited, too, at the start. They told ghost stories the way Max, Seb, and Tyler do, until they *became* the story.

But this isn't a clique, it's an army. Everyone in the entire school seems to be excited for Bloodbath. So hopefully it's as harmless as it sounds.

Something warm and wet trickled down the insides of his eyelids, painting words that he could see in the dark.

When they faded, three shapes pulled themselves free of the shadows, their features coming into focus until he saw them as clear as day. If only it was.

He studied their scars—some, tiny trinkets from forgotten accidents; others, daily reminders of unimaginable tragedies.

He read those scars like stories. Then he fought against the blood matted in his lashes until his eyes peeled open.

As he reached out, they ran from him, toward a house that suddenly filled his vision. Its shattered roof tiles and crumbling chimney scratched the clouds that dared to drift past, while headless stalks swayed in the front yard.

"It's coming."

The whisper snaked up his spine, turning to a wail that filled his head like a bomb blast.

"I know!" he screamed back—over and over until he finally burst a hole in his dreams.

42

I'm not in control anymore. If I ever was.

I'm lost. Hopeless. And yet, I can't tear myself away from them. Away from her.

That's why I go with them to Bloodbath—because, however many good days we have left, I want us to spend them together.

A statue of an angel towers over us, its crumbling face illuminated by portable spotlights. Most people are crammed between the graves, but a few perch on headstones, their feet thudding thoughtlessly against the inscriptions.

"Assholes," Max mumbles. "I'm killing them first."

Seb laughs as something hard settles behind her eyes.

I shouldn't be surprised that almost the whole school is here. The buzz as the final three days ticked down to tonight told me all I needed to know about Bloodbath.

Whatever happens next, this feels like the biggest event of the year.

"The smartest thing about this," Tyler says, "is no one ever knows the exact date. It could be in October. It could be in July. Those flyers and the countdown could begin on any given day. That's smart marketing."

"I still don't understand how the school lets you get away with this," I reply.

"It's a win-win," Max shouts over the rising volume of the crowd. "We get to blow off some steam, and the rest of the year we do as we're told. Besides, if you look closer, it's not just schoolkids."

"What do you mean?"

"Bloodbath is open to all, Nate. Everyone needs to unleash their frustration now and again."

I scan the crowd, their caps suddenly pulled low, while unfamiliar eyes glisten in the shadows.

"Welcome!" someone shouts, silencing everyone in an instant. "This is Bloodbath. And anyone can win."

The cheer makes me shudder but no one else looks uneasy. Max, Seb, and Tyler grin at the cloaked shape in front of us, hanging on their every word.

"What's your favorite scary movie?" the person asks, their voice distorted under their hood. "Because this is mine."

They open their arms wide and the crowd cheers again.

Tyler catches my eye and chuckles. "Just run with it. It's fun."

There it is again—"fun." But my definition is different from his, from Max's, from everyone's in this strange town.

I think of the old elementary school—the wood pulled back from that broken door so many times it may as well have not been there. Then I think of the storefronts protected by a single pane of glass.

In Montgomery-Oakes, some places are open to all and others are untouchable.

"The rules of the game are simple," the figure in the cloak booms. "Last person standing wins."

I feel a surge at my back and, when I turn, more people are joining us from all sides.

"I think we're past capacity," I say, and Max shrugs and replies, "And that's only the people you can see."

She touches the nearest headstone, her lips moving soundlessly, then puts one hand on Seb's shoulder and the other on Tyler's. "You ready?"

They nod and turn to me.

"We're a team," Max says. "We work together."

"Of course."

"You kill by bloodying your victims," the cloak says. "Use these wisely."

When we reach the front, whoever is doing this passes a bundle of ten tubes full of liquid to each of us.

I lean forward to take mine, trying to look under their cloak, but they bend lower. Then we are pushed aside by the crowd and I focus on the vials.

Tyler flicks one. "Plastic, so they don't crack in your pocket."

"What's inside?" I ask, peering at the red liquid.

"It's not real blood. If that's what you're worried about."

I unscrew one and sniff it. It smells sweet, but something nasty is already swirling in my stomach.

"A little tip," Seb whispers. "Always have one ready to throw. If you're messing around trying to open these in the dark, you've missed your chance."

I watch the crowd crawl forward. Someone from math class tucks his vials into his pockets, nervously glancing back and forth. A girl who sits next to me in film class empties all ten tubes into a flask before scurrying into the shadows.

The kid who gets closest to Hazel when I watch her on the track slides his ten into elastic loops sewn into his jacket, practicing pulling them out and slotting them back in.

As for us, we wait, no special routine, no tricks. The four of us stand amid everyone else until our hooded host claps their hands and says, "It's time!

"The rules are simple. You have one minute to hide. After that, if you are cut in any of the four target areas, you are dead and out of the game. The target areas are head, heart, throat, and stomach. Any area with blood on it counts as a cut. So . . . happy killing."

The spotlights go off and the crowd counts down, "Ten, nine, eight . . ."

Seb and Tyler join in but Max stays silent. Then, on "one," everyone runs and I'm knocked to the ground.

"Come on," Seb says, pulling me to my feet. "We need to get out of here."

Screams fill the air like sirens, while the thud of footsteps reverberates up my legs.

I'm used to running and yet, in this moment, all I can do is stand completely still as bodies surge past.

"Stop," I say.

"What are you doing?!" Tyler shouts. "We need to go."

"No. We need to stay."

Seb yanks my arm. "Come on!"

But I hold firm, the excited wails of our classmates growing distant, until we're almost alone.

"Clever," says a voice in the dark.

Tyler flings a vial at the sound but it hits a headstone, painting its letters crimson.

"You can't kill me," says the person in the cloak. "I don't play this game."

It sounds like a woman now, their voice distorter packed along with any remaining vials.

"Have fun," they say. "I wouldn't stay here for long though. They always circle back."

"Thank you," Seb says, one hand hanging in the air until Max slaps it down and says, "Stop waving at the creepy person."

The stars cast a silver glow over everything but I still need to focus as we creep away, with the ground uneven and strangers potentially lurking behind every gravestone.

"That was smart," Max tells me. "Everyone always runs, which means they are out there somewhere. We should have time to think."

"If we wait long enough," Tyler says, "everyone will kill each other and we can take whoever's left."

"Including each other?" I ask.

"Of course not."

"What normally happens?"

"Usually we die early," Seb says.

I close my eyes and listen to the echoes of our peers drenching one another with blood.

Laughter travels on the wind like the voices of drunken strangers talking three streets away.

Shouts hit hard in the gloom, leaving dents where the air feels harder to reach.

Screams rip through the brief moments of silence, until the gaps between those sounds grow bigger and I can hear my own breathing—fast and heavy and ready for anything.

This was a mistake, but what choice do I have?

I couldn't even be alone, when that should be the easiest thing in the world. I *wanted* them to be my friends. I *wanted* to see more of the girl with the terrifying eyes. Not for any horrors they contained, but for the feelings they stirred in a heart I'd forgotten how to use.

There are whispers a few yards away. Seb hears them, too, pointing at a headstone towering over those around it.

Max nods and strides to her right, while Tyler goes left. Seb signals for me to approach from behind while he walks straight ahead.

For the briefest moment a thought strikes me—*This is ridiculous*—but my adrenaline washes it away as I creep toward the whispers that are turning to giggles.

This is too easy. It's almost as though they want to be caught. Soon I will see them, these kids who are playing the game all wrong.

The next thought comes too late—It is *too* easy, which means . . .

A shadow escapes the darkness and lunges at Tyler, pinning him to the ground. Before I can open my mouth, a vial is dragged across his throat.

A second shadow approaches Seb from behind, creeping in and out of the tombstones.

"Don't," someone whispers by my side. "It's too late."

Max steps forward, then crouches in the dry leaves, gesturing for me to do the same.

"It's a trap," she says. "We need to go."

I look up just as two shapes grab Seb by his arms while the giggling girls emerge from their hiding place. They are still laughing as one of them opens a vial and presses it against our friend's heart.

As the blood spills over Seb's shirt, the ghost of the boy from Murder Road bursts into my head and I fall back.

When I turn, more of my classmates appear from the shadows, laughing as they wipe away their fake wounds. Then they transform, forcing me to stare into the faces of all the people killed on that street.

Their grins spread until their rotting skin splits and maggots spill onto the grass at my feet.

I scramble back, my heels leaving panic trails as Max pulls me away.

"I can't believe we fell for that," she says.

"What?"

"Those girls. We thought we had them, but . . . we need more tricks up our sleeves. Some people plan their plays for months. We've got a future soccer pro in our friendship group. Why the hell didn't we use that?"

Her smile fades the longer she stares at me.

"Are you okay, Nate?"

I pull my shaking hands into fists, wait a few seconds, then whisper, "I think so."

"Don't blame yourself," Max says. "They deserved the kills. I like smart players."

"Seb and Tyler . . ."

"They'll be fine. They know the rules."

I need to remind myself that this is a game and no one is dead. But it's hard when everything feels so real.

"You look happy."

In that exact moment, Max's joy falters, and she tucks both hands under her arms. "We all need to forget sometimes. I'm still grieving, but . . . this has always been one of my favorite nights of the year."

"What now?"

She pulls me to the ground as someone runs past screaming, followed by someone holding what I hope is a fake axe dripping with blood.

"People take this very seriously," she says.

"Will Seb be angry that I got him killed?"

"Stop worrying. Dying is part of the experience. We never come close to winning."

"Who does?"

"Does that matter? Come on. We've got someone to visit."

I follow her in silence, hiding every now and again but more often walking past people already painted red.

Sometimes their faces change as they slip past, their features morphing into those I've seen in newspapers and online when learning about decades-old horror stories. But, when I blink, they look like themselves again.

Eventually, Max crouches next to Mrs. Taylor's grave; her flowers are starting to wither, and her order of service is battered by the rain.

"Hi, Bella. I told you I'd come."

I stand back while Max has a one-way conversation with her former neighbor. Or maybe it's *not* one-way. Who knows what she can hear tonight?

"I can't believe she's in there," Max says.

It takes me a few seconds to realize that she's talking to me.

"She's not. Not really. Her body is but . . . the rest of her . . . that's free now."

Max tilts her head, one side of her mouth rising in a confused smile. "That's a nice way to think of it."

It's what grieving people want to hear—that whoever they are crying for is somewhere better. They want them to be among the clouds or on the breeze or floating amid the dust motes that dance in the early-morning sun.

They don't want them to be a body in the ground or a memory turned to dust. There's nothing romantic about that.

"Is this why you wanted to come tonight?" I ask. "To be with Bella?"

"It's one of the reasons. I knew she didn't have long, but it still hurts so much. I thought this might help."

"Has it?"

"I think so. The last time I saw her, I said, *See you soon*. Never *goodbye* . . . as if my choice of words could stop fate."

A twig cracks behind us and something wet drips down my forehead. When I turn, I see the girl with the blood-filled flask merge with the shadows.

Max wipes the thick red ooze from her eyes and licks one finger. "Cornstarch, cherry juice, syrup, and food coloring. In case you want to make your own."

"Who's behind the cloak?" I ask.

"No one knows. At least, no one's telling."

"There were a lot of flyers. That's too much work for one person."

Max shrugs. "You might be on to something. But this is one mystery we're not interested in solving. Once we know who's behind Bloodbath, it will probably end. So, we don't go digging."

She lies next to Mrs. Taylor's grave, crosses her arms, and stares at the stars.

"It's a convenient place to die," she says, as I lie next to her and listen to the screams.

"We've done some weird things together."

"You say 'weird,' I say 'interesting.'"

"I'm glad you spoke to me on my first day."

Max rolls on her side and stares at me. "Me too."

We stay like that for ages, just listening.

This place, these people, this choice our parents made—I'm happy with all of them.

Who knew when we moved here that I would be lying next to a newly found friend in a graveyard splattered with fake blood, while the final few contestants in an absurd competition fight to the "death"?

Whatever happens next, I'll always have tonight.

I stare into Max's eyes, an invisible barrier between us. If she breaks it, I'll kiss her. If she doesn't, I could wait like this forever.

"Hey," she mutters, her lips slowly pulling back into a smile.

"Hey."

She moves closer, just a fraction, her head tilting as I ask, "Are you sure?"

When she nods, the space between us vanishes, and all my bad thoughts turn to dust.

Eventually, Max giggles and asks, "What took you so long?"

Too many reasons.

"I don't really . . . do that."

"Well, you do now," she replies, before she sits up, her head arching toward the darkness. "I know that voice."

She holds a finger to her lips and I listen as someone approaches—two people, arguing in passive-aggressive whispers.

"I'm bored," one says. "Can we die already?"

"I want to win," says the other.

Max turns to me and mouths *That's Helen*.

I watch them pass, not a speck of red on either, then open a vial and pass it to Max.

"Revenge is sweet," I whisper.

She takes the blood from me, touches Mrs. Taylor's grave, and says, "Close your eyes, Bella."

Then she pulls her hood low over her face, creeps up behind them, and pours blood over the heads of the mean girls.

Theirs is my favorite scream of the night.

43

I don't want to go back to the angel statue. I want to stay here, with a Max who is bubbling with the excitement that comes from fake-killing your middle school nemesis. But endings are inevitable.

Seb and Tyler stand separate from the crowd, grinning when they see us.

"We thought you might still be playing," Seb says. "Apparently there are only two people left."

An image of me chasing Max around the cemetery flashes through my mind.

"Not a chance," Max replies. "But I did kill Helen Keane."

"Nice," Tyler says.

"Sorry we couldn't save you," I say, and he shrugs.

"No drama. I wouldn't have rescued you either."

Tyler looks from Max to me and back. Then he points at her and whispers, "You kissed."

"Bullshit," Max replies, but I'm already blushing.

Seb smiles and nudges my shoulder with his. "I think it's cute."

A scream rips through the crowd and I follow the fingers until a shape bounds out of the darkness. Behind him, gaining with every step, is the person with the axe.

I wait for the mass of people to part, but they hold firm because they know. The kid isn't getting that far.

He stumbles, rolls onto his back, and holds his hands against his face.

The masked figure looms over him, the axe rising slowly into the air. It doesn't glisten in the moonlight because it's fake. That's what everyone is telling themselves.

"Do it!" someone yells, while Tyler hops from one foot to the other and Max's fingers rest gently in mine.

The figure lowers the axe just as slowly as it rose, letting it hover an inch from the kid's face. A single droplet separates from the red smeared across the weapon's edge, bulging at the bottom like a water balloon before it splats against his forehead.

"Bloodbath!"

Wings explode in the night sky, the harsh scream of an owl followed by the nervous chatter of foxes.

The creatures that call this place home are used to the company of the dead. But tonight, we have stolen that solitude.

Whoever just won this ridiculous game stands with their arms outstretched, soaking up the cheers, then removing their mask.

As it falls to the ground, I catch their eye and quickly release Max's fingers.

This year's Bloodbath champion stares at me, a satisfied smile spreading across his face.

"I know that guy," Tyler says.

So do I.

44

"Hey, little bro," Rowan says.

This close, the plastic axe looks harmless. But I don't want to think about how many nightmares it has inspired tonight.

"What are you doing here?" I hiss, just as Max steps forward and offers her hand.

"You're Nate's brother?"

"I am," Rowan replies. "It's nice to meet you."

My words stop short, swallowed by the nausea that bobs in my throat. Anxiety twists like barbed wire in my stomach, burrowing deep into hundreds of holes from which I'll never pull it free.

"Why are you here?" I mumble, but the question is lost in a crowd that wraps itself around my brother and pushes me away.

Only Seb hears me. Only he grips my shoulder and says, "Don't be angry with him for coming. It's a town tradition."

How can Seb understand, when he would give anything for *his* brother to be the winner?

As I watch Rowan soak up his latest dose of adulation, I think of the competitions he used to win, all the medals and trophies he doesn't bother unpacking anymore.

When the crowd parts slightly, I see Tyler standing a few yards from my brother, his stare fixed, his fingers twitching by his sides.

Don't do it, I think. *Please don't.*

Tyler edges closer, saying something to Rowan that I can't hear. Then he steps back and hurries over to us.

"What did you say?" I ask, trying to make my weak words sound strong.

"Just congratulations," Tyler replies. "But seriously, guys. Do you know who that is?"

Seb shakes his head and Max stares more intently, trying to figure out the answer before it's handed to her.

"That's Rowan Campbell," Tyler says, and, when no one reacts, "He saved those kids from Murder Road."

"Shit," Seb whispers. "Are you sure?"

Tyler taps something into his phone. When he holds it out, my brother's face beams back. It's his school photo from junior year, the one the media used when they told his story—at least, the part they knew.

Max stares at me until my face is on fire. "Is that true?"

"Yes."

"Holy shit!" Tyler says, pacing between the tiny stone squares in the ground.

When I look over, Rowan tilts his head and I want to punch him so hard that, for once, I knock him down.

But he doesn't fall easily. Just ask everyone at Bloodbath. Just ask anyone he's ever left beaten or tapped out.

"Did you ask him?"

"Of course not," Tyler replies. "But if you want to formally introduce us . . ."

"No!" I say, loud enough for the people still milling about to turn, process, and dismiss me as unimportant.

"Why didn't you tell us?" Max asks.

"Tell you what? That I used to live near Murder Road? That I grew up listening to those fucking stories?"

"I'm sorry," Max mumbles. "But your brother . . ."

"Is a hero. I know. I've heard it more times than you could ever know. But being a hero comes with complications."

"You *wanted* to tell us, though, right?" Tyler says. "That's why you showed us the article."

"No."

I watch my brother disappear with the remaining participants. How many of them recognize him? And how many think he's some college kid with a few hours to kill?

When I look back at my friends, I see it—and terror grips my limbs.

"You want me to tell you about it. You want to know what it feels like living that close to a nightmare. And you"—I turn to Tyler—"you want to see for yourself."

"I don't," he lies.

"I wish I could believe you."

Max takes my hand. "Then believe us."

The whispers stir then swirl in my head. He did this on purpose and I hate him for it.

"I'm sorry," I say. "I need to go home. And we shouldn't hang out anymore."

"Don't be ridiculous," Tyler says. "I was starstruck. It's no big deal."

"Why are you so worried?" Seb asks. "You think we want to go anywhere near Murder Road? You think we'd willingly take a . . . what . . . three-hour drive just to end up dead?"

"People do," I say. "People a lot less obsessed with urban legends than you."

Max watches me in silence and I wish I knew what she was thinking. Does she regret recruiting me? Does she feel betrayed? Or does she think this explains why her town's demons are coming to life—because I'm some kind of ghost whisperer?

"Let's sleep on it," I say, hoping they can, knowing I won't.

"You could have told us," Tyler says as we leave. "We're not like other people."

I know. That's what upsets me the most.

45

They came, even when you told them not to. My brother learned that the hard way.

He'd been talking to a guy online—Jacob Something—and that guy listened to everything Rowan said and went to Murder Road regardless.

He took friends, because he believed in safety in numbers. But sometimes, more people only means more bodies.

Five of them broke into the house and, if it weren't for Rowan, none of them would have gotten out.

That was my brother's origin story—the night he changed forever.

"Idiot!" he said, over and over, until twelve-year-old me wandered sleepily into his room.

"Go back to bed!" he snapped, anger replaced by guilt as he knelt next to me and whispered, "I need to go out for a while. Don't tell Mom and Dad, okay?"

I watched him from my window as he ran to the end of our street, stopped, doubled back. He paced the sidewalk, talking to someone who wasn't there. His lips were still moving when he glanced up and I waved.

He stared at me until the Rowan I knew began to crumble and something different broke through—a mask made from anger, frustration, and fear. Then he turned and ran toward Murder Road.

My room narrowed, the sound of Hazel's music next door

growing distant before it was snuffed out entirely. I tried to find the hum of our parents' conversation through the floorboards, but the more I searched, the deeper I fell into silence.

I knew I couldn't go with him. I knew the rules. But I went anyway.

I crept downstairs and out the door, just as Rowan had. But *I* didn't pause to argue with myself. I didn't let the fragments of those horror stories grow into roadblocks. I marched quickly and foolishly into the street we were told to avoid.

There was the house with the bloodstained girl, next to the home of the boy who was banned from the pet store. After that came the scene of the sweet-sixteen massacre, then old Mr. Lewis's place, where a man in his nineties killed his entire family despite struggling to hold his own spoon.

I stopped for a moment outside the Witchells' house, shuddering at the thought of those twins, trapped inside their dreams as a killer loomed over them.

I knew the fate of every single building I passed until I saw my brother kicking that door, while smoke billowed into the night sky and flames snapped at the shadows.

Rowan rammed his shoulder into the thick wood but it didn't budge. Then I saw the look we're so familiar with now—the one he gives to an opponent right before they fall.

For the briefest moment, as crackles filled the air, I remembered toasting marshmallows over campfires; Rowan and Hazel dancing in the tumbling ash, while Mom sang and Dad smiled at their tiny kingdom.

Then the screams and splutters pulled me back to reality as the door burst inward and five blackened bodies rushed out.

Sirens suddenly soared, as though they were waiting, knowing full well that no one ever got to Cherry Tree Lane on time. But as Rowan stumbled over to me, his bloody knuckles leaving a trail for the emergency services to follow, I knew he'd rewritten that story.

"I couldn't let it happen again," he muttered.

No one ever explained how the boarded-up house caught fire with five out-of-towners inside. If they ever told their side, it didn't make it onto the news.

My brother did—that high school photograph, sound bites from classmates, a few mumbled comments before a better story came along.

That's what Tyler, Seb, and Max know now: that Rowan is a lifesaver, that he stopped—for a while at least—the pattern that gave Murder Road its name.

What they don't know is what happened next because death is inevitable and when you mess with that, there are consequences.

46

Rowan's light is off when I get home. After a night like this, he needs to burn some of that adrenaline, and I picture him charging down the lanes that connect this town to all the others, a fake axe strapped to his back, daring a car to hit him.

He will feel close to immortal right now. He may have won Bloodbath but he's just like the rest of us—one stupid decision or moment of bad luck away from being over.

I stare up at his window, anger pulsing through my veins, all the words I wanted to scream at him fizzling out only for new ones to rise in their place.

"Hey."

I stare into the gloom until I can make out my sister's shape in the living room.

"What are you doing?"

"Waiting for you."

When I sit, she joins me on the sofa, gently resting half her blanket over my legs. I think back to the pillow forts we made when we were kids, always guarding the entrance from a brother who had no intention of breaking in.

"You didn't want to come tonight?"

Hazel sighs. "How do you know I wasn't there?"

I picture the kid who always comes in second in track and wonder if my sister could have outrun everyone tonight—even Rowan.

"If you were, you cleaned up quick."

"It's not really my thing," she says. "It's not really your thing either."

"No, but . . ."

"Peer pressure?"

We both laugh and I miss the sound of our sister's happiness. That's one of the only things we didn't bring with us from the last place.

Hazel touches my head, her finger coming away red. "You should shower before Mom sees you."

I haven't looked in the mirror yet, and I picture all the Montgomery-Oakes kids leaving bloodstains for their parents to find.

"It's clever," I say. "It gives the people here something to escape into. For one night only, they can be the monster."

"Is that a good thing?"

"Sometimes." I stand and lay the blanket back over my sister. "Don't wait up for him."

Hazel shivers, then moves back to the comfy chair.

Her face is lit by the glow of her phone, so I leave her to it.

My reflection in the landing mirror sends a bolt of panic up my spine, and I shake my head hard to flush it out. If I stare too long, the things lying twisted inside me start to stir.

I walk past our parents' bedroom door, Mom's snores silenced by Dad's frustrated whispers. Then I go to Rowan's room, where a flyer for Bloodbath is pinned to his corkboard, along with photos of the friends who have grown up without him.

Is his photo on the walls of the people he saved? How do they remember him—the boy who refused to be the reason for a tragedy? And do they have any idea that, while they lived, others weren't so lucky?

47

Can we meet? I want to talk in person.

Max's message came at 3:45 A.M., so she was awake even later than I was.

Eventually, when I knew Rowan wouldn't come home until the sun was up, I fell into a vicious kind of sleep, everyone I know drenched in blood, decomposing hands bursting from the ground and coiling around my ankles, screams yanking me awake only to drop me back into the darkness.

I knew this day would come, and yet I still want to nudge it away, minute by minute, for as long as possible.

Hazel sits alone at the table, pushing soggy Cheerios around her bowl.

"What time did you go to bed?" I ask, the gray circles around her eyes thicker than ever.

She stands, licks her finger, and rubs it against my forehead. "You missed a bit."

"It will come off eventually."

"What will?" Mom asks, brushing my arm as she passes.

"The blood," Hazel says.

Our mother doesn't react. Instead, she makes two coffees and places one where Dad always sits. Different kitchens, same dining table hierarchy.

I try not to stand still for too long, making myself a moving target so Mom can't see my stains.

"Where's your brother?" she asks.

Hazel and I exchange looks just as Dad walks in.

He asks the same question, like Rowan is suddenly the most important member of the family.

"Probably out for a run," I say, and Mom mumbles, "Probably."

I read Max's message again, then say, "I'm going out too."

Hazel's eyes fall and I picture her rushing excitedly from our previous house. I know what it's like when there's nowhere to go and no one to see. You can leave but it's not the same. Every step is a reminder that you are going nowhere; every person you pass is on their way to someone else.

"You've been busy," Dad says. "I'm proud of you."

I hold his gaze until he looks back at Friday's paper. He can make one day's news last a week. Then I eat the breakfast Mom has discreetly placed in front of me, cursing her for taking that tiny moment in which to forget.

When no one is looking, I send my reply to Max, then shower for the second time in eight hours.

Crimson swirls disappear down the plughole and I imagine the Montgomery-Oakes sewers, thick with everyone's fake blood.

I expect to see Rowan on my way to the town square, but there are only a couple of dog walkers and three elderly ladies laughing as they march past.

I'm happy going slow. The quicker I get to Max, the sooner I must answer the questions that will have been swimming around her head all night.

Max sits on the bench, her face a sheet of half-written apologies. She looks up and smiles at every passerby, then bows her head when she's alone again, her fingers knotted and one leg bouncing on the spot.

The sound of the doorbell from Mr. Taylor's candy store travels on the air and Max glances up, too quickly for me to hide.

I wave, turning my lurk into a stride as she stands like this is a job interview.

"Hey," she says. "Thanks for coming."

"No worries. How are you?"

"Fine. Last night was . . ."

When she doesn't finish the sentence, I mumble, "I know."

Max pushes her shoulders back and tucks her hair behind her ears. "I've been googling your brother."

"Should I be jealous?"

Half a laugh slips from her mouth before she says, "No."

Mr. Taylor's bell rings again and I look past the multicolored displays to the unfamiliar woman behind the register.

It's too soon for him to be back here, handing out smiles with every paper bag, and I wonder how he's coping. Certainly not like Max, who has a unique way of grieving.

I picture the two of us lying beside Bella's freshly dug grave—smiling, kissing, waiting to kill Helen Keane—and wonder if that will be the best memory I take from this place.

"Have you ever worked in Mr. Taylor's store?"

Max glances across the square, then shakes her head.

"How is he?" I ask.

"He's okay. He's still painting Bella's portrait. He wants it finished for her birthday."

Is it still your birthday after you're gone? Or is it something different—an occasion that stings some and destroys others?

"That's nice."

"Is it true?" Max asks. "That your brother saved five people from Murder Road?"

"Yes."

It's not that simple. The better answer is "kind of," but "yes" is enough for now.

"What happened?"

"Some high school kids thought it would be fun to chase an urban legend," I say, letting the words settle, watching the sheen get chipped from Max's smile.

"They were from out of state. My brother had been talking to one of them online for a while. I think he liked telling someone how it felt growing up next to such a horrible place. But when the guy and his friends ignored Rowan's warnings and went there anyway . . ."

Images of that night flick through my mind like the sketches in the corners of Hazel's diary. If you shuffle the pages too fast or too slow, the story falters. But if you get it just right, you see everything.

There's the next house on the list engulfed by flames. There's my brother pulling fools from the wreckage. There's his anger, bursting out in empty speech bubbles as sirens and shouts fill the air. There are the people he saved, helped into the back of ambulances, peering out like the final scene of a horror movie.

They are the lucky ones. But aren't we all? The question is: Is it good luck or bad?

"Did all those people really die?" Max asks. "One house at a time? Because some boy whose mom was murdered cursed the entire street?"

She shivers at the thought, then again when I say, "Yes."

"And your brother stopped it."

She sounds so certain that I don't want to correct her. I prefer Max's version of the story. I like the idea of Rowan saving both the day and our future.

"He didn't stop it," I say, one last tinkle from Mr. Taylor's store filling the air before all I can hear are the screams.

Max touches my hand and I don't care if I'm cold or clammy. I hold her hand tightly until I take a deep breath and say, "Would you run away with me? If I asked you to?"

"What?"

"We've done a lot of running. When you mess with a curse, you put a target on your back."

"Are you talking about Rowan?"

Max pulls her hand away as I say, "We're a family, so . . . if he has to run, we all do."

"And you want me to come with you?"

"Or just the two of us."

She laughs, even though nothing about this is even remotely funny.

"I can't tell if you're being serious, Nate. But, if you are, I have a life here. I'm in school, I have Henry, and there's no way I'm leaving Mom behind. So, no. If you asked . . . and even if you didn't . . . I wouldn't run away with you."

"I know."

"Then why say it? It's weird. Don't go ruining that opinion I've got of you now."

"What opinion is that?"

Max sits down again, sighs, then says, "Let's save that for another day. I wanted to talk to you about something else. Tyler won't tell you, but . . . he really wants to go."

"Where?"

"To Murder Road. He's been reading up on it nonstop since he met your brother. He's kind of starstruck and . . ."

"Kind of stupid?"

"Exactly. I'm only telling you because you might need to follow in your brother's footsteps."

"What do you mean?" I ask, although I already know.

"You need to save Tyler. Convince him not to go. I know you already tried, at the cemetery, but you need to try harder. I think meeting your brother flicked a switch in him and you can turn it off."

I think of all the words our brother used to keep those kids away; all the times he thought he'd succeeded only for them to find another way to ignore him. Then I picture Tyler's joy when he talked about the place that we used to call home.

"He's going to go. He's already made up his mind."

Max's lip trembles as she says, "So stop him."

"Do you like this town?"

"I do," she replies.

"Do you want to leave eventually?"

"I don't know. Maybe. But Mom's happy here. Henry needs me more than ever. And I have great friends, so . . ."

I watch her until it hurts, taking in every tiny piece of Max's perfect face. Everything I want to tell her pushes against the walls in my mouth until dust fills my throat.

"There's another way," I tell her. "To keep you safe."

"What is it?"

I glance around the square, at the people shifting from store to store like stop-motion figures, at the perfectly cut lawn where a ball hasn't been kicked for years, at a girl who slots seamlessly into this scene.

It wasn't supposed to happen like this. I was supposed to be quiet, small, avoidable. But Max found me regardless.

"I'll take you there," I say. "To Murder Road."

"Are you serious?"

"It's only one day," I say. "It's not like Bloodbath, where the date changes every time. If you go on any of the other days . . . it's almost normal.

"If you want to know where I came from, if Tyler wants to see for himself, we'll go together and I'll tell him every screwed-up story, until there's no chance he'll want to go back."

Max stares past me, the questions she's asking herself answered by blinks and nods, until she says, "Fine. If you're okay with that."

I'm not. But what choice do I have?

"When do we go?" she asks.

"Shouldn't you talk to Seb first? Make sure he's up for it too?"

"He is," Max replies softly.

I close my eyes, the Hiding Boy's chant stirring deep inside. "We've got just under a month until Death Day."

That's what they call it in the forums—the first day each resident, new and old, marks on their calendar. It doesn't happen every year. Sometimes there's a decade or more without tragedy. But, as they tell you online, you should never forget that date—just in case.

"You know us," Max says. "We don't wait any longer than we have to."

"Next weekend then?"

"Okay. Do we need anything?"

After the Face in the Glass, the Caretaker, Bloodbath, it's nice to finally be the one in control.

"No," I say. "Just trust me. I'm going to do what my brother couldn't."

48

"What do we tell our parents?" Seb asks at school the following Monday and, without missing a beat, Tyler says, "College open house."

"Won't they want to come?"

Tyler laughs. "With the terrible twins running around there's no chance of that."

"My mom . . ." Seb begins.

"Tell her it's for me and you're coming for moral support. She'll love that."

Tyler's excitement bounces off the Hell Hole's walls. At least he had the decency to pretend to listen to me at the cemetery. Max and I already knew, but now it's more obvious than ever: He was going whether we went with him or not.

"It's a three-hour drive," Max says. "If we leave early enough, we'll be back before dinner."

"That depends on what happens while we're there," Tyler says.

He chuckles as he nudges Seb, but his friend doesn't bite.

"For the record," I say, "I don't want to do this."

Tyler's grin falls away and he picks at the remains of his lunch.

The distant hum of our classmates in the lunchroom suddenly hushes and Max mumbles, "What will you tell *your* parents?"

I picture Mom's and Dad's stony faces as we drove away from Murder Road, and from every town we've left since. Each journey has taken us farther from that place, and now I'm going back.

"Like you said, we'll be home for dinner, so I won't have to tell them anything."

"And your brother?"

"I don't need his permission."

Rage prickles my skin as I picture Rowan standing victorious in the cemetery, boldly showing the hand I was desperate to hide.

I hoped we'd have more time, but I can't avoid our history any longer.

49

The same picket fence that I helped Dad hammer into the ground surrounds our old house.

In the front yard, the rosebush Grandma bought for our parents' anniversary droops toward the lawn, at least twenty buds preparing to bloom.

The others stay back while I stare at a home that isn't mine anymore—a car we could never afford gleaming in the driveway; an open garage full of tools on one side and sports equipment on the other.

There's movement behind the large bay window that Rowan used to line his Avengers on, his precious figures safe until I was old enough to clamber on the sofa and play with them in my own way.

I shouldn't stare for long. Eventually, whoever lives here now will think I'm one of *those* people: the ones who spy on the "weirdos" who live on the edge of a nightmare. What kind of people are happy to raise their families here, to grow old here, to live, laugh, and love here?

That's what those people want to know, while turning blind eyes on all the terrible things in their own neighborhoods.

We didn't just let it happen. We tried to help. At least, Rowan did. And look where it got us—a fractured family with no true home, hopping from one town to the next, leaving nothing but broken hearts and empty spaces.

The front door opens and my sister strolls out, shouting goodbye before grabbing her bike from the grass and rolling it past me.

"Hi," she says, her features rearranging until it's not Hazel at all, it's the girl who lives here now, looking up at me with both confusion and delight.

"Hi," I say. "Is this your house?"

She nods, her stare hardening.

"It's nice. I used to live here."

"Really?"

Her suspicions crack just enough for intrigue to poke through, but I don't blame her for doubting me. She *should* be wary of strangers. She's grown up with the stories, just like I did.

"Yes," I say. "Look here."

I bend down and point to the fence post closest to the gate. In tiny letters, carved with the penknife I borrowed from my brother, the word *Nate* is still visible through the paint.

"That's my name."

She doesn't offer hers in return. Smart girl.

"I should go," she says, looking at Max, Seb, and Tyler on the other side of the street before pedaling off.

I watch the house for a few more minutes, wondering what would have happened if we'd never left. Then I go back to my friends and lead them silently to Cherry Tree Lane.

Tyler touches the street sign, Seb glances nervously at the houses that look almost normal in the sunlight, and Max hovers next to me, her little finger brushing mine.

"It looks safe, doesn't it?" I say. "But it isn't. Decades of horrible things have happened here. And you wanted to come? You wanted to see what all the fuss is about?"

I'm channeling all the times our parents tried to tell us off, and judging from the looks on their faces, it's working.

"This one here, it's where it all started. The OG horror story. The one with the bloodstained girl who escaped somehow, while her mother lay in a real blood bath. Her brother ran to the house at the end of the street and cursed every asshole who ignored his mom's daily cries for help. That was the night the Hiding Boy was born."

Max puts more air between us and I wonder if I'm going too far, but they need to know this stuff. It's history.

I take them past one house after another, remembering all the stories I was told on sleepovers or around campfires or when Rowan was bored; the tales recounted in the articles that have been tormenting me for weeks.

All the way to the fifth house from the end—the one made famous by our brother.

Before that night, it was shuttered and ignored. But those kids still found their way in. They still thought it would be fun to coax out a killer.

Now its burned-out frame is covered in freshly fitted plywood sheets, just like the four directly next to it.

I turn to number 19, where they found the remains of Derek Thornby almost three years ago. Then I flash back to the bathroom stalls and the janitor's closet in the Hell Hole, those horrible moments when someone was stalking me. They were fearless then, but they wouldn't stand a chance here.

The final five houses on Murder Road all have boarded-up windows, but Tyler only has eyes for one.

"There it is," he says, stepping into the shadow of the last house on the street.

It's bigger than the others, the tip of its ramshackle chimney piercing the gray clouds above it.

When we lived in this town, the front door of this house was a rich red with a knocker in the shape of a lion's head. Despite not being cleaned for years, that bronze would shine in the weakest light like forbidden treasure.

Before they knew better, little kids would dare each other to knock on that door. Once they learned the truth behind the legend, they kept their dares to themselves.

"This is the place the Hiding Boy ran to," Tyler says. "It's where the curse started."

"And you wondered why I didn't want to bring you."

"So why did you?" Seb asks.

"Because if you're going to mess with this shit, at least find a tour guide who knows what they're talking about. You come here at the wrong time, and you die."

"Okay," Max says. "We get it."

Police tape is fixed firmly to the thick slab of timber that now covers the red front door.

Crumbling bricks and storm-ravaged tiles fill my sight and I recall the feeling of dread whenever I saw this ancient slab that looms over Cherry Tree Lane, threatening to crush the whole of Belleview.

Tyler's feet dance forward then back, his body swaying; he's like a kid at Christmas. He wants to get closer, to touch a real urban legend. He wants to go home with another story to tell.

"Can you guys feel that?" he asks. "It's kind of electric. Like it's humming."

"That's *you,*" I reply. "You are projecting your excitement onto something else. *You're* the thing that's buzzing."

If enough people project, you get unexplainable scenarios or, sometimes, mass hysteria.

"I don't think so," Tyler says, edging closer.

"You want to go in?" I ask, and his face shoots to me.

"Are you sure it's safe?"

I walk through the open gate, then pull back the moss creeping up the back wall.

They did a great job boarding up all the windows they could see, but Max isn't the only one who knows about hidden passages.

A long panel of glass runs about a foot off the floor and I take a rock from the ground, wrap it in a cloth, and swing it hard at the window.

Splinters spread in every direction, exploding in on themselves when I hit it a second time.

"Nate!" Max says. "What if someone catches us?"

"The police have put their sign up. They've tried their best. If people break in regardless, that's on them."

"You mean us," Seb whispers.

"Exactly."

I make sure the frame is completely free of glass, then slide through feetfirst, careful to land as softly as possible on the shards that crack beneath my sneakers. The stale air fills my nose, and I grip it tight then shout up, "Breathe through your mouth. It's nasty down here."

That would put some people off, but Tyler's head is already visible as he forces his body through, resting his hands on the sheets I've quickly laid over the broken glass, then stands next to me in the half-light.

"Fuck," he whispers. "I'm actually *inside* the house where the Hiding Boy got his name. This is awesome."

He's changing in front of me, the enthusiasm he feels about his silly small-town legends growing when faced with something bigger.

"What's down there?" Seb asks.

"It's fine," Tyler shouts up. "You need to get in on this."

My heart quickens as Seb pauses; then he crawls through the gap and lands with a grunt.

Tyler doesn't laugh at his friend's awkwardness. They have barely spoken since I got in the car.

"Is it safe to come down?" Max asks, tossing her knapsack at my feet.

I find a paint-stained blanket, smoothing it over the sheets for added protection from the glass, then I nod.

As she slides through, I pull out my flashlight and shine it across the room.

Shelves hang like collapsed bridges all around us, their piled contents buried in dust, while the wretched waft of death lurks in the corners.

One time, Hazel found a dead raccoon in our basement, and I watched as Dad wrestled its stiff body into a bag. Every time I reached out to stroke it, Mom slapped my hand away.

"Who used to live here?" Tyler asks. "There's no mention of it online."

"No one," I say. "It's always been empty; even before this place got its name. Way back in the nineteen sixties, it was the house at the end of the street that kids avoided on Halloween."

"That's creepy," Max mutters, shining a flashlight on the stairs that I shuffle over to.

"We can't be here long," I say. "We go up, we look around, then we leave. That okay with you?"

I stare at Tyler until he gives a single nod.

The creak of the steps sends something scuttling into the shadows, and I pause with my hand on the door handle, its iciness creeping down my arm until I take a deep breath and twist it.

The wood sticks in the frame and I push until it gives way with a low thrum. Then I step aside and watch the others hurry into the kitchen.

My heart is pounding as I walk into the stale-smelling living room, and I picture Rowan charging into the place four doors down without a thought for his own safety.

I should have stopped him. I should have seen in that moment, before he left our house, what hid behind his anger. I should have stood in front of him or found the strength I'd never had. I should have called our parents or been the first to that door.

I should have told him that not everyone can be saved; that people must live and die by their own decisions, no matter where the seeds of those choices were sown.

But I didn't do any of those things, and now we are here.

"What do you think they did?" Seb asks. "Those people Rowan saved? Do you think they started the fire?"

"Of course not," Tyler spits. "They pissed off whatever monster has made this street its playground. They came to Murder

Road thinking it was all fun and games and they were nearly burned alive. What do you think, Nate?"

I smile, edging toward the basement door just as my brother appears behind me.

"I think you're probably right," I say, and then, as Rowan passes me the candle, we chant, "Let their sacrifice be your last."

"What's going on?" Max asks. "Are you screwing with us?"

"No," Rowan says, pulling me backward and locking the door from our side.

"Nate?" Max's voice is so small. "What's happening?"

I don't answer. But I can't leave either. Not until the screaming starts.

Part 2

"Is this a joke?" Seb asks. "Max? Are they still there?"

I press my ear to the door and listen for that asshole's breathing, but all I can hear is Seb hyperventilating and Tyler laughing in the corridor.

"Which bit of this is funny to you?!" I yell, and he pokes his head around the corner and says, "All of it. You do realize what they're doing, right? Nate is trying to scare us. That's all."

But that's *not* all, because I saw his face before he slammed the door and that wasn't the boy I knew. It was someone I'd never seen before. Someone who terrified me.

"You don't need to do this," I whisper. "We can go home and forget all about this place."

"No, we can't!" Tyler shouts. "Don't listen to her, Nate. It will take more than a locked door and a surprise appearance from your brother to frighten us."

Seb presses his hands against the thick plywood covering the windows. "Did you bring anything that could help us escape?"

I shake my head and Tyler shrugs.

"There must be something around here," Seb mumbles, but as I check each room, I realize the place has been cleaned out. Whether it was by scavengers or by something else, the entire house is empty.

There are no table legs to snap off, no tools tucked under the grimy sink. There is literally nothing here. Except us.

"Please, Nate. I'm sorry if we went too far. And Rowan,

if you're there, we can leave you alone. We can go back to Montgomery-Oakes and forget this ever happened."

The silence is sickening and I think I'm going to throw up.

Then something crackles in the distance and, when I turn, I'm alone.

"Seb? Tyler? Where are you?" I step into the hallway, then peer up the staircase to the second floor. "Are you guys there?"

I hear the crackle again, so distant that I close my eyes to pull it closer. It sounds like radio static, softly tickling my brain. Then it's so loud that I clamp my hands against my head.

If I lessen the pressure, even for a second, the sound bursts through, so I press harder and focus on my breathing until each release is long and steady, like wind washing over the bay.

I listen for the sound, not trusting my own mind, then slowly move my hands until I'm sure it's gone.

I could call again, but where are *their* calls? Why aren't my friends searching for me?

The stairs are long and wide, patterned tiles filling the vertical slats. I rest one foot on the peeling wood, expecting it to bend under my weight. But it's solid and I slowly creep up until I reach the top.

There are four doors on the landing, all closed. Something crashes against the one directly behind me and I leap away then turn, ready to fight.

As I step closer, claws scratch at the space between the wood and the frame, before distant groans snake up my spine.

"Max," someone says. "Can you hear me?"

"Tyler?"

"Help me. Please."

The scratching stops, shadows flickering in the dimming sliver of light. Then the landing darkens, every speck of sun slicing through the boarded-up windows suddenly swallowed whole.

The groan nestles in my ears like an idling truck. Then a wail breaks through—a millisecond of something unbearable that holds my limbs in a death grip.

"What the fuck?" I say, wisps of breath dissolving before my eyes.

The same tiny claws rap at every door, as the wail comes again and I picture blood gushing from my ears.

Then one of the doors bursts open and Seb stumbles out.

"He's here," Seb whimpers.

"Who is?"

"He came back."

Seb's finger curls upward until he's pointing at the space behind me.

"Look," he whispers. "He won't hurt you."

I grip his shoulders, fighting the urge to turn.

"Focus on me," I say. "It will be okay."

"Look!!" Seb snarls, his hands at my face, twisting my head until the shape fills my vision—a shadow that rests above the murkiness around it, like a black hole deep inside a cave.

There's a sting as Seb's arms jolt back to his sides, something warm trickling down my cheek, and I clamp my eyes shut.

"I'm sorry I couldn't save you," he mumbles. "I'm so sorry."

He's looking past me, at the shape I refuse to let in. But I can feel it—the suffocating iciness caressing my throat, the threat hovering inches from my skin.

"Please forgive me," Seb says, his body brushing mine as he steps past.

For a moment, his breathing is calm and his words are steady as he says, "It's okay now."

Then a rush of air knocks me back, my eyes springing open just long enough to see another door fly open and my friend dragged through, one hand reaching out to me before he is swallowed by the black.

Seb

He came to my house and smiled at my parents and now what? He's a psychopath? Are we the idiots who fall for this when it's staring them in the goddamn face?

"Max!" I yell. "Tyler!"

I saw Nate's expression as the door slammed, and that's not the look of a "nice guy." His grin twisted and his limbs stiffened and the light behind his eyes was snuffed out.

Why did he bring us here?

A swarm of terrible answers fills my head, so I picture Miss Kittle's cramped office, her patchwork armchair, her fingers forming a steeple below her chin.

I hear fragments of her voice, like broken words on poorly tuned radios. Then I focus on the last thing she told me.

Eventually, you will have to stop knocking on my door and start opening new ones.

It was supposed to be inspirational, but it only made me more scared. And now I'm here, in someone else's darkness, not a single door in sight.

A rotting stench fills my body and I gag; then I clamp my nostrils tight, breathing through my mouth as I take one tiny step forward.

Something scrapes back and forth across the hardwood floor, a shape slipping in and out of the shadows.

"Hello?"

It stops, replaced by a hissing sound.

Ssssss. Ssssss. Sssssseh.

"Who's there?"

Ssssseh. Ssssseh.

"If that's you, Nate, I'm warning you . . ."

Ssssseh. Ssssseh.

I creep toward the sound, then freeze as something shuffles back.

When I crouch, two huge eyes stare out of the gloom and I stumble.

"Where's the door? Where's the fucking door?!"

Ssssseh.

I feel my way around the room, careful to avoid the corner where the hisses grow louder. Then my hand finds something in the darkness—something cold and clammy that snatches itself away.

I swallow hard, trying to unblock my throat as terror fills my chest.

"I'm sorry," I whisper. "I'll leave you alone."

But the shape rises, bones cracking as it leaves its hiding place, my heart hammering against my ribs when I realize who it is.

"Joshua?"

My brother lifts his spindly arms, beckoning me into a hug I've wanted for nine years. Then his freezing fingers pierce my skin and I'm not here anymore, wherever here is.

I'm back in that damn car, its tangled seat belt carving sores into my neck, while bolts of pain shoot through my legs.

Blood fills the footwell where my brother's sneakers twitch, but I can't look at him. Not even when he forces his hand into mine and says, "I love you, bro."

Instead, I watch smoke billowing from the hood and listen for the sirens that I desperately hope are not too far away.

Tyler

Say "adrenaline rush" and people think roller coasters, bungee jumps, low- to mid-level scary situations. Maybe they think scoring the winning goal or saving a last-minute penalty.

But science isn't that simple.

Adrenaline rushes start in the brain.

Find yourself in a heightened state and it's all about the amygdala. If that bad boy spots danger, he's straight on the phone to the hypothalamus.

That's your brain's command center, and once the hypothalamus is involved, it's all systems go.

Signals are sent from your body's HQ to the medulla, which gives those adrenal glands the thumbs-up to release adrenaline into the body. That's why you breathe faster, why you sweat, why your heart rate increases, why you suddenly feel like you can deadlift a house.

When I'm panicking, I think about science, because there's a reason for everything.

That's how I cope as I walk alone in the black, trying to find my friends and get the hell out of here.

The other option—the one starting to seem most likely—isn't one I can think about unless I want my amygdala to lose its shit.

So, Murder Road is real and Nate is . . . what? I don't know that part yet, but let's go with "a very bad person" and revisit when we have all the info.

Here's what I know for certain: People die on this street. Lots of people. And all because a boy whose mom was murdered by her abusive husband rocked up here and cursed every house that let it happen.

Kudos to the kid that it worked. I've cursed my sisters countless times and nada. But they aren't actually evil, so that's probably fair.

Using humor in stressful situations has been proved to reduce anxiety. A good old belly laugh can aid muscle relaxation and enhance your intake of oxygen-rich air. The problem is, the air in this place is swimming with the remains of God knows what, so I'll make the jokes and someone else can laugh at them.

"If you can hear me!"

My voices echoes off the high walls and vibrates in my shoulders, until I close my eyes and breathe as calmly as I can.

I asked for this. I saw the infamous Rowan Campbell come out of nowhere to win Bloodbath and I got starstruck. Next thing I know, I'm following a guy I've only known for a few months into an actual haunted house and, what? I'm surprised when weird shit happens?

But then I'm not surprised; not really. Of all the emotions I am feeling, that isn't one of them.

"Max! Seb!"

Something moves behind me and I spin, desperate not to see the Hiding Boy staring back. That's the warning sign, the countdown to doom. Once you see the ghost of the child who started this mess, it's curtains for you.

But something different steps out of the shadows. It's me, only, it's not. His features look skewed, like stickers stuck on wonky.

When I take a step back, this bizarro version of me edges forward. When I lift my right hand, it raises its left.

When I turn, I see other shapes—all wearing my clothes and my face but all altered in almost-imperceptible ways.

Ghost houses have halls of mirrors but, when I reach out, my hand moves past the place I half expect glass to be, until I'm touching skin.

"Fuck!" I shout, falling into another "me," who pushes me back toward the first.

Wherever I turn, I'm blocking my own path, and not even my hypothalamus knows what to do.

It's sending garbled messages and incorrect commands, and I collapse, pulling my knees into my chest and waiting for this to stop because there's only one of me. I know that. I do.

Yet frosty fingers rest on my shoulders and my arms and my legs, until I'm being pulled in so many different directions that it feels like I'm breaking apart.

Max

"Seb!" My fists hum as they slam against the door, and then I kick it over and over until I slide to the floor, exhausted.

What is this place? Who are these people?

Nate was alone and harmless. He was the new kid who needed a friend. And then, one day, he was more than that. I liked him and I thought he liked me.

Do your research, Max. Background checks are a girl's best friend.

The memory of Mom's voice stirs something in me—a fight wrapped in wire. If I can get to it, I can win.

Mom knows better than me that, these days, anyone can be a monster. She knows because she's met some, always in public spaces, always before they show their true colors.

Evil is measured in increments and I hate Nate for hiding his so well.

"Nate," I say again, softer this time. "Can you hear me?"

The silence rings in my ears and I shake it away.

I search my bag for my phone but it's not there—the memory of tossing my knapsack down to him taunting me as I try to formulate a plan.

We're used to this. It's what we do. And yet, it's nothing like that. For so long we searched for urban legends, failing and failing and failing until, one day, a kid with a cool T-shirt turned up.

"Was it *you,* Nate? Are you the one who made the Face in the Glass come true? Was it you and your twisted brother who blew smoke through those school vents?"

I want to scream in his face and tear his eyes out because we have never hurt anybody. We're good people.

"I trusted you!" I yell. "I let you in and you fucking betrayed me!"

A faint whisper sneaks through the air and my back presses hard against the cold plaster.

I need my friends back.

"Whoever is doing this," I shout, "you don't have to. No one needs to get hurt today."

Yes, they do.

The whisper slices through the silence, splintering into smaller sounds that hiss in the darkness.

"I'm going home. We all are."

If I speak the words, they become real—a promise I dare not break.

"Tyler!" I shout. "Seb! If you can hear me, please do something."

I leave a gap for them, for hope, for rescue, but it only expands until I rise and try to slide my fingers behind the boarded-up window on the landing.

I force them as deep as I can, biting back the sting of wood splinters piercing my skin. But, intentionally or otherwise, they've turned this place into a prison.

Seb

The wrong person died that night. It should have been the one whose veins were filled with liquor.

He said sorry to us once, in the courthouse, before he was led away. And I wanted to leap over the benches and slit his throat.

I wanted to tell him that "sorry" is what children say when they break something their parents used to think was important. "Sorry" isn't a word for murderers.

I close my eyes and imagine a different place, because this isn't real. I'm not here—trapped all over again in a crushed car, while Joshua's last breaths splutter out of him along with the blood that trickles down the dashboard.

"This is all in my head," I chant, until the hiss comes again and I slam my hands against my ears and roar.

The noise erupts like a volcano, its lava washing over everything until I'm back in the room, a memory of Max's wide-eyed panic forming then fading in the half-light.

The ghost of my brother sits on the floor opposite me, infected wounds peeking from the rips in his jeans.

"You're dead," I whisper.

He opens his mouth and I try to pull his voice from the wreckage of my grief. But that memory vanished long ago.

Mom and Dad rarely filmed their grown-up son, so when I think about the sounds he made, the laugh he had, they are the noises of a boy I never knew.

A single guttural click escapes his decaying lips; then his

mouth closes and music drifts through the gap in a door I can see clearly now.

Even this faint, I know that song. My brother listened to My Chemical Romance every day. The lyrics of "The Kids from Yesterday" grow louder until it feels like the speaker is somewhere in this room, hidden alongside other torture techniques.

"What is this?" I ask. "Are you trying to break me? You think I'm not broken already?"

My dead brother stands, heat surging up my legs as his crooked shadow covers them. Then my skin feels like it's on fire as the song gets louder, until I can't hear the tune anymore, just an unbearable beat smashing my eardrums to pieces.

"Stop!" I scream. "Please! Just stop!"

But he doesn't, because whatever looms over me, its dirty fingers twisting inches from my face, it's not Joshua. It is something terrible.

Tyler

"Kill them. Kill them all."

The whispers scuttle through my ears like rats and there's a reason for everything, a solution for almost everything, and yet here, now, I have nothing.

"What do you want?" I ask, and the voices merge into a malevolent choir as they say, *"Kill the imposters."*

I hold my head in my hands and think of the others. What are Max and Seb seeing right now? If they are still alive.

Stop, I think. *Just stop. They are looking for you and you're looking for them and, eventually . . .*

The hand gripping my right shoulder squeezes tighter, until a sharp sting flares under my shirt. Then something digs into my left thigh . . . my hip . . . my chest . . . until an army of claws are forcing their way deep into my body.

I tense my muscles and fight back, pushing them away long enough to scramble to my feet. Then they double in size and fall onto me again, until all the air is pushed from my lungs and I let them drag me across the grimy floor.

A low-hanging light hums over the kitchen table and my eyes search every crevice of the room, trying to find the smallest sign that Seb or Max has been here. But it's just me . . . and me . . . and me.

They lift me into a seat, five others taking their places around the table, and then another version of my reflection steps forward, a gleaming knife laid across his outstretched palms.

"*Take it,*" he whispers.

The others start chanting the words until my trembling fingers reach out and grip the warm handle.

Then the shape holds its arms out and says, "*Me first.*"

The others giggle and chitter as I play with the heavy blade. Then the shape's face changes, its smile losing its rough edges, the blank space behind its eyes glowing warm. The others copy it, until everyone looks exactly like me.

"*Make sure you get it right,*" they say. "*You don't want to kill the wrong one.*"

I hold the tip of the blade against my finger and push, waiting for the pain, the blood, the regret—any sign at all that I haven't lost myself in this house.

Then I pull every ounce of rage and panic and fear into the center of my soul, using it as kindling for a fire that must soar. Because I'm not dying here today. And my friends aren't either.

That's why I roar for them, bellowing into the darkness until the entire house shudders.

Max

I charge downstairs, following the sound.

"Tyler?"

"I'm here."

The smell of lavender fills the living room, but I block it out and burst into the kitchen, where Tyler is sitting at a dining table, the fingers of one hand splayed wide and a knife held high in the other.

"What are you doing?"

He turns to me, his eyes blank, his lips trembling, then lowers the knife until it almost touches his skin.

"Where did you get that?"

Tyler's eyes flick to the corner of the room, then back to me.

"Is someone here?" I ask. "Can you see them?"

"It's me," he whispers. "I'm there . . . and there . . . and there."

The tip of the blade points at each empty chair in turn; then it slams into the space between Tyler's thumb and forefinger.

"Where did you get the knife?" I ask again, because none of this was here before. There was no table, there were no chairs, there were no empty bottles where bottles now line the kitchen shelves. Did I somehow miss it all—these everyday objects temporarily lost in the gloom? That's the only explanation I want, because the alternative . . .

"Do you know who I am?" Tyler asks, moving the knife between each finger and the next, faster and faster, all the time staring at me.

"Stop!" I plead, but the knife only goes quicker.

"Which one am I?!" Tyler yells and then, softer, "Which ones do I kill?"

My hand hovers in the space between us. If I touch him, will this stop? Or will that knife sever his skin or turn on me?

I can't take that risk. Instead, I kick over the chair closest to me, then another, not stopping until all five are lying on the dirty floor.

When I turn, Tyler has one hand in front of his face, a thin trail of blood creeping down his arm.

"What happened?" he asks, letting the knife crash onto the table before stepping back.

"You saw something. I don't know what, but I think it made you do this."

I tear a strip from my top and wrap it around Tyler's hand, pulling it into a knot that makes him wince.

"It was me," he says. "I could see all these versions of me around that table and . . . I thought I'd lost myself."

"You haven't. And that's a good thing because we need you. What is this place? And how the hell do we get out?"

"Where's Seb?"

"Something took him. That's why you need to remember whatever you can about Murder Road. We need to fight back."

Tyler shakes his head and looks past me. "People keep dying here, a different house every time; different killers; different methods. Whatever the Hiding Boy found in this house that night—they formed one hell of a tag team. But . . ."

"But what?"

"The legend," Tyler mumbles. "It says the Hiding Boy possesses someone, they do his bidding, then everyone dies."

"So?"

"So, *I'm* not possessed. Are *you*?"

I shake my head, picturing the panic on Seb's face as he was pulled into the darkness.

"That's a good thing, right?"

Tyler's eyes widen. "Not necessarily. But it does mean we can focus on whatever screwed-up spirit haunts this place. The song, the story, it's playground stuff. Don't be swayed by what you think you know about Murder Road, Max. This thing gets into your head. It makes you doubt everything."

Tyler faces the door that Nate escaped through. "You hear that, boys? I know you're not the big bad. You're just the big bad's bitches."

He rattles the handle but it holds firm.

"Any idea how we get out of here?" I ask.

"First off, we stick together. Whatever this is, it's most dangerous when there's no one to kick the chairs away." Tyler touches my shoulder as he strides past. "Thanks for that, by the way."

"No worries."

"Secondly, we find Seb because, like I said, strength in numbers. And thirdly, well that's obvious."

I picture the three of us back in the Hell Hole and focus only on that. Then I follow Tyler into the hallway and say, "We don't die."

Seb

I grip the crinkled photo from my brother's school essay, wiping away the tears that wash over his face.

I want to be home now, building Lego with Dad and happily answering Mom's never-ending questions.

That's all it would take to make them happy, and I'm so sorry I failed.

I saw things in them that weren't their fault. I treated them like a burden rather than a sanctuary. And now I'm going to break them all over again.

"Please look after them," I say, to whatever is or isn't listening.

When you've lost a brother, you can't say that you doubt the existence of God. You must keep that story alive for the good of everyone else, to ensure their platitudes remain relevant.

I guess I'll find out soon enough.

The boy sits on the chair in the far corner of the room, his legs swaying in knee-length shorts, his smile unmoving, like a waxwork with a mechanical body.

He hums softly to himself, a lullaby that prompts fragments of ancient memories to break through my fear, but I do my best to focus on Joshua's picture.

He is the only kid I want to see right now, not this creepy child with slicked-back hair and fingers that fold slowly into his palms as he counts them off.

Everything is choices—the ones we make and the ones we don't.

There's the choice to drink and drive; the choice to go for an evening ride with your little brother just for the hell of it; the choice to make friends with a lonely-looking new kid; the choice to follow him into an abandoned house despite everything inside you screaming no.

Choices define everything. And mine have been almost universally bad.

But there's Tyler . . . and there's Max . . . and I'll always be happy about that.

The last finger falls on the boy's left hand and he drops down and walks toward me.

Then my brother stands by my side, his heavy hand on my shoulder. When I glance up, his skin isn't rotting anymore. It's the way it used to be, covered in freckles that he said were one big family—some tiny like distant cousins, others large like our parents and me.

"I miss you," I whisper, because whatever happens next, I have a few good choices left.

The smell of lavender follows me up the stairs, but she isn't here. Not the real Bella. She's in a box nearly two hundred miles away, and there is only one Tyler.

Everything else is a trick we cannot fall for.

I don't tell him what I can smell. Instead, I focus on vengeance, because when we get out of here, I'm coming for Nate and Rowan and, if necessary, their entire family.

How stupid must we have been to fall for their crap? I search my memory for cracks in his story, for moments he gave himself away. But he's good. I'll give him that. He's got sad and lonely new kid down to a T.

That savior complex is going to wear you out, Maxine.

Mom again—more wise words from a woman who trusts me to travel out of state with three guys because I've convinced her I'm a great judge of character.

She met him too. Just once. And only for the briefest time. But he stood in front of her and she saw nothing wrong. No red flags. No masks slipping under scrutiny. He tricked a woman who can't be tricked.

And he sat in Bella's living room, alone with her while Henry and I made tea. I trusted him with my brightest treasures, and I will never forget that.

"You *can* get out," I say. "If Rowan really did save those kids—whatever the reason—it means there's hope."

"Maybe," Tyler says. "But *they* were rescued by someone on the outside. I think we're in this alone."

He tries each door in turn, all of them locked.

"This is the one Seb was pulled through," I say. "I got a glimpse of what's in there and . . . I don't think I want to go inside."

"But we have to, right?"

I nod, watching as Tyler pulls something from his pocket and lays it on the carpet, where large brown stains merge with the ugly pattern.

"Lock-picking kit," he says. "I got it for my birthday."

"Why?"

"You're asking me that now?"

A mischievous grin dances across his face and I wish I could smile back. But he didn't see Seb reaching desperately for my hand as he was pulled into the shadows.

"What did the other versions of you look like?" I ask.

"Like me," Tyler replies, "but not quite right."

"Are you okay?"

"We can psychoanalyze what happened here when we're home."

His hands shake as he tries to place the thin metal pins in the lock.

"I'm fine," he says. "If you let me be."

"Okay."

When his hands rise again, they are steady, his brow creased in concentration.

"Did this come with instructions?"

Tyler huffs. "Wiggle it until there's a click."

"How many times has it worked?"

"I've practiced on some old padlocks from Dad's shed. They all open eventually."

We don't have that long. But I keep quiet because he's doing more than I am.

I watch his fingers gently caress the lock for a few more minutes, then swallow my nausea when it finally submits.

Tyler slowly turns the handle until whatever is inside is only a push away.

"Are you ready?"

No. But what choice do we have?

My nod comes out like a tremor, and when Tyler opens the door, light sprays onto the landing.

"Are you sure it was this one?"

Seb's eyes rolled back into his skull fill my mind as I say, "Yes."

Tyler steps inside and I follow. A thick layer of dust rests on the furniture, while the windowsill is full of photo frames with nothing inside.

A picture hangs over the fireplace, elaborate swirls carved into a gold frame and five people staring back at me.

The man has one hand on the back of the woman's neck, while her hands rest on the shoulders of two children. The third child sits in the center, untouched and unsmiling.

"Seb?" Tyler whispers. "Can you hear me?"

There's no reply, and I think of the highway only a few miles away. The hum of it should rest on the wind, the way it does in Montgomery-Oakes, the way it did on Nate's old street.

But this place is a vacuum, devoid of all noise except for the whispers of ghosts and the screams of their victims.

And yet . . . a faint murmur rests in the walls, growing as I press my ear against it. One straight line of sound that travels through the patterns on the wallpaper.

The carpet is thick and springy under my feet, the baseboards a rich brown; no sign or stench of decay.

Tyler lifts a vase from the table, a lone stem beheaded and withering in the heavy light of a chandelier.

"This place is different," he says, as the lavender finds its way back to my nose.

I focus on the hum, following it from one wall to the next, until I stop at the family portrait.

When I push the frame, it tilts slightly to the right and the noise increases.

"There's something here," I say, stepping back and watching Tyler as he lifts the picture off the wall.

A narrow tunnel stares back at us, fuzzy at the edges, the murmur echoing in the deep.

Tyler moves the table, then stands on it, pulling himself up and peering inside.

"Seb?" he whispers, and the hum changes, another sound buried in its frequency, words that crackle and fall like conversations written with sparklers.

"Seb?" he says again. "Are you there?"

Yes.

I stumble back until I'm pressed against a door that's suddenly closed. Then I watch as Tyler wiggles clumsily through the gap, his sneakers the last thing to vanish.

"What are you doing?" I ask.

"Rescuing our friend," he replies, his voice low and tinny. "Are you coming?"

I glance around the room, at the portrait of a family that makes me shiver, at a door I dare not try to open, and then I clamber into the darkness.

Tyler

It's easier to pretend with Max around. But, as I edge through the tunnel, I feel them returning—the horrible doubts and snarling voices.

"Max?" I call.

If she followed me, she's too far behind to respond. If she *didn't* follow me, that's another matter entirely.

This house is a complex equation I don't understand. But I've already reunited with one person, so if we can find Seb, we can focus on getting out of here.

The tunnel takes a sharp right, but there's no sign of an end. If anything, it's narrower here, my shoulders sticking before I force them through, the temperature increasing, the oxygen leaving gaps in my lungs that they clamor to fill.

After this, I'm focusing on what's important—my family and friends. The other *F*—my future—that can wait. I'm done beating myself up about decisions we shouldn't have to make when we're so young.

All that matters, right now, is that I decide to live.

The space around me shrinks again and I can't go any farther. Instead, I shuffle back, but I can't budge.

"Max?" I say again, softer this time, afraid that a shout might take up the last available space. "Are you there?"

"I'm coming!" she calls.

"Don't. There's no room."

"What?"

Her words shrink into a distance I can no longer see, and when she speaks again, I can barely make out her words.

"Where are you?" I call.

Shallow breathing fills my ears, and then a hand touches mine, its fingers stroking my trembling skin before it grips my wrist, hisses, then pulls me deeper into the darkness.

Max

Ashes swim in the gray, resting on mounds that pull at my feet like quicksand.

Then Tyler is walking toward me with Seb under his arm.

"I found him," someone says, but that's not the voice of my friend. The words shatter into a thousand echoes and the space around me narrows until I'm on my hands and knees.

Seb stands over me, his lips moving soundlessly; then he points as freezing breath rests against my neck.

Seb's smile is a rip across his face, thick tears edging down his cheeks while his teeth chitter.

Something brushes my arm then glides past, the ash at our feet parting as the shape turns and settles.

The man next to Seb looks just like him yet so different, and I know instantly who it is.

"Your brother," I say, the words muffled in my ears, neither of them looking at me.

The man holds his hand out and Seb takes it; then the other hand breaks through the darkness, something glistening in its grip.

The blade is forced deep into Seb's stomach; plunged and twisted until blood spills from his lips.

Heavy droplets fall from the knife, pooling in the blank space between us; then he looks at me with wide and hopeless eyes before crumpling to the ground.

The shape of his brother waits for a moment, staring at a body choking on its own blood. Then it breaks apart like the seeds of a dandelion clock, scattered before fading to nothing.

"Seb!"

My voice booms, so I try again, softer this time. "It's okay. You'll be okay."

When I touch him, my hands come away warm and red, and his breathing hitches then stops.

I listen closer, the lightest breeze nuzzling my ear. It's not much, but it's something to fight for.

"Come on. Don't leave me."

I force my air into his mouth, then push on his chest the way they told us at school.

If you're not breaking a few ribs, you're not doing it properly. That's what the first aid instructor said. But so much of Seb is already broken.

I try. I really do. I try even when I know in my heart that I've failed. If I stop . . . something ends that I cannot bear to think about. So, I push and I breathe and I push and I breathe until someone pulls me gently away.

"He's gone," Tyler whispers. The real Tyler.

"Where were you?"

"I don't know."

"I saw you," I say. "Or a version of you. You were carrying Seb out of the shadows and then . . ."

I can't say the rest. Instead, I push Tyler back and start CPR over again.

"Max! He's gone."

When I don't answer, he says, "Did he see the Hiding Boy?"

"I don't know."

"Have *you* seen him?"

Tyler's lips tremble as he drops down next to Seb and grips his hand.

"No," I reply. "But I saw Seb's brother. And I keep smelling lavender. That was Bella's favorite flower. I'm so scared."

Tyler opens his arms and I step into his hug. I don't know what's real anymore. But I'm sure, with every fiber of my being, that the body lying motionless in front of us is the real Seb.

I feel wrong inside, like something small but vital has been taken out. It's exactly how I felt the moment Bella passed away—a knowledge, unspoken but unmistakable, that someone I loved wasn't here anymore.

Only this time, that feeling is wrapped in thorns and washed in bile.

"We're getting out of here," Tyler says. "I promise."

I think of Mom's wedding albums, buried deep in the attic but sometimes not quite where I left them. Then I press my lips against Seb's cheek and, between my sobs, I say, "Don't make vows you can't keep."

Tyler looks at me apologetically until I say, "Pick the lock of every single door. There must be a way out of here."

Then realization smacks me between the eyes as I picture Nate's face, the moment before he left us to die.

"Downstairs. We leave the way we came in."

"How did you get out of the tunnel?" he asks. "I thought you were behind me."

I was. And then I wasn't.

"I don't know. I think this house has its own rules. How did *you* get out?"

His eyes fall to the floor as he shakes his head.

We don't have time for this, so I run downstairs and wait for him to catch up.

Eventually, Tyler rests his tools against the cellar door then furrows his brow. "I can't get in. They've sprayed something in the lock."

He shines the flashlight that Nate dropped into the gap and something gray and solid glares back. Then he takes five steps backward before charging at the wood, his body reverberating as he bounces away and the door stands firm.

"Back to plan A," I say. "We try all the rooms upstairs."

"Like the one full of ghosts?" Tyler replies. "I don't think so."

"What then?"

He paces the room, one finger in the air as he flicks his thoughts away like flies. Then he shakes his head and sinks to the floor.

"We're not leaving him here," Tyler mumbles into his hands. "When we go, we take Seb with us."

"Of course."

He doesn't move, though. He sits with his head down, whispering things I don't want to hear.

My head is full of them too. Likely outcomes. Worst-case scenarios. Two phrases that, today at least, feel like the same thing.

"What are you afraid of?" Tyler asks, his face cast in shadow.

"Why?"

"Because I don't know who I'm supposed to be. And this place knows that. Do I take the soccer scholarship or do I focus on physics? Should I choose a college close to my family so I can see the boys grow up, or do I pick the one that's best for me, even if that means crossing the entire country? And what do I say to all the kids I coach—the ones who put genuine smiles on my face? How do I leave that Tyler behind when it's my favorite version?"

I stare at the fallen dining chairs.

"I saw Seb's brother, but I didn't see any other versions of you. Are they here now?"

Without looking up, Tyler shakes his head.

"Where were you when he died?"

"Lost somewhere in this fucking hellscape."

"Okay."

The word grows in our silence until the lavender fills my nostrils. I don't fight it anymore. If that's the best they've got, bring it on, because Bella could never scare me.

But she isn't the person who appears from the shadows.

"Dad?"

My father's smiles were all sparkle and no substance and that's no different now. Except, he's not dead, so this isn't even a ghost of him. It's another trick I won't fall for.

"Hey, Max."

His voice is caramel that Mom's warning breaks into tiny pieces—*That man could make a kill list sound like a love letter.*

She's right. He's smooth and convincing and full to the brim with bullshit. But, like I said, this isn't him.

"What are you expecting from me?" I say, my words fired at whatever lurks behind these illusions. "You think I have daddy issues? You think I'm that weak? Well, fuck you!"

"Who taught you to talk like that?" Dad asks. "It certainly wasn't me."

"No. You didn't teach me anything. Actually, that's not true. You taught me that Mom is a queen and we're better off without you."

"You don't believe that," someone says.

"You're a liar."

"You're so jealous of us."

The voices dart between the flecks of light like they are playing Murder in the Dark.

"Who's that supposed to be?" I ask.

"You know exactly who," a woman replies.

She smirks at me, my father's wife, the woman whose children run to her side and pull faces while Dad ruffles their hair.

"We're the family you always wanted," the woman says, and I swing for her, all five of them vanishing and reappearing on the opposite side of the room.

I can't see Tyler anymore. Is he watching me, desperate but unable to help, or is he suffering another of his own twisted nightmares?

"I don't want you," I say. "Just like you didn't want us."

"I'm sorry if it hurts you, baby," Dad replies. "I was a different person then."

"That's the kind of bullshit that only assholes say."

He frowns and his fists tense. "What did I tell you about that kind of language?"

"You've never told me anything worth listening to."

His smile falters, his wife softly rubbing his back while the children pull on his legs.

"I used to look across the bay and wonder what you were doing," I tell him. "I used to think that was important but it's not. You're nothing to me."

"I'm your father."

"No."

"How dare you . . ."

His hands are at my throat before I can move, squeezing my skin until white spots fill my eyes.

As the room dims, I watch his children and his new wife, all grinning at me while my head explodes. Then I think of Mom, waiting for me to come home so we can eat dinner and watch our shows.

I think of the person who has kissed me good night for as long as I can remember. I think of the woman who worked three jobs to ensure Santa never forgot me. I think of the superhero who turned the wreckage of her one-sided marriage into the best life I could imagine.

I think all those things, and so much more, as I turn the dying embers of my fight into a flame.

The kitchen starts to shake, the empty bottles lining the shelves crashing to the floor.

"If not you, then him," Dad says, morphing into a version of Tyler with hollow eyes and teeth like crumbling stalactites.

Then the real Tyler is running to me, crying, telling me he won't let me die too. He doesn't see the jagged bottle, its shards cracking under his feet. He doesn't see the arm pulled back like a slingshot. He doesn't see our story shifting until it's too late.

His hands clutch his chest and he stumbles but doesn't fall. Instead, he sways on the spot, then turns his palms over and says, "Mom has all our handprints in lockets."

He laughs to himself, then sits as I push against the wound.

"Sorry I couldn't save you," he says. "We should have done the Corpse's Grip instead."

He chokes on his chuckle while his heat fills my hands.

"At least our story won't die," he mutters. "We're an urban legend now. We died on Murder Road."

"No. We're not dead yet."

"Seb is."

"But we're not leaving him here. Right?"

"Whatever you say."

Tyler's eyelids flicker and I slap him across the face. "Stay awake."

"I think I'm already asleep," he whispers. "This feels like a nightmare."

The glass covering the kitchen floor crackles as I rush across it, and then I hold one of the chairs over my head and slam it against the table. It shatters on the second swing and I frantically search for something the perfect size.

Shards pierce my skin as I push through the glass but the pain only drives me on. Then I'm sliding the thinnest strip of wood I can find into the frame of the cellar door, cursing when it breaks in two.

"There must be something!" I shout, running back into the corridor and smacking one of the thick chair legs against the boarded-up front door.

"Stop," Tyler says. "Come here."

"I *can't* stop. You need help."

"Then help me."

Tyler's outstretched arm falls to the floor and I crouch next to him, his fingers clammy and quivering, while ragged breaths fill the suddenly stifling air.

"I need you to remember some things," he says, grunting as he wipes my tears away. "Just in case."

"No."

He laughs, then holds his chest. "You can't say no. I need you to tell my family that I love them. Tell my sisters that I wouldn't be the same without them, tell our parents they are legends, and tell my brothers . . ."

Tyler's body judders then settles as he blinks hard and whispers, "Tell them I was planning on being the best big brother they could imagine."

"You still will be."

He laughs again, then shakes his head and says, "You don't have to keep pretending, Max. I know what's happening."

I slide my hand out of his and run into the hallway, and then I scream until my throat is sore and my head is pounding.

I scream until Tyler's eyes close and don't open again.

I scream until there is nothing left to save.

Then I go to him, as faint mumbles dance across his lips, and I listen to whatever he wants to say.

There's a thud somewhere deep in the house, then another.

I stand and wait for whatever comes next, because I'll fight to the death if I have to.

There's a crash and the shadows come again. It's my father and one of his children, coming back for one last try. Then a face breaks through the gloom—an uncertain smile and a hand soft against my cheek.

"You're safe now," someone says, but I don't believe them.

I hold Tyler until they gently release my fingers; then he is carried away by people with quick hands and quicker tongues.

"Are you hurt?" they ask, but I let them find out for themselves.

A small boy stands in the corridor, scuffed knees poking out of his shorts and sadness filling his washed-out face. His eyes slowly close and he turns away from me, his edges fraying then fading to nothing.

When I turn, I see a girl in the doorway, one hand gripping the frame and one leg swaying between outside and in, between safe and not.

I know her from somewhere. But she steps back as other people help me outside, into a gallery of sun-kissed collages, my eyes stung by the light.

As I sit on the sidewalk, strangers watching me from a safe distance, I remember Nate standing outside his old house and the girl who lives there now.

She waves before a man takes her hand and leads her away.

"It started with a bloodstained girl," I say, to no one, to everyone.

I don't know everything about Murder Road, but I do know that. And as I watch the person who might have saved me walk home, I wonder if it could have ended with a girl too.

Part 3

50

They take Seb out last, zipped inside thick black plastic.

They slide him into the back of an ambulance and gently push the doors shut, as if they are scared to wake him.

When they took Tyler away, the sirens blared. But Seb leaves in silence.

I study the people on the other side of the police tape, searching for two faces that I'm sure are long gone. Then I look for the girl who rescued us, even though I know she has already been ushered home, her parents desperately trying to erase what she saw before it stains.

I focus on the things I know, because everything else makes my head hurt.

"I can't keep pulling dead kids from these houses."

When I turn, two police officers are standing on the sidewalk, one of them giving me the death stare.

"When will they learn?" she asks. "How many times have we boarded up these places now?"

When her colleague doesn't answer, she says, "This is the fifth time in less than three years. They should knock the whole damn street down."

I study the ash-stained building that Rowan pulled those kids from, then the three directly next to it.

"Excuse me," I say. "What exactly happened in *those* houses?"

One of the officers laughs as the other turns away. "Are you serious? Like you don't know."

"I'm sorry, but . . . I'm not sure I do. They were all abandoned, right?"

"Of course they were," the officer says. "Eventually—too late, if you ask me—people realized that you didn't risk living in the untouched houses."

"Untouched?"

"Untouched by the Hiding Boy. But they still came. Some got out. Most didn't. I guess now, if you believe the story, your friend was the final sacrifice."

"Enough!" Her colleague pushes past, leans close to me, then whispers, "Why did you come here?"

"We were tricked . . . by Rowan Campbell and his brother."

"Rowan Campbell? The hero of Cherry Tree Lane?" The officer shakes her head and chuckles. "I doubt that very much."

I don't argue with her. I'm too tired and too broken to start a pointless battle with a stranger. Instead, I try to make sense of one more thing.

"I always thought the deaths only happened on a specific date."

"That used to be the case," the officer replies. "But I guess something changed, because the last five houses, they've all become murder scenes in the space of three years. It's out there, if you read the right reports. But whoever stirs this stuff online—they've muddied our facts with their fiction.

"I figured the last few victims knew the truth but came anyway. You don't travel that far for nothing. They weren't from here, that's for sure." She looks at the people behind the tape and gives them a sarcastic wave. "They keep their distance these days."

It was a trap. Nate used what we thought we knew about Murder Road and left us to die.

"I'm sorry about your friends," she says. "I hear one of them might make it."

I tense every muscle in my body until the officer touches my shoulder and whispers, "You'll need to come to the station to give a statement. And we can call someone to take you home, okay?"

I nod. Even though that's not going to happen.

When she turns back to her colleague, I slip between the cop cars and ambulances until it's just blank space between me and wherever I want to go.

I go back to Nate's old road and watch the house he used to live in. One day, I'll thank the girl who lives here now; the one who saw through a monster. For now, I go to Seb's car, holding tight to the keys I took from the landing carpet.

I can't sit in his seat. Instead, I rest my feet among the half-finished water bottles on the passenger side and pull his phone from the glove box.

When I type in his code, our smiling faces fill his home screen, and I stumble onto the curb and retch.

He's gone . . . and it's all because of me.

Don't blame yourself for the actions of assholes. Mom's voice fills my head and I wish it were that easy. But the moment that knife plunged into Seb is on repeat and I can't turn it off.

"I'm sorry," I sob. "I'm so fucking sorry."

I stare at the photo of the three of us—before Nate, before this. Why didn't I realize that's all we ever needed? We were perfect, and I ruined it.

I jolt at the sound of a siren, quickly scrolling through Seb's phone until I find Nate's number.

"Hello?"

His voice is a rock dropped deep into my soul, sending waves of panic and rage high into the air.

"Hello? Seb?"

I want to scream, *He's dead!* But instead, I whisper, "It's me. You failed, Nate. We got out."

There's silence, muffled sounds, then, "I don't believe you."

"That's up to you," I say, my heart stalling as I add, "But I'm looking at Seb and Tyler right now, and we won't stop until we tear you down. You lied to us."

"It's not that simple," Nate says. "If you knew the truth . . ."

"I'm pretty sure whatever you have to say won't make up for the fact that you locked us in a house from hell!"

I hold one hand in the other, desperately trying to stop the shaking. Then I carefully put the phone back to my ear and say, "We're going to the police. Right now."

"Bullshit."

"I dare you to not believe me."

I hang up before he can say another word. Then I press my hands against my mouth and scream, over and over until the birdsong creeps back and sweat drips down my forehead.

If none of us is dead, Nate failed. If he failed, he'll come back.

Let their sacrifice be your last. That's what he and Rowan said before they ran.

I search online for any clues that other people have died here, at the times the police officer referred to.

If you look for "Murder Road," you only see the patterns people want you to see. But if you search for "Cherry Tree Lane," and you go past all the blog posts and forums and conspiracy theories, you find the truth.

They were right. People have been dying here every nine months or so for the last few years. If you drew a line from Nate's first house to his last, would it cover all the places these people came from?

I should have asked what hospital Tyler was taken to. I should call my mom. I should do so many things that I don't think I can do, because I need to end this. Me. The almost-final girl.

Screams rip through my skull and I smack myself on the side of the head, trying to force them out.

I'm scared to blink, because my eyes are growing heavy and I can see fragments of the moments when Seb was pulled into the darkness, when he collapsed in front of me, when Tyler rammed the knife between his fingers, when the fractured bottle was forced into his skin.

I leave the car and walk farther into town. If I stay where I am, the police will find me, and that can't happen yet. A sign declaring that Belleview is the town "where happiness is found" looms over me, an image of the sun ironically faded white by the real thing, rust creeping from the corners.

When I look closer, I see that tiny scratches cover the metal—*Ready or not. Whatever you do. The Hiding Boy is coming for you.*

There are names too. *Harriet Souter. Eloise Witchell. Tammy Witchell. Hayley Osborne. Frank and Josephine Oswald. Derek Thornby.*

Those are just a few of them, the names sprawling across the sign like two-word horror stories.

I shudder at the thought of someone carving Seb's name here one day and quickly walk on.

There is a park Nate might have played in; a school he might have gone to. I find a row of stores with half their fronts boarded up and the other half barely surviving.

There is nothing magical here. There is only horror and whatever exists on its edges.

When Seb's phone rings, I crouch on the sidewalk and steady myself.

"Hello?"

"Where are you?" Nate asks.

"We're sightseeing. No wonder you moved to Montgomery-Oakes. This place is a dump."

If I pretend to be okay, if they can't hear the terror clawing up my insides, or the ghosts of everyone I've lost fighting for my attention, this might just work.

"I'm glad you got out," he says.

"Fuck you."

I hear laughter down the line, but it's not Nate. Then a deeper voice—Rowan's voice—fills my ears. "We're sorry it had to be him."

"Glad." "Sorry." These words don't belong in their mouths.

"I know what you're trying to do," Nate says. "You want to

lure us back there. But we know that street a lot better than you do, Max. I'm so sorry about Seb."

"What are you . . . ?"

"It had to happen. There was no other way."

"Liar! There's always another way!"

"I wish that were true."

Nate's voice cracks before Rowan says something I can't make out over the static.

"We're near the grocery store," I say. "Come by yourself."

If I can separate Nate from his brother, maybe I can at least work out why this happened. If Rowan comes with him, he'll see that I'm alone and probably kill me on the spot.

There's silence for a long time, but I don't hang up. I listen to Nate's stilted breathing, his sobs, his sniffs, until eventually he says, "If I'd been honest with you from the beginning, would you have run away with me?"

"Would Seb still be alive?"

"I don't think so."

"Then there's your answer."

"I really *am* sorry, Max. I know you don't believe me, but . . ."

"If that's true, at least tell me why."

I picture Nate's hand pressed over his phone as muffled words slip through. Then he sighs and says, "Okay. I'll tell you everything."

The shadows worked silently, crowbars glistening in the moonlight while heavy breaths bloomed then splintered like the wood slowly cracking before their eyes.

When the board covering the door gave way, wings slapped the sky and a distant howl sliced through the muggy air, leaving a sliver of icy terror to stroke their spines.

Four of the shadows stepped back, while one crouched by the rusted lock, humming a lullaby until it finally stood, arms outstretched, then bowed.

The front door clung to its warped frame as they pushed, and then it sailed softly open, allowing them to hurry through before creaking closed.

As they lit their candles, the darkness shrank to the edges of the hallway, like the blur of old-fashioned photographs, ready to snap back the moment the flames were snuffed out.

The five friends came into focus, all with the same fragile smile. If they hadn't known one another so well, they might have seen relief or happiness or excitement. Instead, they saw only terror.

Their words were fractured, their faces like crumbling Halloween masks, their bodies leaning toward the door they had just broken through.

But they stayed, until the fear was replaced by a nervous excitement that showed itself first through tics and giggles, then through voices shattering the silence.

They shouted and they laughed and they bounded from one room to the next. Then they blew every candle out and sat in a circle, chanting words they had read online, feeling braver than they had any right to feel.

They didn't hear the whispers stirring above them. Or the scratching behind doors no one thought to lock anymore.

Their chatter drowned out the creaks that houses make when you're not alone, heavy feet resting almost silently on each step until there was no escape.

The flames came fast, pushing them into a front door that wouldn't budge.

They screamed until thick smoke forced its way deep into their throats and throttled every sound.

Then they wished, silently, desperately, hopelessly, that they had listened to the boy who warned them not to come.

When the front door burst open, four ash-stained shapes ran through, while a fifth cowered in the corner.

"Come on!" Rowan bellowed, pulling on their limp arms then reaching beneath their shoulders and yanking them up.

"What's happening?" the boy muttered, and as he staggered into the light, Rowan replied, "You're an idiot. That's what happened."

For a few seconds, hacking coughs and the snarl of greedy flames were the only noises on Cherry Tree Lane; then sirens filled the air, the flashing lights on the vehicles suddenly lining the curb revealing anxious faces peering through cracked curtains.

Rowan lay on the overgrown grass, staring at the stars and thinking about the time he got really into astronomy. Like so many things, it was a passion that quickly burned out, the books he pleaded with his parents to buy now lost in his siblings' wardrobes.

When he tried to laugh, it came out as a splutter that turned into a call for help—a paramedic rushing to him and asking questions he must have answered . . . somehow.

His mother's voice broke through the commotion, her warm hands on his face as she checked him for damage.

"Is he okay?"

"I'm fine," Rowan replied. But she ignored him, nodding emphatically as the medic said the same thing, with more words, less rage, and the proviso that she drive him straight to the hospital.

When Rowan protested, his mom locked eyes with him and said, "I've seen This Is Us. *We are going to the hospital right now. And we're not leaving until I'm convinced you are one hundred percent safe."*

He grinned, because his weird-ass mother loved him and she didn't care who knew it. Then his entire family clambered into their car—Nate too scared to speak; Hazel's head against their father's shoulder; his parents asking the same question over and over.

"Why did you run into that house?"

"Because someone had to!" he yelled, as they pulled into the emergency room parking lot, and nobody asked after that.

He had the same nightmare whenever he was ill, his pillow and quilt expanding until they were as thick and heavy as elephants' legs.

It didn't sound scary when he said it aloud. He'd tried to explain it to his parents, how something sickly stirred in his stomach whenever he touched his tangled sheets; how he'd cower where his bed met the wall, his quilt kicked to the floor, while panic scurried around his brain.

That nightmare came with every fever and every sickness until it crept into his waking hours. Flashes, like déjà vu, that snapped him out of even his favorite moments.

He wondered if some dreams grew on people like mold.

When he was ten, he accepted it was part of him. Not nice, not welcome, but familiar.

He didn't think there were worse things. He assumed that was the recurring nightmare he'd been given by whoever, or whatever, decides these things.

He was wrong. Because that night, as he searched for sleep on a hospital mattress that was too flat, his head on a pillow stuffed by someone with no concept of comfort, whispers slithered through his ears like snakes.

"You ruined everything. Now you must pay."

Rowan bolted upright and stared at the bodies around him, some softly snoring, others deathly still. Gurney wheels rattled on the corridor tiles, softening as elevator doors pinged open, fading as they crunched closed.

Then someone whimpered from the farthest corner of the room, where flat white sheets were forced onto the only empty bed on the ward.

Rowan's feet hung a few inches from the floor, then slid into the slippers his mother had brought from home.

He watched the patients around him, praying that one of them would wake up and stop him from doing what he had to. He listened as the clock hanging above the door clicked through three whole minutes; then he stepped forward.

The whimpering grew louder, until Rowan felt the tremors in his throat. When he reached up, hot tears smeared his cheeks.

"Hello?" he whispered. "Is someone there?"

The noise stopped as Rowan's foot touched whatever was huddled next to the bed. Then a hand reached out, dried blood under its twisted nails, its arm a skinny trail that he followed all the way to the boy's angry face.

"You shouldn't have saved them," the boy snarled. "You owe us now."

Rowan stumbled backward, his head smacking against the metal bed frame as the boy lunged for him.

"They let my mother die," he said. "They all have blood on their hands."

As he reached out, something dark and thick splatted on the floor, and Rowan pushed himself back on his heels, while the people in the beds around him began to stir.

The boy leaned forward until his breath burned Rowan's ear. "They weren't supposed to live."

Limbs spasmed under the flattened sheets, then empty faces rose from their pillows, bony fingers pointing at Rowan until he felt the boy's breath retreat.

"You owe us," he repeated, as Rowan finally broke free from his nightmare, the other patients rubbing confusion from their eyes, while the warning drifted through his mind like a distant wail kept alive by the wind.

Rowan tried to keep the terrors a secret, but he couldn't hide his screams.

At first, his parents attempted to soothe him like they always had. They thought their whispered words and tender touches were enough, but the worst nightmares evolve.

Eventually Rowan told them that—in between those suffocating moments when he was forced to smile for the cameras and pretend to be a hero—he was tormented by the Hiding Boy.

"It's real," he told them. "All of it. There is a ghost, there is a curse, and I screwed it all up."

"You saved people's lives," his mom replied.

"But at what cost?"

Every night, Rowan's terror filled the house, until his father preempted the inevitable knock at the door by telling their neighbors that his son was suffering from lucid dreams.

It wasn't a lie. And it earned them a sliver of relief. But, behind closed doors, Rowan would smash his fists against his skull while begging for respite, his baseball cap pulled low over his head to hide the failed attempts to destroy a nightmare.

Rowan told his grandmother everything. She watched him with hollow eyes and a faint smile that could turn to panic without warning.

It felt good, telling her. And it felt horrible.

Sometimes, the deep lines on her face shifted, and he was convinced that she understood. But, whenever she spoke, it was to ask when she could go home or where her "other" husband was—the one in the photo that had pride of place on her care-home windowsill.

"The best day of my life," she would say in her more lucid moments, beaming at the versions of her and her husband on the first day she used that word.

Rowan wished he could have been there somehow, to remember that occasion the way she no longer could. He didn't realize how much he loved his grandmother's memory until it was shattered beyond repair.

"Who's that?" she asked one day, pointing at the space next to Rowan's chair.

"There's no one there, Grandma," he replied, but his spine grew cold as she shook her head, fierce determination replacing the fog.

"That boy's not happy with you."

Rowan stood and slowly stepped aside, careful not to frighten her any more than she already was. Then he knelt in front of her and kissed her bony hands.

"There's no one there," he said again.

When he glanced up, her eyes were clear. "Remember when we went to the beach and all our clothes washed away?"

He chuckled at the memory, then listened as she painted a perfect picture of his father dashing into the ocean to save whatever he could, while his mom calmed Nate, who thought the water was about to swallow his entire family.

Their grandma stood at a safe distance, saying things that made Hazel giggle, and when their dad finally stumbled back to the sand, he had three socks, a skirt, and Nate's Avengers *T-shirt.*

"He rescued some clothes," she said. "But you saved people."

"What?"

"You saved them, Rowan. If what you've been telling me is true, that means someone else must die."

He had grown to like those times, when his grandmother would suddenly start talking like they were kids; when her face lit up and he knew she was still in there. At some point, they had stopped being scary—brief moments to treasure rather than terrible reminders of what she'd lost. But not that day.

With eyes as clear as he'd seen them in years, with a voice as strong as it had ever been, his grandma said, "I'll do it. I'll be the sacrifice."

"What?"

"I'm ready to go, Rowan. I want to help you."

"No."

As a cloud fell over her eyes once more, he vowed to stop telling her about his nightmares. But it was too late.

Whenever they came to visit, there were sporadic moments of clarity when his grandma fought to be heard.

"Stop!" his mom shouted, the ferocity reflected in her own mother's reply.

"I will not!"

Rowan waited to be chastised, but as the weeks went on, he realized why he was never blamed for unloading on the frail old woman who had suddenly rediscovered her fight. It was because his mom had been doing the same.

After a few months, his grandma was so full of her family's fear that she had no choice. She had to protect them, first by navigating the malevolent mazes of dementia, then by making the ultimate sacrifice.

Rowan's mother waited until she slipped back into the traps in her mind, then asked if she meant it.

"Meant what?" their grandma would ask. "How many bedrooms do I have at home?"

Relief swirled with guilt until Rowan's mother broke clean in two.

"What the hell do I do?" she pleaded with her family. "I've come to dread the moments when she's her again. I'm a terrible daughter."

"No," her husband replied. "She's a wonderful mother. All she wants is to help us."

That night, as they watched Rowan convulsing in his bed, mopping sweat from his forehead as murmurs turned to screams, she chose a side. She would be a good mother too. She would save her son from the nightmares that were tearing him apart.

Rowan's mom and grandma went alone. He didn't ask what happened, because he didn't want to know.

Eventually, when they had searched all the usual places and his parents gave the answers that they'd scripted to perfection, the police and nursing home staff assumed she'd wandered into the ocean.

The truth was far worse. She had been driven to Murder Road and left alone in the house Rowan should never have entered. Her body disappearing just like her mind.

There were no screams; no reports of anyone else involved. One minute she was there; the next, she was gone.

They held a funeral in their garden, standing over an empty patch of grass while their dad hammered a tiny cross into the ground.

But that night, the terrors that had tormented Rowan for months came for the entire family.

One by one, they woke up panting, clutching their chests while the words reverberated through their pounding heads.

It couldn't be a willing sacrifice. It had to be someone who wanted to live. There were five houses left when Rowan got involved so, now, he owed them five bodies—all unconnected by blood; all innocent.

And if they tried to be clever again, their nightmares would tear them all apart from the inside out.

Rowan's dreams became prophecies.

Whenever he closed his eyes, he saw the last house on the street, looming over the rest of Murder Road like a volcano about to erupt. He knew, now, that ancient building with its bloodred door was both where it started and where it would end.

The Hiding Boy's victims cowered in corners of Rowan's mind that he refused to explore. Mostly, they sat quiet; sometimes they stirred. The worst was when they screamed, their wails leaving migraines in his head that lasted for days.

Rowan couldn't be trusted, so the victims were chosen for him.

On the worst nights, he would dream of the next untouched house and see a person's face pleading at the window.

That was when he knew who would die. His only job was to get them there.

It was easier than he thought, to convince people he'd only just met to come with him to Murder Road. Rowan's words were so well rehearsed, and the desire to see the origins of an urban legend so strong in so many, that only once did he have to use force.

The rest of the time, eventually, he could convince whoever had been chosen to walk willingly into a trap.

Rowan's family remained in Belleview after the first death.

But the guilt clawed at his mother the longer they stayed, until she convinced his father to run and keep running. As though the terrible things they did were lessened by leaving them in the rearview.

No matter how much pain Rowan let others inflict on him, no matter how many times he pleaded for forgiveness when the rest of his house endured their fitful but never unbearable sleep, he knew there was only one way to end it.

Complete the curse.

Five houses. Five victims. The last one taking their final breath in the place where the Hiding Boy was made.

51

"Holy shit," I say, "I'm . . ."

The next word stalls in my mouth because *am* I sorry? After everything Nate and his family have done? And yet, images of Bella crash into my head as I imagine Nate's grandma willingly walking to her own death.

"You've killed five people?"

There's silence for a long time; then Nate breathes down the phone and mumbles, "It's not as simple as that."

"Yes, it is. I understand that your grandma did that of her own volition, but you said the street demanded five bodies after that. So, was Seb the last one?"

"I hope so."

"Don't screw with me, Nate. You're the one with all the answers."

"I'm not. We thought we'd given that place what it wanted when my grandma sacrificed herself. Now, after five more deaths, we can only hope it's satisfied. Monsters can change the rules with no warning."

"I know," I say, thinking of how Nate twisted what we thought we knew about Murder Road to get us here.

"I only killed one person," Nate says. "If you believe I got Seb killed."

"Fuck," I reply. "Did you really just say that?"

"I brought him here, but it's the house that killed him. Before we messed with the curse, something malevolent would always turn someone else into a monster. It could be the kind old man, the nanny, the DJ at a sweet sixteen. Someone no one would ever suspect suddenly went full slasher movie on an entire household. But, after Rowan broke that door down, whatever cursed this place took full control. We send someone in and it does the rest."

I try to calm my breathing as my father's twisted grin coils behind my eyes.

"How did you know Seb was dead? Were you watching?"

"No. He was picked. We've got no choice in that."

"That's crap and you know it!"

"It's true. Rowan's dreams show him who must be sacrificed. That's why I . . . why I was reluctant to make new friends."

"You knew Seb was going to die and you brought us here anyway?"

I want to clamber into the phone and punch him until my knuckles are raw.

"I asked you to run away with me."

I almost choke on my laugh. "Seriously? That's what you're going with?"

Heavy sniffs rustle down the line before he says, "I'm sorry, Max. I fell for you and I figured . . . after last time . . . that my closest friends would be safe. It used to always be someone random."

"Someone 'random' is still *someone*. You won't get away with this."

"Okay."

I don't want to hang up because, once I do, I'm terrified he'll never answer his phone again. Wherever they are running to, it would be a lot easier to follow if we can somehow track Nate's cell.

"I didn't want to do it," he says at last. "None of us did. But the rules are simple. Five bodies. One for each of the houses that hadn't seen a homicide when my brother got involved."

"Did you take one kill each? Is that how you sleep at night—by sharing the murders between your fucked-up family?"

"We don't share them out," Nate says. "And we definitely don't 'sleep at night.' The first three sacrifices didn't mean much to us. They were just people we'd seen walking around whatever town we lived in at the time, or someone who served one of my parents in the grocery store.

"Once Rowan started dreaming about them, and he knew for certain they were the next victim, he'd plant some seeds, drop Murder Road into the conversation, and let curiosity or stupidity do the rest. We didn't used to go with them. It's too risky. All they needed was the house number and a gentle nudge."

"What changed?"

"Rowan dreamed about someone more important. And we had to change our game plan."

"That's all we are to you? Pieces to move around a board?"

"It wasn't Seb," Nate says. "It was in the town before this one. My sister fell in love. We'd been so careful not to create connections, just in case. But, after three victims that meant nothing to us . . . we got sloppy."

His words twist like thorns in my stomach. How can he be so nonchalant about the people they have led to their deaths?

"Rowan didn't tell us who needed to die. He knew what would happen if he did. So, he lured Hazel's boyfriend away on his own, took him to the penultimate house on the list, and locked him in. When Hazel found out . . ."

A car door slams on the other end of the phone and Nate starts to whimper.

"My family is more broken than you could ever imagine, Max. Everything we have been forced to do kills us a little more. But what Rowan did to that guy . . . the grief and heartbreak he forced on our sister . . . that was the worst thing until . . ."

"Until me?"

"Exactly."

"Go and live in the damn woods!" I shout. "Don't speak to anybody. There must have been some way to keep people safe."

"You think we haven't tried that? If we don't play by the rules, the terrors come harder than ever—forcing us out of our hiding places. It's unbearable pain, Max. It's soul-shredding, skin-ripping agony."

I picture Seb's icy hand in mine. "That sounds a lot like grief."

"It's worse, but I'm glad you'll never understand. I'd hate for you to experience those terrors."

I laugh again because he has no idea what he's done. "You think I won't have nightmares about today for the rest of my fucking life?"

He stays silent for a long time. Then he whispers, "I'm sorry. When we arrived, I kept to myself, watching for people who deserve to suffer. But we don't have any control. We can't force a target onto someone's back. It has to be an innocent. So, no murderers, no villains, no bullies.

"I thought, after my sister's boyfriend, that I was safe to step a little closer to you. I didn't think we'd be that unlucky again; not with all the people in this town. Sometimes I tried to push you away, but I liked you . . . I *like* you . . . and ignoring that was more painful than anything else."

"You don't *like* me . . . and you certainly don't love me," I spit back. "If you did, you'd have found a way to save us."

"My sister calls her dead boyfriend every day," Nate mutters. "She listens to his voicemail then leaves messages that she always deletes. Apologies, love letters, rants, breakdowns. I watch her face crumble every single time she hears his voice. I know what love is, Max. I really do."

I stare into the gray sky, light rain resting on my face, and hate myself for not seeing through his act. The signs were there. They always are. But I ignored any that snuck through because, for a while at least, I liked him too.

"I'm so fucking naive," I say. "I thought the urban legends were coming true when you arrived, but they weren't."

"I'm sorry," Nate replies. "That was Rowan. I didn't know right away. When we did the Face in the Glass, I had no idea he was the one banging and scratching the car. But I saw him at the abandoned school and I knew then that something wasn't right.

"He was planting seeds of his own, convincing an urban legend club that his brother was special somehow.

"I told him I wouldn't do it. I pleaded with them to find another way. But when Rowan turned up at Bloodbath, that was him making sure you all knew exactly who I was.

"By then, he'd seen enough to know we could get you to Murder Road, provided you all thought it was safe.

"Once I knew Seb was the sacrifice, I accepted it. Reluctantly. You'd be safe, the pact would be complete, and we wouldn't have to live in torment any longer. Before you judge me, Max, ask yourself: What would you do to protect your family?"

He hangs up before I can answer, sirens skating on the air as I hold my head in my hands and pray.

"I'm so sorry," I start.

The rest of my words crumble and I pull my knees tight into my chest, while Seb's phone lights up with his mom's number, and I wait to be found.

52

One officer watches me in disbelief, while another writes everything down. They don't say anything until I'm back in the corridor and they are huddled over the front desk.

Every few seconds, someone peers at me then looks away.

What must it be like working as a police officer in Belleview, where one street has seen more horror than most cities?

When Mom finally arrives, she pulls me into a hug that I wish could last forever. I breathe in her perfume and her shampoo and every sliver of home, and let everything that is holding me together fall apart.

"Are you okay?" she asks, stepping back and looking me up and down.

"Yes. Can we go to the hospital?"

"Of course. But first . . ."

She looks over to the desk and we follow the officers back into the room, where I say everything again.

Mom stares at me the whole time, her thumb frantically brushing against mine. Then she signs something and we leave in silence.

In the car, I rest my hand on hers and say, "Focus on the road please, Mother. It would be ironic if I survive that only to die in a car crash."

She laughs until I can't control my sobs. Then she pulls over and we both cry by the side of the road.

"What are Seb's parents going to do?" I ask. "They've lost everything now."

I imagine bruises where Mom's fingers grip mine, but I don't want them to move. She's protecting me and I'm so grateful for that.

"I know you'll want to help them," she says, "and you will, in time. But first you need to help yourself. I can't imagine what you've been through."

"Do you believe me?"

Mom squeezes harder and says, "Yes."

We wait for ages at the hospital, in chairs designed for torture, eating food that coats my teeth in something I can't wait to brush away.

They tell us to go home but we don't.

Tyler's parents arrive first, his little brothers excitedly exploring every inch of the waiting room until they are swept up in their father's thick arms. They complain by kicking the air, then giggle when he kisses their necks.

His mom falls into mine and they stay like that for a long time. His dad is too busy to look sad, but in the moments when his newest sons are settled, all the life drains from his face.

They disappear soon after, only reappearing to collect the sisters that come two hours apart, drowsiness dragging on their eyes and open-mouthed children using their shoulders as pillows.

"We can take them," Mom says. "If you need a break."

But Tyler's dad shakes his head, holding tight to all the children he can, while their other one lies behind too many doors to count.

An army of Tylers stands over me, their eyes hollow, their smiles jagged like they have been made with box cutters.

One by one, their hands reach out, and I crawl deeper into the corner until there is nowhere to escape. Eventually, one long fingernail strokes my face, its razor-sharp point piercing my skin.

It follows the warm trail down my cheek, then brings it to its mouth, where a wart-filled tongue laps at it like a kitten devouring milk.

A low hum comes from deep inside its skull, and then blood pours from its eyes, drenching my sneakers and quickly rising past my knees.

I hold my breath, waiting for it to reach my head; then a hand reaches out of the dark red liquid and Seb bursts through.

"It's okay," Mom whispers as she strokes my face. "It was only a dream."

Was it a dream? Or was it a terror?

I listen for the whispers of the dead, but all I can hear are the clattering wheels of hospital gurneys and the chatter from the nurses' station.

"Tyler is awake," Mom says. "The surgery was a success and they said you can see him."

I leap up, one leg giving way and forcing me back into my chair.

"Take it easy," she says. "There's no rush."

But I need to see for myself. I need to know this isn't another trick of the dark.

I stop outside his room and Mom takes my hand and whispers, "It's okay."

Then I step in, looking past the smiling faces of his parents and his sisters and his impossibly cute brothers, at the boy who didn't die.

"Hey," Tyler says.

I run to him, my hand hovering an inch from his. "Is it okay to touch you?"

"Of course. But not too hard. And definitely not here."

He touches the spot on his chest where the bottle went in, now hidden beneath his hospital gown and whatever they used to repair him.

I press my face softly against his, and then I whisper, "I'm so sorry."

When I pull away, he shakes his head and says, "Don't apologize for things that aren't your fault. That what Seb used to say."

He's already using past tense, and Mom's hand on my back stills my shudder.

"We've got a lot to talk about," Tyler's mother says, "but, for now, we eat."

His brothers cheer as she pulls a box of cupcakes from under the bed, but the rest of us keep our happiness hidden.

"When can you come home?" I ask.

"It shouldn't be long," Tyler's dad says. "But he needs rest, so no more chasing monsters."

Despite what we thought, they were the ones chasing us, but I don't correct him.

We sit with Tyler and his family for another hour; then Mom rubs my shoulder and nods at the door.

"I'll see you soon," I say, watching as he gently lifts my hand off his and whispers, "I'm safe now."

Mom spends half the journey arguing with the radio, her favorite songs cut off by traffic reports and random people talking.

When the static sprays loudly into the car, I stiffen, only settling once at least two new tunes have played.

We drive past all the towns we ignored on the way here; the places I will visit one day, to find the homes of all the people Nate's family has ever lied to.

I want their stories to be the first thing you find when you look for Murder Road. I want the truth to be top of everyone's search. And I don't want anyone to ever suffer in those houses again.

"When you're ready," Mom says, "I'm here. You know that, right?"

"Of course," I reply, although I don't think I will ever tell her what I saw there.

I'll tell her she was the inspiration for my fight. She'd like that. But she doesn't need to know that I saw a twisted version of my father and his second-chance family. I'm done wasting so much time thinking about him.

53

Seb's mom walks around her immaculate front room, moving things that don't need moving, brushing away specks of invisible dust.

His father slouches in the chair opposite me and I glance at the dining table, then away.

I wish it weren't bare. I'd give anything to see him sitting where he always sits, the sound of Lego bricks being rummaged through as I strain to hear Seb's mother.

But the only sound is a sigh here and a cough there, noises that don't fit in a house where nothing is out of place.

Seb's smiles beam at me from fifty different photos, some real, most fake, but all of them cherished by parents who will never see a new one.

"The police told us everything," Seb's mom says. "So, don't feel that you have to."

How can she say that so calmly? How can she hear those impossible words and simply accept them? How can she be so calm for me when I want to scream how unfair this is for her?

"I wanted to come," I reply. "I'm so sorry this happened to you."

"I know," she says, "and we're grateful."

Seb's dad clears his throat and his wife looks at him, her eyes full of hope while unspoken words pull on her lips. But he doesn't say anything.

He sits with his head down, staring at the patch of carpet singed when Seb had a sleepover and we almost did a séance.

We only lit three candles before he knocked one over; I can still see him frantically stamping out the flame with his mismatched socks.

I smile at the memory, then sip my tea.

"How are *you*?" Seb's mom asks.

"I'm okay."

"It's all right if you're not."

That's what Miss Kittle says. I've taken Seb's place in her office and I want so much to ask what he shared in there. Instead, I must tell her how *I'm* feeling. I heal whatever hidden wounds I have with confessions and self-analysis.

"I know."

Mom says I'm not grieving properly because I'm too busy trying to help others. But what if they are the same thing?

"I miss him," I say, and his dad whimpers.

His wife crouches next to him and he pulls her into a hug. Then I nod at the most recent picture of Seb and let myself out.

I have two more houses to visit—one that I want to, and one that I don't.

Henry puts out his bottom lip when he opens the front door; then he wraps his arms around me and says, "I said I wouldn't be sad as you've got enough of that already. I need to make you happy."

"You *do* make me happy," I reply, and he steps back, grins, then says, "Well that's all right then."

Bella's portrait hangs proudly in the living room, a lavender-filled vase on either side.

The smell brings flashes of something I quickly snuff out. I sometimes wonder, if we hadn't been rescued, would a version of her have tried to break me? Or would it have been increasingly angry versions of my father?

"How have you been?" I ask, and Henry gives a deep sigh and says, "I'm getting there."

The room looks too big without Bella's bed in it, and I wish I'd been here to help him arrange the things that now sit in boxes by the front door.

"I'm donating a lot of her clothes to charity," he says. "But I'm keeping a few things, for posterity."

"You keep whatever you wish," I reply. "Keep it all if you want to."

"We have to let some things go."

He stares at me for a bit too long and I wish I could go somewhere without being put under a microscope. I'm okay. Not perfect, but nowhere near as broken as everyone seems to think.

What happened was messed up. I haven't gone a night without it breaking into my dreams. But I won't let it define me.

"I was so angry when Bella passed away," Henry says, "and *I* knew it was coming."

"I thought you were making me happy," I reply, and he chuckles and says, "Okay. Come with me."

Like so many times before, I follow him down the garden path and into his studio. That's what I call it. He calls it a shed, but it's so much more than that.

He's tidied away most of his canvases, but his easel still takes pride of place in the center.

"Have a look," he says.

I step tentatively forward, then lift the corner of the cloth.

"You'll like it. I promise."

I pull the rest of it off and wait for the picture to settle. Then I stare at something beautiful.

"It's me."

Henry stands by my side and says, "It is."

"Do I really look like that?"

"Yes."

I can't take my eyes off it.

"Did you do this from memory?"

"And with a little help from your mom. She supplied me with a few photographs and I worked my magic."

He stutters over the last word, but he shouldn't.

"I wasn't sure if you'd pick up a brush again, after Bella died. I thought you'd go into angry-artist mode."

He full-on belly laughs, and I copy him.

Then he puts his arm around me and says, "She wouldn't have wanted that."

"Can I have it?" I ask.

"When it's finished. It won't be long."

"Thank you," I say, losing myself in the eyes of the girl I hope I can be again one day, when that house is finally brought to the ground.

54

I shout a lot. I rage at a mother who doesn't deserve it. I cry when no one is looking and, sometimes, when there are too many eyes to escape.

"If you want to hit something," Tyler says, "make sure it doesn't bruise."

He stands behind the punching bag and grins. Then he spreads his arms and says, "What are you waiting for?"

"I'm waiting for you to get out of the way."

He chuckles and steps aside, crouching in the training room as I strike the heavy leather until my arms burn.

"Feeling better?" he asks, the weight in his left hand tiny compared to what he used to lift.

"Much," I reply, as he reaches for something bigger. "Remember what your physical therapist said. Don't rush it."

He tosses the dumbbell from one hand to the other. Then he grabs the closest soccer ball and starts doing kick-ups.

"I can't wait to be back on the field," he says, and I think of everything he told me when he thought he was about to die.

I hope he told his family those things anyway. But I won't embarrass him by asking.

In the corridor, Helen Keane nods at me and I nod back. That's as close as we'll come to being friendly, but when you've survived a night on Murder Road, your classmates no longer feel like enemies.

Tyler and I leave via the side door and find the nearest bench, laying our lunches across the table and picking the best bits from each.

We don't eat in the Hell Hole anymore. As small as it is, it felt horribly huge without Seb.

Instead, we enjoy the sunshine, or the rain, or whatever the weather has in store for us that day.

"Have you been yet?" Tyler asks.

"No."

"You don't have to, you know."

But that's not true. It's the only thing left on my list, and until I've scratched it off, it will haunt me like everything else.

I watch a new kid walk awkwardly through the crowd and sit with his back against the wall, an overflowing trash can his only company.

He catches my eye, a tentative smile creeping out; then he opens a book and nibbles on the edge of his sandwich.

"What are you thinking?" Tyler asks.

He knows. And he's letting me decide either way. Just like he did with Nate.

"We're good as we are," I say, because it's better to be safe than sorry.

55

A for-sale sign stands outside Nate's old house. He never brought me here, but it didn't take long to find his address.

When the whole town knows you sent one of their own to die, they stop keeping your secrets.

It looks like any other house. But don't they all?

As I walk along the gravel path, curtains from the home next door twitch then fall back into place. The front door is freshly painted, yet, if you look close enough, the thick letters break through.

MURDERERS!!

That's what someone wrote the week after Nate and his family left town, a few hours after my first live stream.

I wonder what would have happened if they'd still been here. Would whoever targeted this place have been as brave, or would they have waited until it was safer to insult the monsters in their midst?

I'll never forgive myself for trusting him. Mom, Tyler, Henry, Miss Kittle—they all say it's not my fault. But I don't believe them.

Every night, I replay the moment I spotted Nate across the corridor and felt like I'd struck gold. If only someone had pulled me back just long enough for him to disappear into the crowd, over and over until he tricked someone else into liking him.

But my friends had nothing to do with it. This is all on me.

There have been potential sightings, from as close as the next town to as far away as Europe. Who knows how long you have to run when everyone is chasing you?

All we can do is keep the story trending.

I hold my phone up, go live, then say, "This is their last known whereabouts. As you all know, they left here the same day we were attacked; the same day we lost our best friend.

"They're gone now, so please stop targeting this place. But if you know anything, leave your details in the comments.

"I doubt Nate will find another school. But they will surface eventually. And someone will catch them."

One by one I hold up the photographs of Nate's family, from the bastard I thought I knew, to the girl winning a track meet in a town halfway between here and Murder Road, to Rowan's school photograph from the year he pissed off a demon.

His mom's photo used to hang on the coffeehouse staff board; his dad's is a Facebook profile picture from an account that hasn't posted for eight years.

"We used to pretend to chase urban legends," I tell whoever is watching. "But I'm chasing something else now . . . and I need your help."

The curtain moves again, a girl about my age holding her phone out until I can see my face looking back. She nods and I hope, with all my heart, that this works.

It won't be immediate. Nate and his family will go off-grid until they feel safe enough to hide in plain sight. But, even if they have repaid their debt to that malicious street, I won't let them sleep soundly.

I want them to know that we're waiting for them to slip up. And they will.

Cold breath creeps across my neck and I hear the faint groan of my father.

I hold steady, ending my stream and waiting for her to come.

The scent of lavender drifts on the air, sunlight washing over my skin, and the sounds of my past wiped clean.

56

Henry sits next to Seb's mom on her sofa, their hands wrapped around steaming mugs as they quietly discuss plans for the weekend.

Seb's father opens a cleaned-out ice cream tub, multicolored Lego bricks cascading onto the table like hailstones, and I marvel at how quickly his fingers work.

He doesn't need instructions anymore. That's how many times he has built and rebuilt the castle that sits in the corners of half the photos on these walls.

So much of their life is broken, but at least this small piece of their story can be put together again.

"We're thinking the market in Winchester," Henry says, his voice filling the room. "We could grab lunch at that café Bella loved."

Seb's mom grins as her husband looks away from his work just long enough to reply. "Sounds good."

Baby steps—that's what Henry said we need; not only the parents robbed of their sons, but the man grieving his soulmate, and the teenagers thrust into a waking nightmare.

It isn't always like this. Sometimes we sit alone in separate houses, screening our calls, lifting whatever holds back our tears and letting them wash over us. But we always return to one another.

This is the only club I belong to now—the one with five members and no name.

When the doorbell rings, Seb's dad stands and lets Tyler in.

"Here he is," Henry cheers. "Player of the match . . . again."

Tyler shrugs, trying his best to brush off the praise that fits him like a glove. Then he sits next to Seb's father and quietly joins in.

We can never replace what was lost. We wouldn't want to. But hopefully we can fill some of the cracks that, if ignored, will grow into craters.

As Henry smiles, I picture Bella in the space he always leaves next to him, her head resting on his broad shoulder. Then I imagine Seb dancing around the living room with a boy I will never know.

I search their parents for glimmers of their past, placing my hand in Seb's mother's and letting her squeeze for as long as she wants.

I fight off whatever else tries to break through. Not because I am strong, but because I have these people who refuse to be beaten. We will live. We will fight. And we will win.

Six Months Later

Crowds make hiding so much easier. And this crowd is bigger than most.

Dad stands away from us, a hood pulled low over his face.

"He should look up the word 'inconspicuous,'" Hazel mutters, "because that is not it."

There's a rumble deep within the crowd that quickly grows into a cheer, as the bulldozer judders along the road before settling on the sidewalk.

Mom pulls her sleeves over her hands and bounces softly on the spot, while our father's head darts from left to right.

It's a miracle we've never been caught, with parents who cannot keep their shit together in public spaces.

When the first bricks crumble and fall, I see the surge of elation and imagine being part of it. It must feel good to be this happy. But that's not why we came.

"She's not here, little brother."

I make fists that I imagine pummeling Rowan's face until he can't even think about smirking. Then I smile at the boy who has turned to look at me from his dad's shoulders.

He has the perfect vantage point to bring us down, but he is only here to see a horrible house razed to the ground. He's just a kid, and kids love destruction.

Dust billows into the sky as the roof collapses, and tired-looking police officers hold their arms out as someone attempts to break the cordon.

"One last idiot wants to die," Rowan says, and the woman next to him turns and looks a little too long.

I step forward because, as we agreed, it's every person for themselves today. Then I keep edging through until the police tape flickers in front of me.

As the front loader pushes the walls in on themselves, whispers break through the dust cloud, scratching at my ears then scrambling for other places to hide.

They should flatten every house on Cherry Tree Lane. But, for now, whoever decides these things is making do with the one Seb died in; the one the Hiding Boy ran to on the night his rage forged an unbreakable curse.

At least it's over now. If you think of it like that—if you remove the names and the faces from each horror story—you can almost find a happy ending.

That's what I tell myself when I cling to the strands of sleep wrapped tight around my fingers. Words I could never say aloud. Words she wouldn't understand. But the only words that I've got.

For a moment, we watch each other. But Max's brow unfurrows as the sun creeps behind a cloud and she turns to her mother and smiles.

There are new colors in her hair, yellow and green and purple, and my skin warms with the memory of her hand in mine.

Tyler stands next to her, surrounded by strangers I will never officially meet. The sisters, brothers, and parents who are now his armor.

"I'm sorry," I whisper, to the people I can see and all the ones I can't.

There are no ghosts standing forlorn on the sidewalk, watching their refuge crumble. Like all the others, Seb is wherever his parents put him.

"It had to be someone," Dad told me.

But I wish it hadn't been him.

Hazel tugs gently on my shoulder and we fall back.

Mom is already in the car, the engine running, while Dad peers longingly at our old neighborhood, and I think of all the ways it could have been different.

If our brother had never run into the house that night, would I still have met Max one day, somehow? Or was it always meant to be like this?

She hates me. I know that. *I* hate me, too; for what it's worth.

I hate all the things we've done just to drag ourselves back toward "normal" and, let's face it, that's the last thing we can ever be.

Rowan's thigh presses against mine as he clambers in and I can feel his lightness. For so long, he was weighed down by the reality of being the wrong kind of hero; one who created a mess that could only be cleaned up by a villain.

Now, with no nightmares, no prophecies, no dreams about that decaying house, he is neither, and he is happy.

As we pull away from Murder Road, we shiver—some out of habit, others due to fear—and I crane my neck to see her one final time.

Then I put my headphones in and watch Max's old live streams. She's persistent, that's for sure. But she won't catch us.

The world doesn't work like that. It soon tires of other people's horror, until only the victims are left screaming.

We should know. We've heard more than most.

The light of my sister's phone catches my eye, the goofy grins of Hazel and her boyfriend filling the screen before she swipes it away.

Her finger hovers over his number for ten long seconds before she finally selects it.

Mom flinches at the sound of the muffled voicemail message, but I keep my headphones on until Hazel hangs up without saying a word, then opens her recently deleted photos.

There are only a few pictures in the folder, and sadness hits me as I imagine how many she used to take, back when she had moments she wanted to remember.

Hazel selects one and I don't understand.

You can't run forever!

Then another.

He's coming for you!

The third photograph is of the article about the sweet-sixteen massacre.

The fourth detailing the horrific double homicide of the Witchell twins.

The final image is the story about Derek Thornby—the second person that Rowan convinced to walk willingly into an untouched house on Murder Road.

"It was *you*?" I whisper.

Hazel pulls a bag from between her feet and takes out her diary.

Guilt burns in my chest as I think of all the times that I've read those pages. Then it turns to panic as she shakes the book and another clipping falls out.

She carefully unfolds it until I see the name—Isiah Malone—and the same face that fills Hazel's phone screen.

The headline reads:

MISSING TEEN'S BODY FOUND ON "MURDER ROAD"

Hazel glares at me, then whispers, "You don't know all my hiding places."

"I'm so sorry."

She nods. "I was only reminding you that we had a job to do. I'm sorry, too, Nate. But . . . he wasn't going to die for nothing."

We've become horrible, twisted, vile versions of ourselves. But not my sister. She found love and Rowan stole it from her. We shattered her heart into a million unsalvageable pieces because we had no more ways to fight back.

But does that make *us* the twisted ones? Or the ghost who chose his own victims?

Hazel turns away from me, and no one else says anything because, sometimes, even our family knows better than to stoke a fire.

Did they know already, as I stood in the garden burning those warnings? As Hazel filled the space beside me with a tiny sacrifice of her own?

She did what she had to, to make sure that I did the same.

It takes a while to drive to our new home; so long that fatigue pulls on my eyelids and, eventually, Rowan forgets to nudge me awake.

The Hiding Boy stands in the center of my vision, his fingers forming a steeple painted red. He steps forward, his eyes finally dry, his snarl replaced by a soft smile.

I wait for the wails to fill my skull, for my skin to burn and peel, for the souls of all the people we have led to their deaths to come for me . . . like they always do. But the boy turns and walks away.

It's over, I tell myself.

Then something coils around my ankles, so fast that I can't even think about pulling free.

Nails burrow into my skin and I'm yanked backward, my face smashing against the ground then splitting as I'm dragged over a carpet of jagged bones.

I scream but my mouth is empty, the agony filling my brain until I jolt and Dad says, "We're here."

"You okay, Nate?" Rowan asks, but I'm looking past him, at the street we now call home.

At the end, where there used to be an empty lot, is a house

with a ramshackle chimney and crumbling roof tiles. A thick red door sways on its creaking hinges, a slice of black growing and shrinking in the wind.

I blink, desperate for it to disappear, and I keep blinking, as the house we just saw being demolished stretches farther into the darkening sky.

Acknowledgments

I owe so much to my incredible wife, Rachel, whose love and support are priceless. Your belief in me has never wavered, and I am so pleased that we are on this journey together.

Thank you to our amazing boys, Charlie and Lucas, who keep me grounded, inspired, and young at heart.

To my agent extraordinaire, Claire Wilson—it has now been seven years since you sent the email that changed everything. Thank you for seeing something special in my writing back then and for championing my books with unrivaled enthusiasm.

Thank you to my US agent, Pete Knapp, who continues to go above and beyond. Despite being more than three thousand miles away, you make it seem like you are right on my doorstep whenever I need you.

My editor, Eileen Rothschild, provided such incredible feedback and support as I pulled this story into shape. In some ways, this was the toughest book I've written so far, and I am so grateful that, with your help, the story I've had in my head for so long made it onto the page so effectively.

I'm lucky to have had four covers designed by Kerri Resnick, and this one, like all the others, is exceptional! Thank you for getting to the core of my stories with such fantastic designs.

Thank you to everyone at Wednesday Books who has been involved with *One House Left,* with special thanks to Lisa Bonvissuto, Rivka Holler, Zoe Miller, Devan Norman, Melanie Sanders,

Eric Meyer, Gail Friedman, and Char Dreyer. Thank you for everything you do, both seen and unseen. I truly appreciate the wider publishing team, without whom we would be lost.

Thank you to Stuti Telidevara at Park & Fine Literary and Media, and to Safae El-Ouahabi and Sam Coates at RCW.

To each and every incredible teacher, librarian, and bookseller who has helped my stories find new readers—thank you! I will always be amazed by the success this fledgling English author has had in the US, and I know that is down to the work and support of so many people.

And to everyone who reads my stories—I am only able to write more books because of you, and I am eternally grateful!

Mum—as always, thank you from the bottom of my heart for the life you gave me. The older I get, the more I realize how hard you worked to provide me with everything I needed and more.

This book is dedicated to my grandmothers. I was blessed to have known these two strong, loving, selfless women, and my life is far richer for having had you in it. I wish with all my heart that you could have held my published books in your hands, and I will never forget the belief you both had in me—long before I believed in myself.